every

last

word

Also by Tamara Ireland Stone

Time Between Us

Time After Time

every
last
word

Tamara Ireland Stone

HYPERION

Los Angeles | *New York*

So Long Lazy Ray words and music by Joe Rut copyright ©

Printed in the United States of America
First Edition, June 2015
10 9 8 7 6 5 4 3 2 1
G475-5664-5-15091

Library of Congress Cataloging-in-Publication Data
Stone, Tamara Ireland.
Every last word / Tamara Ireland Stone.—First edition.
pages cm
Summary: "Consumed by a stream of dark thoughts and worries that she can't turn off,
a girl coping with Purely-Obsessional OCD learns to accept herself and take control
of her life through her experiences in poetry club"—Provided by publisher.
ISBN 978-1-4847-0527-8 (hardback)—ISBN 1-4847-0527-0
[1. Obsessive-compulsive disorder—Fiction. 2. Self-acceptance—Fiction. 3. Poetry—
Fiction. 4. Love—Fiction. 5. High schools—Fiction. 6. Schools—Fiction.] I. Title.
PZ7.S8814Ev 2015
[Fic]—dc23   2014041978
Reinforced binding

Visit www.hyperionteens.com

THIS LABEL APPLIES TO TEXT STOCK

For C. And all the other special minds

six months earlier

I *shouldn't be reading the notes.*

Hailey trims a rose and passes it to me. As I attach the note to the stem with sparkly pink ribbon, I read it. I can't help it. This one's a little over-the-top, but it's still sweet. I give it to Olivia and she drops it in the classroom-specific bucket.

"No way! You guys . . ." Olivia snorts, laughing hard as she turns the card over in her hand. I guess she's reading them, too. "I can't tell who wrote this but . . . poor boy. This is so cheesy."

Someone's attempt at heartfelt poetry makes its way around the circle. Alexis falls back against my bed in hysterics. Kaitlyn and Hailey double over on my rug. Eventually, I join in.

"This is mean. Let's not read them," I say, hiding the rose in the middle of the bucket, wanting to protect this anonymous guy who put his heart on the line for some girl in his calculus class named Jessica.

Olivia grabs the stack of cards in front of me and starts thumbing through them. "God, who are these people and how do we not know any of them?"

"We're not losers?" Alexis offers.

"It's a big school," Hailey counters.

"Okay, back to work. The flowers are wilting." Kaitlyn's still laughing as she snaps back to her role as the leader of our Valentine's Day fundraiser. "Olivia, since you like the notes so much, switch places with Samantha."

Olivia shakes her head, and her ponytail goes flying. "No way. I like my job."

"I'll switch. My hand's getting tired anyway," Hailey says, and the two of us trade spots.

I grab a rose out of the bucket and pick the scissors up off the floor. The instant I slide my fingers through the handles, this thought hits me out of nowhere, and before I have time to react I feel my brain sink its teeth in and latch on tight, already preparing to fight me for it. My hand starts trembling and my mouth goes dry.

It's just a thought.

I let the scissors fall to the floor and I shake out my hands a few times, looking around the circle to be sure no one's watching me.

I'm in control.

I try again. Rose in one hand, scissors in the other, I squeeze my fingers together, but my palms feel clammy and my fingers are tingling and I can't get a solid grip. I look up at Kaitlyn, sitting directly across from me, watching her face twist and blur as a wave of nausea passes over me.

Breathe. Find a new thought.

If I cut it once, I'll keep going. I know I will. I'll move on to the next rose, and the next one, and I'll keep cutting until there's nothing left but a huge pile of stems, leaves, and petals.

After that, I'll massacre those syrupy sweet, carefully written notes. Every single one of them.

God, that's so twisted.

Then I'll take the scissors to Olivia's ponytail and cut right through that hair tie.

Shit. New thought. New thought.

"I need a glass of water," I say, standing and hoping none of them notice the sweat beading up on my forehead.

"Now?" Kaitlyn asks. "Come on, Samantha, you'll hold everything up."

My legs are wobbly and I'm not sure I can trust them to get me downstairs, but somehow the scissors are gone and the banister is in my hand instead. I head straight into the kitchen and run my hands under the water.

The water is cold. Listen to the water.

"Are you okay?" Paige's voice breaks through the chatter in my head. I hadn't even seen my little sister sitting at the counter, doing her homework. That's when I spot the knife block, full of knives. And a pair of scissors.

5

I could slice right through her hair.

I take big steps backward until I slam into the refrigerator. My knees give out and I slide down to the floor, gripping the sides of my head, burying my face in my hands to make it dark, repeating the mantras.

"Sam. Open your eyes." Mom's voice sounds far away, but I obey her words, and when I do, the two of us are nose to nose. "Talk to me. Now."

I look over at the staircase, wide-eyed.

"Don't worry," she says. "They won't find out. They're upstairs."

I hear Mom whispering to Paige, telling her to take a bag of chips up to my room and keep my friends distracted.

Then she grabs both of my hands so hard, her wedding ring digs into one of my knuckles. "They're just thoughts," she says calmly. "Say it, please."

"They're just thoughts." I can echo her words but not the steadiness in her voice.

"Good. You're in control." When I look away from her she grips my arms harder.

"I'm in control."

She's wrong. I'm not.

"How many thoughts does the brain automatically deliver in a single day?" Mom moves on to facts to help me center myself.

"Seventy thousand," I whisper as tears splash onto my jeans.

"That's right. Do you *act* on seventy thousand thoughts a day?"

I shake my head.

"Of course you don't. This thought was one in seventy thousand. It's not special."

"It's not special."

"Good." Mom pinches my chin and lifts my head, forcing me to look at her again. "I love you, Sam." She smells like her favorite lavender-scented lotion, and I inhale it, feeling a host of newer, prettier thoughts overpowering the darker, scarier ones. "Whatever you're thinking, it's okay. It doesn't mean *anything* about you. Got it? Now tell me."

The two of us have been here before. It hasn't happened in a long time, not like this, but Mom slips right into her assigned role as if it's second nature. She's well trained.

"Scissors," I whisper, dropping my head to my chest, feeling dirty and sick and humiliated. I hate telling her these awful thoughts, but I hate the thought spiral even more, and this is my ticket out. I'm well trained, too.

"The roses. Olivia's hair and . . . Paige . . ." Mom doesn't make me finish. She wraps her arms around me and I grab ahold of her T-shirt, sobbing into her shoulder, telling her I'm sorry.

"You have nothing to be sorry for." She pulls away and kisses my forehead. "Now stay here. I'll be right back."

"Please don't," I beg, but I know she won't listen. She's

doing what she has to do. I dig my fingernails into the back of my neck three times, over and over again until she returns. When I look up, she's crouched down in front of me again, holding the scissors flat in her hand.

"Take them, please."

I don't want to touch them, but I don't have a choice. My fingertip connects with the cold metal and I let it slide over the blade, lightly, slowly, just tickling the surface. When I feel the handle, I curl my fingers through the holes. Mom's hair is dangling in my face.

I could cut it. But I would never do that.

"Good. It's just a pair of scissors. They triggered a few scary thoughts, but you won't act on them because *you*, Samantha McAllister, are a good person." Her voice sounds closer now.

I drop the scissors on the floor and give them a hard push to get them as far away from me as possible. I throw my arms around Mom's shoulders, hugging her hard, hoping this is the last time we go through this but knowing it isn't. The anxiety attacks are like earthquakes. I'm always relieved when the ground stops shaking, but I know there will be another one eventually, and again, I'll never see it coming.

"What am I going to tell them?"

My friends can't know about my OCD or the debilitating, uncontrollable thoughts, because my friends are normal. And perfect. They pride themselves on normalcy and perfection, and they can't *ever* find out how far I am from those two things.

"Paige is sitting in for you on rose duty. The girls think

you're helping me with something in the kitchen." Mom hands me a dish towel so I can clean myself up. "Go back upstairs whenever you're ready."

I sit alone for a long time, taking deep breaths. I still can't look at the scissors on the far end of the kitchen floor, and I'm pretty sure Mom will hide all the sharp objects for the next few days, but I'm okay now.

Still, I can hear this one thought hiding in the dark corners of my mind. It doesn't attack like the others, but it's frightening in a totally different way. Because it's the one that never leaves. And it's the one that scares me most.

What if I'm crazy?

more than anything

Lane three. It's always lane number three. My coaches think it's funny. Quirky. A *thing*, like not washing your lucky socks or growing a rally beard. And that's perfect. That's all I want them to know.

I step up to the top of the block and twist at the waist, shaking out my arms and legs. Squeezing my toes tight around the edge, I look down at the water and run both thumbs over the block's scratchy tape three times.

"Swimmers, take your marks." Coach Kevin's voice echoes off the clubhouse walls at the far end of the pool, and when he blows his whistle, my body's response is purely Pavlovian. Palm over hand, my elbows lock as I press my arms into my ears and throw myself forward, stretching and reaching and holding the position until my fingertips slice through the surface.

And then, for ten blissful seconds, there's no noise at all except the sound of water *whoosh*ing past my ears.

I kick hard and lock in my song. The first one that pops into my head is a happy tune with catchy lyrics, so I start my butterfly stroke, throwing both arms over my head in perfect synchronization with the beat. Kick, kick, throw. Kick, kick, throw. One, two, three.

Before I know it I'm touching the opposite end of the pool, doing a tight turn, and pushing hard off the wall. I don't look up or left or right. As coach says, right now, at this moment in the race, no one matters but you.

My head leaves the water every few seconds, and when it does, I can hear the coaches screaming at us to get our chins down or our hips up, to straighten our legs or arch our backs. I don't hear my name, but I check myself anyway. Today, everything feels right. I feel right. And fast. I increase the tempo of the song and kick it into gear for the last few strokes, and when my fingertips connect with the edge of the pool, I pop up and steal a glance at the clock. I shaved four-tenths of a second off my best time.

I'm breathing hard as Cassidy gives me a fist bump from lane four and says, "Damn . . . you're gonna slaughter me at county this weekend." She's won the county championship three years in a row. I'll never beat her, and I know she's just being nice, but it feels good to hear her say it anyway.

The whistle blows again and someone dives off the block

above me, signaling my turn to exit. I pull myself up out of the water, peeling off my swim cap as I head for my towel.

"Whoa! Where on earth did that come from?" When I look up, I'm eye to eye with Brandon. Or, more accurately, eye to *chest* with Brandon. I force myself to keep looking up, past his thin T-shirt and to his eyes, even though the temptation to check out the way his shorts hug his hips is almost more than I can resist.

During my first summer at the club, Brandon was just an older teammate with an insanely fast freestyle who always put up the most points in meets and taught the little kids to swim. But for the last two summers he's returned from college as a junior coach—my coach—and that makes him strictly off-limits. And even hotter.

"Thanks." I'm still trying to catch my breath. "I guess I just found a good rhythm."

Brandon shows me his perfect teeth, and those crinkles next to his eyes are even more pronounced. "Would you do that again at county, please?"

I try to come up with a funny comeback, something that will keep him smiling at me like this, but instead my cheeks get hot while he stares at me, waiting for me to reply. I look at the ground, chastising myself for my lack of creativity while I watch the water drip from my suit, forming a puddle underneath my feet.

Brandon must follow my gaze because he suddenly gestures

at the row of towels strewn across the wall behind him and says, "Stay there. Don't move."

A few seconds later he's back. "Here." He wraps a towel around my shoulders and slides it back and forth a few times, and I wait for him to drop the ends, but he doesn't. I look up at his eyes and realize he's staring at me. Like . . . maybe he wants to kiss me. And I know I'm looking at him like I want him to, because I do. It's all I think about.

His eyes are still locked on mine, but I know he'll never make the first move, so I take one brave step forward, then another, and without overthinking what I'm about to do, I press my dripping wet suit against his T-shirt, feeling the water soak it through to his skin.

He lets out a breath as he balls the ends of the towel in his fists and uses it to pull me even closer. My hands leave his hips and find his back, and I feel his muscles tense beneath my palms as he tips his head down and kisses me. Hard. And then he pulls on my towel again.

His mouth is warm and he parts his lips, and oh my God, this is finally happening, and even though there are people everywhere and I keep hearing the whistle blow and the coaches calling out behind me, I don't care, because right now I just want to—

"Sam? You okay?" I blink fast and shake my head as Brandon releases the towel and I feel it fall slack at my sides. "Where'd you go, kid?"

He's still standing two steps away and not even the slightest bit damp. And I'm not a kid. I'm sixteen. He's only nineteen. It's not that different. He adjusts his baseball cap and gives me that ridiculously adorable smile of his. "I thought I lost you for a second there."

"No." You did the exact opposite of losing me. My chest feels heavy as the fantasy floats up into the air and disappears from sight. "I was just thinking about something."

"I bet I know."

"You do?"

"Yeah. And you have nothing to worry about. Push yourself like *that* at county and keep swimming year-round, and you'll have your choice of college scholarships." He starts to say something else, but Coach Kevin yells for everyone to take a spot on the wall. Brandon gives me a chummy pat on the shoulder. A coachlike pat. "I know how badly you want this, Sam."

"More than you could possibly understand." He's still two steps away. I wonder what would happen if I *really* opened up my towel and wrapped him up in it

"Sam. Wall!" Coach Kevin yells. He points at the rest of the team, already gathered and staring at me. I squeeze in next to Cassidy, and when Coach is out of earshot, she elbows me and whispers, "Okay, that was cute. That thing with the towel."

"Wasn't it?" I shoot her a surprised look. At the beginning of the summer, Cassidy called him "Coach Crush," but over the last few weeks she's become increasingly irritated with me for not giving up.

"I said it was cute, not that it means anything."

"Maybe it does."

"Sam. Sweetie. Really. It doesn't. He grabbed your towel and dried you off a bit. But that's it. Because he has a girlfriend. In college."

"So?" I lean forward, trying not to make it obvious that I'm looking for him. He's over by the office, drinking a soda and talking with one of the lifeguards.

"So. He has a girlfriend. In *college*," she repeats, stressing the last word. "He talks about her all the time, and it's obvious to everyone except you that he's totally in love with her."

"Ouch."

"Sorry. It had to be done." Cassidy piles her long red hair on top of her head in a messy bun and then grips my arm with both hands. "I'm not telling you anything you don't already know." She comes in closer. "Look around, Sam," she says, gesturing to a long line of our teammates. "There are plenty of fish in the fancy-private-swim-club sea."

I look around and see boys in tight Speedos with solid abs and muscular arms, their skin tanned by the Northern California sun, their bodies lean and solid after three months in the water, but none of them are anywhere near as flawless as Brandon. Even if I did find one of them remotely attractive, what's the point now? Summer's nearly over.

Cassidy tilts her head to one side, pouting dramatically. She brings her fingertip to my nose and sighs. "What am I going to do without you, Sam?"

My stomach clenches into a tight fist as she voices a thought that's been haunting me since the first day of August. Like all my summer friends, Cassidy has never known me outside the pool. She has no idea who I am when I'm not here, so she doesn't know how backward she has it.

"You'll be fine," I say, because it's true. Me? I'm not so sure.

My psychiatrist nailed it back in June, when I practically floated into her office and announced that I'd taken my last final. She strode over to the minifridge, poured sparkling apple cider into two plastic champagne flutes, and said, "To the triumphant return of Summer Sam" as we clinked glasses.

But it's coming to an end. In two weeks, I'll be back in school, Cassidy will be in L.A., and Brandon will be at college. I'll be missing them, along with my early morning dives into lane number three.

I'll be Samantha again. And more than anything, I'll be missing Sam.

five of us

"You look fantastic," Mom says as I step into the kitchen.

I'd better. I spent the last hour putting myself together for the first day of school. I left my hair down and ironed it straight. I'm wearing a sheer top over a white camisole, skinny jeans, and the wedges I begged Mom to buy me. My eyes are lined, my lips defined, and my foundation is effectively masking the stress-induced breakout on my chin.

"Thank you." I hug her tight, hoping she knows I'm not thanking her for the compliment alone. It's for everything she's done for me this summer. For coming to all my swim meets and cheering so loudly, she's hoarse every Sunday night. It's for all those late-night talks, especially over the last week when Cassidy left for L.A., Brandon went back to the East Coast, and the first day of school began to loom over me like an ominous storm cloud.

Mom's wearing that encouraging smile she always plasters on when she knows I'm nervous. "Stop looking at me like that, please," I say, fighting the urge to roll my eyes. "I'm fine. Really."

My cell phone chirps and I pull it from my pocket to check the screen. "Alexis wants a ride to school today."

"Why?" Mom asks as she fills a bowl with cereal for Paige. "She knows it's against the law to drive with passengers in your first year." Of course Alexis knows the law, she's just surprised I'm following it since most people don't.

I text her back, telling her I can't give her a ride because if my parents found out, I'd lose my car. I hit SEND and flip the phone around so Mom can read the screen. She gives an approving nod.

I shove the phone back in my pocket and hitch my backpack over my shoulder. "Have a good day, sixth grader," I say to Paige as she spoons a big bite of cereal into her mouth.

As I head for the garage, I'm still texting back and forth with Alexis, who's begging me to change my mind. I finally drop the phone into the cup holder as I pull out of the driveway, ending the discussion without ever telling her the real reason I won't pick her up today. Or any time in the near future.

Earlier this month, on my sixteenth birthday, Dad took me to the DMV to get my license, and when we got home a few hours later, there was a used Honda Civic parked in our garage. It was totally unexpected, and it meant so much more

21

than regular transportation to me. It meant Mom, Dad, and my psychiatrist thought I could handle it.

I was dying to show off my new car, but Alexis, Kaitlyn, Olivia, and Hailey were all out of town on their respective family vacations, and Cassidy was grounded, so I just drove around by myself for the rest of the afternoon listening to music and enjoying how the steering wheel felt in my hands.

But every once in a while, I'd glance down at the odometer, fascinated by the way the numbers changed. I felt this strange charge whenever the last digit hit the number three.

When I finally pulled into the driveway that evening, the last digit was resting on a six, so I backed out again and drove around the block a few times until the odometer stopped where it belonged. And now I have to do that every time I park. I'm not about to let Alexis and the rest of my friends in on my secret, so I'm happy to have the law as an excuse to drive alone.

As I pull into the student lot, the odometer is on nine, so I have to drive all the way to the far end by the tennis courts before I can park on a three. As I cut the ignition, my stomach turns over violently and my mouth feels dry, so I sit there for a minute taking deep breaths.

It's a new year. A fresh start.

The anxiety eases as I walk through campus. Avery Peterson squeals when she sees me. We hug and promise to catch up later, and then she returns to Dylan O'Keefe and grabs his hand.

He was my obsession for the first three months of freshman

year, starting when he asked me to the homecoming dance and ending when Nick Adler kissed me at a New Year's Eve party a few months later and promptly replaced him.

A few steps later, I spot Tyler Riola sitting with his lacrosse buddies at a table on the far end of the quad. He had my undivided attention for the first part of sophomore year, until I started dating Kurt Frasier, the only guy who wasn't a one-sided fixation. I liked Kurt. A lot. And he actually liked me back, at least for a few months.

Kurt was hard for me to shake, but Brandon finally took center stage in my mind when summer started. I picture him in his Speedo and, as I turn the corner, I wonder what he's doing right now.

I stop short. That can't be my locker.

The door is wrapped in bright blue paper and there's a giant silver bow tied around the middle. I run my hand across it. I can't believe they did this.

I glance up just in time to see the crowd part for Alexis. As usual, she looks like she just stepped off the cover of *Teen Vogue*, with her long blond hair, striking green eyes, and perfect skin. I can hear her high heels tapping on the concrete as her designer sundress swings with each step. She's holding a giant cupcake with purple and white frosting.

Kaitlyn is on her right, looking equally pretty but in a completely different way. She's exotic-pretty. Sexy-pretty. She's wearing a tight-fitting top with thin straps, and her dark wavy hair is cascading over her bare shoulders.

Hailey peels away from the pack and speeds toward me with her arms spread wide. She throws them around my neck and says, "God, you have no idea how much I missed you this summer!" I squeeze her tighter and tell her I missed her, too. She looks amazing, still tanned from her summer in Spain.

Olivia's now within arm's reach, so I grasp big chunks of her newly dyed jet-black hair with both hands. "Okay, this is totally working for you!" I tell her, and she pops her hip and says, "I know, right?"

As my friends close in, all the people around us stop what they're doing to gather in a little tighter. Because that's what happens when the Crazy Eights do *anything*. People watch.

We started calling ourselves that back in kindergarten, and it kind of stuck. There were eight of us until freshman year, when Ella's family moved to San Diego and Hannah transferred to a private high school. Last year, Sarah landed the lead in the school play and started hanging out with her new drama club friends. And we were down to five.

That's when I started to realize that friendships in odd numbers are complicated. Eight was good. Six was good. But five? Five was bad, because someone's always the odd girl out. Often, that's me.

"Happy birthday, gorgeous!" Alexis says, bouncing in place as she gives me the cupcake.

The smile on my face grows even wider. "My birthday was two weeks ago."

"True, but we were all talking about how much it must suck

to have a summer birthday. None of us even got to celebrate with you." I'm surprised Alexis hasn't mentioned this earlier. I saw her twice last week, and both times we talked about the spa day her mom is planning and the new convertible she's getting for *her* birthday.

"This is so perfect, you guys," I say, holding up the cupcake and then pointing to the bow on my locker. "Seriously. Thank you."

There's a chorus of *You're welcomes* and *We love yous*. And then Alexis steps forward. "Hey," she whispers. "Sorry about all the texts this morning, but I have to talk to you about something and I was hoping to do it in private."

"What's up?" I try to make my voice sound light, but the second she said the words "I have to talk to you," my stomach twisted right back into that tight knot I've been trying to loosen since the parking lot. Those words are never good.

"We'll talk about it at lunch," she says. And just when I was starting to feel like this was the best first day of school ever, I'm now dreading lunch.

Kaitlyn steps in to hug me. "Are you shaking?" she asks. *Breathe. Breathe. Breathe.*

"Too much coffee this morning, I guess." The warning bell rings and I turn to my locker and start dialing the combination with trembling fingers. "I'll see you guys later."

Once the Eights are gone, the rest of the crowd takes off to first period. I set the cupcake on the empty shelf and grab the door to steady myself.

Taped on the inside of my locker door, I see all the photos and mementos I've saved over the last two years. There are pictures of the five of us dressed up in the school colors for spirit week, and the four of us surrounding Kaitlyn when she won homecoming princess last year. There's a copy of the noise ordinance we got when Alexis's parents left town last Halloween and we threw this epic party people talked about for months afterward. Scattered around, covering any sliver of paint, are my ticket stubs. It's an impressive, eclectic collection—ranging from bands no one's ever heard of to names like Beyoncé, Lady Gaga, and Justin Timberlake—thanks to Olivia's dad, who owns an indie record label and always gets us seats in the VIP section.

I use the small mirror to check my makeup and whisper, "Don't. Freak. Out." Then I close the door and stare at the wrapping one more time, letting my fingertip trail across the surface, running my thumb across the silver bow.

"That was really nice." The voice is so faint, at first I wonder if I'm hearing things. I turn to see who spoke, but her locker is blocking her face.

"Excuse me?" I hope she didn't see me pathetically fondling the bow.

"You have really nice friends." She swings the door closed and walks over to me, pointing at the wrapping paper. I almost reply "Not always," but I catch myself. It's a new year. A new start. And today, I do have really nice friends.

"How'd they get your locker open?"

"They all know the combo. It's kind of a birthday tradition. We've been wrapping each other's lockers since middle school. This is only the second time they've wrapped mine, but you know, those were big birthdays. Thirteen and now . . ." I reach for the silver bow again. "Sixteen."

Why am I telling her this?

I look around, realizing that the corridors are now empty. "I'm sorry. Do I know you?"

"Apparently not." She points to the end of the row. "My locker has been there since freshman year, but we haven't formally met or anything. I'm Caroline Madsen."

I take her in, starting with her feet. Brown hiking boots. Baggy, faded jeans. An unbuttoned flannel shirt that might be considered cool if it belonged to her boyfriend, but I'm pretty sure that's not the case. Underneath it, her T-shirt reads, WHAT WOULD SCOOBY DOO? That makes me laugh to myself. I continue up to her face. Not a stitch of makeup. A purple-and-white-striped ski cap, even though it's the end of August. In California.

"Samantha McAllister." The final bell rings, signaling that we're both officially tardy on the first day of school.

She tugs on her shirtsleeve, uncovering an old, beat-up watch. "We'd better get to class. It was nice to meet you, Sam."

Sam.

Last year, I asked the Eights to call me Sam. Kaitlyn

27

laughed and said that's her dog's name, and Olivia said it's a guy's name, and Alexis declared that she would never, *ever* go by Alex.

I watch Caroline round the corner, and by then, it's too late to correct her.

keep a secret

We're eating lunch under our tree in the quad when Alexis takes a dramatic breath, places her palms flat on the ground, and leans into the circle. "I can't stand this anymore. I have something to tell you guys."

Kaitlyn rests a hand on Alexis's back, like she's offering silent reassurance. "It's about my birthday this weekend," Alexis says, and the rest of us squeeze in tight. "We've been planning to go to this amazing spa in Napa for months now, right? Well, I guess my mom should have scheduled the appointments earlier, because when she called two weeks ago, they told her there was a wedding this weekend and everything was booked solid." She sighs dramatically. "She could only get three appointments."

"Whatever. We'll go to another spa," Olivia says.

"That's what I suggested. But my mom said she called all

the high-end places, and none of them could accommodate all of us on such short notice. Besides, this is her favorite—she's been going there on special occasions for years—and she's always wanted to take me."

"Can we go on Sunday instead? Or the following weekend?" I ask.

Alexis looks at me and her eyebrows knit together. "Saturday's my birthday, Samantha."

She takes a sharp inhale as she removes two envelopes from her bag. She hands one to Kaitlyn and the other to Olivia. "I've been thinking about this nonstop over the last week, and I finally decided it was only fair to pick the two people I've known the longest."

"You've known all of us since kindergarten," Hailey says, voicing what I'm pretty sure each one of us is thinking.

"True, but our moms," she says, gesturing to Kaitlyn and Olivia, "knew each other when we were in preschool," and the two of them nod like that explains everything. Then they actually have the audacity to start opening their envelopes in front of us.

Again, Hailey speaks on behalf of us losers. "Samantha has a car now. Maybe the two of us can drive up and meet you for lunch?"

Hailey's pleading expression makes me actually consider it for a moment. But Mom and Dad would never agree. Even if they did, what would happen when we arrived at the restaurant?

It might take me ten minutes to park correctly. What if there's a valet?

I can't drive.

"I thought about that," Alexis says. "But she won't drive with passengers. Right, Samantha?" My face gets hotter the longer they stare at me.

I shake my head. Alexis glances around the circle, shifting the blame to me, using nothing but her eyes.

The thoughts start gathering, butting up against the caution tape surrounding my brain, strategizing and preparing to rush in and take over. I hold them off, telling myself all the right things, repeating the mantras, taking deep breaths, counting slowly.

One. Breathe.

Two. Breathe.

Three. Breathe.

It's not working. My face is getting hotter and my hands are clammy and my breathing feels shallow and I need to get out of here. Fast.

I pull my phone out of my pocket and pretend I just received a text. "I have to run. My new lab partner needs my notes from class." I pack up my untouched sandwich, hoping no one asks about the lab partner I don't actually have.

"You're not upset, are you?" Alexis asks sweetly.

I bite the inside of my lower lip three times before I make eye contact. "Of course not. We get it, right?" I direct the question at Hailey, acknowledging the two of us as allies, stuck on the bottom rungs of Alexis's social ladder.

And then I walk away as slowly as possible, ignoring the fact that every muscle in my body wants to run.

When I feel the first sign of a panic attack, I'm supposed to go to a quiet place with dim lighting, where I can be alone and get my thoughts under control. My psychiatrist has burned these instructions into my brain in a way that makes them second nature, but instead I duck around the corner out of sight and stand there, my back against the science building, my face pressed into my hands, like I can achieve the same effect if I can only block out the glare of the sun. Eventually, I start walking through campus and let the path take me wherever it leads.

It leads me to the theater.

I've been here before for the annual talent show, the band recital, school plays—basically, the slew of events we're forced to attend because they take place in lieu of class. The five of us always ditch our assigned row and sit together in the back, snickering to ourselves and poking fun at the people on stage, until one of the teachers gets tired of shushing us and sends us all outside, as if that's punishment. We sit on the grass, talking and laughing, until everyone who had to stay and watch the entire performance finally files out.

I hunker down in a seat in the center of the first row, because it's actually darkest here, and I'm already feeling calmer, despite the fact that Alexis just force-ranked her best friends and put me on the bottom. On the bright side, I no longer have to waste so much time wondering where I fit.

The bell rings and I'm about to get up and head for class, when I hear voices. I crouch down lower, watching a group of people walk across the stage, talking to each other in hushed tones. A guy's voice says, "See you Thursday."

The last person emerges from behind the curtain. She's about to disappear on the opposite side when she stops and takes a few deliberate steps backward. Resting her hands on her hips, she scans the theater and sees me in the front row.

"Hey." She walks over and sits with her legs dangling over the edge of the stage.

I narrow my eyes to get a better look at her in the dark. "Caroline?" I ask.

"Wow. You remembered my name," she says as she jumps down and collapses into the seat on my right. "I'm kind of surprised by that."

"Why?"

"I don't know. I guess I assumed you were the type of person I'd have to introduce myself to more than once before it would actually stick."

"Caroline Madsen," I say, proving that I even remembered her last name.

She looks a little impressed. "So did you see the rest of us?" she asks, pointing at the empty stage.

"I guess. I saw a bunch of people go by. Why?"

Her mouth turns down at the corners. "No reason. Just wondering."

But now she has me curious. And besides, this is a great distraction. "Who were they? Where were you coming from?"

"Nowhere. We were just . . . looking around." I start to press her for more details, but before I can say anything, she leans over, stopping a few inches short of my face. "Have you been crying?"

I sink down farther in my chair.

"Guy trouble?" she asks.

"No."

"Girl trouble?" She looks at me out of the corner of her eye.

"No. Not like that. But, well . . . actually yeah, sort of."

"Let me guess." She taps her finger against her temple. "Your locker-wrapping best friends are actually manipulative bitches?"

I look up at her from under my eyelashes. "Sometimes. Is it that obvious?"

"You can take in a lot of information from a few lockers away." She scoots back into her chair and slides down, kicking her legs out in front of her and crossing them at the ankles, mirroring my posture exactly. "You know what you need?" I don't answer her, and after a long pause she says, "Nicer friends."

"Funny. My psychiatrist has been saying that for years."

As soon as the words leave my mouth, I suck in a breath. No one outside my family knows about my psychiatrist. She's not my biggest secret, but she's right up there with the rest of them. I look over at Caroline for a reaction, expecting a biting comment or a condescending stare.

"Why do you see a psychiatrist?" she asks, like it's no big deal.

Apparently I'm not keeping secrets from her, because words start spilling out on their own. "OCD. I'm more obsessive than compulsive, so most of the 'disorder' part takes place in my own head. That makes it pretty easy to hide. No one knows."

I can't believe I'm saying this out loud.

She's looking at me like she's actually interested, so I keep talking. "But I obsess about a lot of things, like guys and my friends and totally random stuff. . . . I sort of latch on to a thought and I can't let it go. Sometimes the thoughts come rapid-fire and cause an anxiety attack. Oh, and I have this weird thing with the number three. I count a lot. I sort of have to do things in threes."

"Why threes?"

I slowly shake my head. "I have no idea."

"That sounds pretty horrible, Sam."

Sam.

Caroline's looking at me as if this whole thing is completely fascinating. She leans forward, resting her elbows on her knees, exactly the way my psychiatrist does when she wants me to keep talking. So I do.

"I can't turn my thoughts off, so I barely sleep. Without meds, I don't get much more than three or four hours a night. It's been that way since I was ten." Now there's a hint of sympathy in her eyes. I don't want her to feel sorry for me. "It's okay. I'm on antianxiety meds. And I know how to control the panic attacks." At least, I think I do. It's been a little harder since the bizarre impulse to slash the Valentine's Day roses.

"I started seeing a psychiatrist when I was thirteen," Caroline says matter-of-factly. After a long pause she adds, "Depression."

"Really?" I ask, resting my elbow on the armrest between us.

"We've tried different antidepressants over the years, but . . . I don't know . . . sometimes it feels like it's getting worse, not better."

"I was on antidepressants for a while, too." It sounds so strange to hear myself admit all this. I've never talked with anyone my age about this stuff.

Caroline reclines into the chair and smiles. She looks pretty when she does. She'd be even prettier if she would just wear a little makeup.

I bet I could help her.

I no longer have plans to be at a fancy spa with my four best friends this weekend. I don't have any plans at all. "Hey, what are you doing on Saturday night?"

She crinkles her nose. "I don't know. Nothing. Why?"

"Want to come to my house? We can watch a movie or something."

Maybe I could talk her into letting me give her a mini-makeover, too. A few highlights to give her hair a little dimension. Some concealer to hide the pockmarks and blemishes. Nothing dramatic, just a touch of color on her cheeks, eyes, lips.

Caroline pulls a pen out of the front pocket of her baggy jeans.

"I'll text it to you," I say, reaching for my phone.

She shakes her head. "Technology is a trap," she says, waving her pen in the air. "Go." I give her my house number and street, and she scribbles it on her palm and pockets the pen again. Then she bounces up from her chair so quickly, I jump in my seat. She backs toward the stage, places her hands on the surface, and with a little hop, she's sitting on the edge again. She leans forward and checks the room. "I want to help you, Sam."

Wait. What? She wants to help *me*? "What do you mean?"

"Can you keep a secret?"

I'm great at secrets. My friends tell me all their dirt, knowing I'll never breathe a word of it to anyone. They have no idea I've been keeping a mental disorder from *them* for the last five years.

"Of course I can," I say.

"Good. I want to show you something. But if I do, you can't tell anyone. And I mean *anyone*. Not even your shrink."

"But I tell her everything."

"Not this."

Caroline waves me over to her. "See that spot over there?" She points at the piano in the corner of the stage. "Come back here on Thursday, right after the lunch bell rings, and wait for me. Don't say a word to anyone. Hide on this side of the curtain and don't come out until I come get you."

"Why?"

"Because." She grabs me by the shoulders. "I'm going to show you something that will change your whole life."

I roll my eyes. "Oh, please."

"It might not." Caroline moves her hands to my cheeks. "But if I'm right about you, it will."

in the deep

The elevator is already waiting. I press 7 and then, because I can't help it, I press 7 two more times. As soon as I open the office door and step inside, Colleen's head pops up from behind the counter and her whole face brightens. "Ah, it must be Wednesday!"

At first, I found her regular greeting mortifying, but then I realized there are never any other patients here, and even if there were, there's no reason to hide. We're all regulars.

"She's running about five minutes late. Water?" she asks, and I nod.

I fish my phone out of my purse, pop in my earbuds, and put on my typical waiting room playlist, *In the Deep*, named for lyrics in a Florence + the Machine song. I think of my naming strategy as a hobby, even though my psychiatrist doesn't see it that way. I don't simply listen to music, I study the lyrics, and when I'm done making a playlist, I pick three words from one of the songs—three words that perfectly encapsulate the collection—and that becomes its title.

I let my head fall back against the wall and close my eyes, ignoring all the motivational posters hanging above me. I mentally transport myself back to the pool two weeks ago, to that moment when Brandon kissed me but didn't, and I feel my face relax as I relive the fantasy again. His mouth was so warm. And he smelled good, like Sprite and coconut sunscreen.

"She's ready for you," Colleen says.

Sue's office hasn't changed in five years. The same books line the same shelves, and the same certificates hang from the walls covered in the same beige paint. The same photographs of the same children stand propped up on her desk, suspended in time like the office itself.

"Hey, Sam!" Sue crosses the room to greet me. She's this tiny Japanese woman with thick black hair that hangs to her shoulders, and she's always impeccably dressed. She looks like she'd be refined and soft-spoken until she opens her mouth.

I'd only been seeing her for a few months when I came up with the nickname "Shrink-Sue." I never actually thought I'd call her that to her face, but one day, it slipped out. She asked me how I came up with it, and I told her it sounded like something badass you'd call out while throwing a judo chop.

Until that point, I hadn't really stopped to question whether or not psychiatrists appreciated being called shrinks. I was only eleven years old. And I didn't want to offend her, but once I'd said it, I couldn't take it back.

But Sue said she liked the name. And she told me I could call her anything. I could even call her a bitch, to her face or behind her back, because there would certainly be times I'd want to. I liked her even more after that.

She sits in the chair across from me and hands me my "thinking putty." It's supposed to take my mind off the words I'm saying and give me something to do with my hands so I don't spend the entire fifty-minute session scratching the back of my neck in threes.

"So," she begins, opening the brown leather folio across her lap like she always does. "Where do you want to start today?"

Not with the Eights. Not with the spa.

"I don't know." I wish I could tell her about my secret meeting with Caroline tomorrow, because that's pretty much all I've thought about over the last two days, but I can't break my promise. Then I think about the rest of the conversation, the two of us bonding over medication and therapy sessions.

"Actually, I sort of . . . made a new friend this week." The words sound so dorky coming out of my mouth, but apparently Shrink-Sue doesn't hear them that way, because her eyes light up like this is the best news she's heard in ages.

"Really? What's she like?" she asks, and I feel myself mimicking her smile. I can't help it. I think about the way Caroline put her hands on my face like an old friend. That look in her

41

eyes when she said she wanted to help me. The whole thing caught me completely off guard.

"Well, she's *not* like any of the Crazy Eights," I say, picturing her long stringy hair and lack of makeup and those chunky hiking boots. "She's kind of awkward, but she's nice. I barely know her, but I already think she sort of . . . *gets* me."

Sue opens her mouth, but I hold my finger up in the air between us before she can speak. "Please. Don't say it."

Her mouth snaps shut.

"This doesn't mean I'm leaving the Eights. You always make it sound easy, Sue, but I can't just 'find new friends.'" I put air quotes on the last words. "They *are* my friends. These are the people that every girl in my class *aspires* to be friends with. Besides, it would kill them if I left. Especially Hailey."

Sue shifts in her chair and crosses one leg over the other, taking an authoritative pose. "You have to make decisions that are best for *you*, Sam. Not for Hailey or anyone else," she says in her straightforward way.

"Sarah made a decision that was best for her, and look what happened."

I'm not about to be on the receiving end of what we all did to Sarah. Shooting her dirty looks as we passed her in the halls, talking about her from the other side of the cafeteria, leaving her out of our plans for the weekend. I'm not proud of myself, but when she dumped us for her drama club friends, we made it feel like an act of disloyalty on her part.

"She's probably quite happy," Sue says.

"I'm sure she is. But being part of the Eights makes *me* happy."

Their friendship might require weekly therapy, but I have fun with them. And I'd be *truly* crazy to say good-bye to parties every weekend, cute guys crowded around us at lunch, and VIP tickets to every major concert that comes to town.

"Either way, this is a really positive step, Sam. I'm glad to see you making new friends."

"Friend. Singular. One person." I hold up a finger. "And no one can *ever* know about Caroline."

"Why not?"

Before I even realize what's happening, my chin begins to tremble. I take a deep breath to steady myself and stare at the carpet.

"Why can't they know about her, Sam?" Sue repeats softly.

"Because." The word comes out all wobbly. "If they kick me out—" I can't finish my thought. I squeeze the back of my neck three times, as hard as I can, but it doesn't help. "I don't have anyplace else to go."

The tears start to well up, but I fight them off, biting the inside of my lower lip, forcing my gaze toward the ceiling. Sue must be able to tell how uncomfortable I am, because she jumps in and says, "Hey, let's change the subject."

"Please," I whisper.

"Did you have a chance to print out those pictures?"

"Yeah." I blow out a breath and reach into my bag.

Dad took a bunch of photos during the county championship

meet and sent them to me. Last week, I showed them to Sue. She spent twenty minutes sliding her fingertip across the screen of my phone, carefully taking in each photo. Then she asked me to pick my three favorites, print them out, and bring them with me today.

"These are great," she says, taking her time to examine each one. "Tell me, why did you choose these three?"

"I don't know," I say with a shrug. "I guess because I look happy."

Her expression tells me that wasn't the answer she was looking for. "What word comes to mind when you see this?" she asks, holding one of the pictures up in front of me. "One word."

Cassidy is squeezing me hard; her nose is all scrunched up and her mouth is open, like she's screaming. Dad took it right after I beat her time by a tenth of a second, breaking her record in girls' butterfly. I was afraid she'd be upset, but she wasn't. "Friendship."

She holds the next one up. My stomach feels all light and fluttery when I see Brandon resting one hand on my shoulder and pointing at the first-place medal around my neck with the other. He kept high-fiving me. And hugging me. All day.

Sue wouldn't approve of the word "love," even though it's the first one that pops into my mind, so I fix my gaze on the medal, thinking about the way he made me push myself all summer, making me believe I could be faster, stronger. "Inspiration."

44

I feel my face heat up and I'm relieved when Sue moves on to the next picture and says, "I was really hoping you'd print this one."

Dad took it with a long lens and you can see every detail in my face. I'm standing on the block in my stance, seconds away from diving in, and even though my goggles are covering my eyes, you can see them clearly. I stare at the picture for a long time, trying to think of a single word to describe what I like so much about it. I look strong. Determined. Like a girl who speaks her mind, not someone who cowers in the dark every time she gets her feelings hurt.

"Confidence," I finally say.

Sue's nod is proud and purposeful, and I can tell my word was spot-on.

"Here's what I'd like you to do. Bring these to school tomorrow and tape them on the inside of your locker door." She taps the last one with her perfectly manicured fingernail. "Put this one right at eye level. Look at it off and on all day to remind you of your goal this year. Which is?" she prompts.

"I'm going to make swimming a priority, so I can get a scholarship and go to the college of my choice. Even if it's far away."

The "far away" part makes me start hyperventilating. I feel nauseous when I think about moving away from here, leaving my mom, leaving Sue. But I force myself to stare at the picture, locking in on that strong, determined expression.

A swim scholarship. Competing at a college level. A chance to reinvent myself.

This girl looks like someone who could do all those things.

"And don't forget," Sue says. "This isn't Summer Sam, who shows up in June and disappears when school starts. This is *you*."

"Is it?" I ask, staring at the photo. It was only two weeks ago, but I already feel like a completely different person.

Sue rests her elbows on her knees, forcing me to meet her eyes. "Yes, it is. And she's in there all year long. I promise. You just have to find a way to pull her out."

by your side

On Thursday morning after first bell, I linger, taking my time at my locker. I keep peering toward the end of the row, looking for Caroline, but she hasn't shown up. I haven't seen her once since we sat together in the theater on Monday. Finally, I give up and race to class.

The last few days have been brutal, with Caroline's words running through my head in an endless loop. I can't imagine what she wants to show me today or how it could possibly change my whole life. And if she's *right* about me? What does that even mean?

Lunch can't come soon enough. As soon as the fourth period bell sounds, I stand up and race past the rest of my U.S. History classmates, bolting for the door. Everyone heads for the cafeteria and the quad, but I take off in the opposite direction.

When I arrive at the double doors that lead into the theater, I take a quick look around. Then I slip inside and go straight to the piano, hiding from view like Caroline told me to.

I keep checking the time on my phone, and I'm starting to wonder if this is all a joke, when I hear voices, quiet but audible, coming toward me. I'm tempted to take a step forward so I can get a look at their faces, but I press my back flat against the curtain and tell myself not to move.

The voices fade away and Caroline pokes her head around the curtain, curls her finger toward herself, and whispers, "Follow me."

"Where are we going?" I ask, and she brings her finger to her lips, shushing me. We disappear backstage, and about twenty feet away, I see a door closing. We wait for it to shut completely, and then we creep forward.

"Open it," she says, and then adds the word "quietly." She rests her hands on her hips and I read her T-shirt: EVERYONE HATES ME BECAUSE I'M PARANOID.

I turn the knob as gently as I can, and soon I'm staring at a steep, narrow staircase. My first instinct is to close the door and turn back the way we came. I shoot Caroline a questioning look and she gestures toward the stairs. "Go ahead. Go down."

"Down?"

She raises an eyebrow. "Well they don't go up, now do they?"

No. They don't.

"Here," she says. "I'll go first." And before I can say another word, she pushes past me and starts down the stairs, and because I can't imagine doing anything else at this point, I close the door behind us and follow her.

The narrow hallway is painted dark gray, and I look up at the ceiling lights, wondering why they're so dim. Caroline and I turn down another hallway just in time to see the door at the far end swinging shut. I stay on her heels until we're standing in front of it.

This is beyond creepy. "What is this place?"

She ignores my question and points to the doorknob. "Okay, I'm going to be by your side the entire time, but this is all up to you from here. You have to do all the talking."

"Talking? To whom? What do you mean, it's up to me?"

"You'll see."

I don't want to see. I want to leave. Now.

"This is bizarre, Caroline. There's no one down here." I try not to look like I'm rattled, but I am. And I can't imagine how anything in a freaky basement underneath the school theater could possibly change my life. My mind's operating on overload now, my thoughts racing, and I feel a panic attack coming on.

What was I thinking? I don't even know her.

I turn away and start heading back the way I came.

"Sam," she says, and I stop, just like that. Caroline grips my forearm and looks right into my eyes. "Please, check it out."

There's something about the look on her face that makes

me want to trust her, like I've known her all my life. And as nervous as I am, I'm even more curious to see what's on the other side of that door.

"Fine," I say, clenching my teeth. I reach for the knob and turn.

The room on the other side is small and painted completely black. Black ceiling. Black floor. Metal shelving units stocked with cleaning supplies line three of the walls, and the other one is covered with hanging mops and brooms.

Caroline points to a section of mop heads gently swaying back and forth against the wall, as if they'd recently been touched. I pull them to one side, exposing a seam that runs all the way up the wall until it meets another one at the top. It's a door. The hinges are painted black and so is the dead bolt, camouflaging everything perfectly.

"Knock," Caroline commands from behind me. I do what I'm told without questioning or arguing or second-guessing.

First there's a click, and then the door swings toward me and I see a pair of eyes in the narrow opening. "Who are you?" a girl's voice whispers.

I glance over at Caroline, but she just gives me this *Say something!* look, so I return to the girl in the doorway.

"I'm Samantha." I hold my hand up. "I mean, Sam." Why not, I figure, as long as I'm making introductions and all. "I was hoping I could come in."

She looks past me, over my shoulder, and Caroline whispers, "She's with me."

The girl makes a face but pushes the door open anyway, giving us enough room to step inside. Then she scans the janitor's closet, like she's checking to be sure the two of us are alone, and I hear the dead bolt snap closed again.

I don't even have time to take in the surroundings because now there's a guy standing in front of me. He's tall and thin, with broad shoulders and a headful of sandy blond hair. He looks a little bit familiar, and I'm still trying to place him when he narrows his eyes at me and says, "What are you doing here?"

I look at Caroline for help again, but she runs her finger across her lips like she's zipping them shut, and I kind of want to punch her right now.

"I'm Sam—" I begin, but he cuts me off.

"I know who you are, Samantha." I study his face again. He knows my name. I don't know his.

"I'm sorry." I'm not really sure why I'm apologizing, but it seems like the right thing to do. I step backward toward the door, feeling for a knob, but there isn't one.

The girl who let me in hands him a thick braided cord and he slips it over his head. A gold key bounces against his chest.

"How did you find this room?"

"My friend . . ." I say, gesturing toward Caroline. He glances over at her and she nods at him. He quickly returns his attention to me.

"Your friend what?"

Caroline's made it pretty clear that she isn't going to do

anything to help me at this point, but that doesn't mean her words can't get me the rest of the way into the room. "I heard that this place might change my life, and, well . . . I guess my life could use some serious changing, so I thought . . ." I trail off, watching him, waiting for his face to relax, but it doesn't.

He stares at me for what feels like a full minute. I stare back, refusing to give in. Caroline must be getting worried, because she wraps both hands around my arm and pulls herself in closer, showing him she's on my side. He crosses his arms and never takes his eyes off me.

"Fine," he says. "You can stay today, this one time, but that's it. After this, you have to forget all about this place, got it? One time, Samantha."

"Got it," I say. Then I add, "And it's Sam."

His forehead creases. "Fine. But it's not like this makes us friends or anything."

Friends? My friends don't call me Sam. "Why would I think we're friends? I don't even know you."

He smiles, revealing a dimple on the left side of his mouth. "No," he says, as if it's funny. "Of course you don't know me." He walks away, shaking his head, leaving Caroline and me standing alone at the back of the room.

"What the hell was that?" I ask her. My voice is even more wobbly than it was a few minutes ago.

She gives me a supportive nudge with her elbow. "Don't worry about it. You did great."

Now that he's no longer blocking my view, I can see where

I am. The room is long and narrow and, like the janitor's closet, painted entirely in black. But the ceilings are twice as high, and even though it's dark, it's not claustrophobic at all. At the front of the room, I see a low riser that appears to be a makeshift stage. Smack in the center, there's a wooden stool.

I count five other people in the room. They're sitting on small couches and oversize chairs facing the stage and set at a slight angle, each one covered in different material—blue crushed velvet, brown leather, red and gray checks—and completely unique. Low bookcases line the room, and small mismatched lamps are spaced evenly around the perimeter. I nervously wonder what would happen if the power went out.

Then I see the walls.

I spin a slow 360 in place, taking it all in. All four walls are covered with scraps of paper in different colors and shapes and textures, all jutting out at various angles. Lined paper ripped from spiral-bound notebooks. Plain paper, three-hole punched. Graph paper, torn at the edges. Pages that have yellowed with age, along with napkins and Post-its and brown paper lunch bags and even a few candy wrappers.

Caroline's watching me, and I take a few cautious steps closer to get a better look. I reach for one of the pages, running the corner between my thumb and forefinger, and that's when I notice handwriting on each one, as distinctive as the paper itself. Loopy, flowing cursive. Tight, angular letters. Precise, blocky printing.

Wow.

I don't think I've ever experienced this sensation outside the pool, but I feel it now, deep in my bones. My shoulders drop. My heart's no longer racing. I can't see a toxic, negative thought for miles.

"What is this place?" I whisper to Caroline, but before she can say anything, the girl I met at the door comes out of nowhere and grabs my arm. She has dark hair and a pixie cut, and now she's bouncing in place like this is the most exciting thing that's happened to her in a long time.

"Come sit with me. There's an open spot on the couch in front." She starts leading me toward this atrocious green-and-pink-plaid sofa in the first row. "How long have you been writing?"

For what feels like the one-hundredth time today, my head spins toward Caroline. She's got a weird grin on her face. "Writing?"

"Don't worry," Pixie Cut says. She tightens her grip on my arm and pulls me closer. "I'm the newest one here and I totally remember my first time. Don't be afraid. You're only here to listen."

She plops down on one end of the couch and pats the cushion on her right. "Sit." I do as I'm told. "Well, you definitely picked a good day," she says. "Sydney's going first and AJ's up after her."

Caroline settles in on my other side. I look to her for clues, and again she gives me nothing.

Everyone gets quiet as a heavyset girl I assume to be Sydney climbs up to the stage and bumps the stool with her hip, scooting it to the side. Wait. I know her. She's in my U.S. History class.

I'd never seen her before this week, but on the first day of school, she strolled into class wearing a black strappy dress with bright red cherries all over it. It looked vintage. But it wasn't her outfit or her confidence that caught my attention. It was her hair. Long, thick, and bright red, like Cassidy's. I'd already been thinking about her all day, wishing the two of us were at the pool instead, and seeing that hair made me miss her even more.

Sydney holds up the top of a Chicken McNuggets container. "I wrote this last night at . . ." She flips the paper around to show us the McDonald's arches and bounces her hand up and down, nodding proudly. "The lid wasn't as greasy this time, so I got an entire poem in," she says, and everyone laughs at what I presume to be an inside joke.

"I call this one *Neujay*." She turns the paper around again and runs her fingertip across the word "Nuggets," and then clears her throat dramatically.

ENTRY
My teeth pierce your bumpy flesh.
Oil, sweet, slipping over my tongue
Sliding down my throat.

DECISIONS

Barbecue or sweet and sour?

Mustard or honey?

I close my eyes

Let fate decide.

Tip, dip, lift

Barbecue.

STUDY

Golden. Shining under fluorescents.

Piled. Grazing each other's edges.

Patient. Always patient.

ADMIRATION

Gold, pink.

Crispy, salty.

What the hell are you made of?

Everyone stands, clapping and cheering, and Sydney holds
her skirt to one side and curtsies. Then she throws her arms up
in the air and her head back and yells, "Yes! Stick me!"

Some guy on the other couch tosses a glue stick at her. She
catches it in the air, removes the cap, and, using the stool as a
table, runs the glue back and forth across the McDonald's logo.

She steps off the stage and I think she's walking toward me,
but she passes our couch and stops at the wall. We all watch as

she smacks what's left of the Chicken McNuggets lid against it. Brushing her hands together, she settles into a spot on the couch behind me and our eyes meet. She smiles at me. I smile back. I don't think I've ever heard her speak until now.

When I turn around again, the guy who let me inside is taking the stage. He perches himself on the stool and picks up the acoustic guitar that's strapped over his shoulder.

How do I know him?

I follow the string around his neck, and picture that gold key hiding behind his guitar.

"I wrote this last weekend in my room. And, okay, I'm sayin' it." He pauses for dramatic effect. "This one sucks."

He stands up, holds his hands in front of him, and lets the guitar fall slack so the strap catches it. He's gesturing toward himself in this go-ahead-let-me-have-it kind of way, and everyone around me starts ripping papers out of notebooks, balling them up, and chucking them at him. He laughs and keeps gesturing with his hands, silently telling them to keep it coming.

I look over at Caroline. She won't make eye contact with me, so I lightly elbow pixie-cut girl. "Why are they doing that?" I ask, and she comes in close to my ear. "It's one of the rules. You can't criticize anyone's poetry, but especially not your own."

He perches himself on the stool and picks up his guitar again, and the second he does, the paper stops flying. He starts plucking the strings, and this melody fills the room. He's only playing a few notes, but they sound so pretty together this way, over and over again. And then he starts singing.

> So long, Lazy Ray.
> Were you a crack you'd be tempting to look through.
> Were you my coat on a cold day,
> You'd lose track of the ways you were worn.
> And it's true.
> I haven't got a clue.
> How to love you.

He's not looking at any of us. He's just staring down at the guitar, picking at the strings. He sings two more verses, and his voice rises higher, louder when he reaches the chorus. After another verse, the tempo slows, and I can tell the song is winding down.

> Like sunlight dancing on my skin,
> You'll still be in my mind.
> So I'm only gonna say,
> So long, Lazy Ray.

The last note lingers in the silence. Everyone remained quiet for a second or two, but now they're on their feet, clapping and cheering and tossing more paper balls at his head as he swats them away. Then they start pelting him with glue sticks.

He manages to catch one as it bounces off the wall behind him, and then he does that musician thing, slipping his guitar around his back in one fluid motion. He's shaking his head as if he's embarrassed by the attention, and pulls a piece of paper out of the back pocket of his jeans. He unfolds it, flattens it against the stool, and rubs glue along the back before he steps down from the stage.

He walks to the other side of the room and, still clutching the paper, bows once. Then he reaches up high on the wall, smacking his words against it.

I'm trying to figure out if everyone else is as taken aback as I am, but they don't seem to be. Didn't anyone else think that was amazing? Because while all of them are clearly enjoying this moment, none of them look quite as surprised as I am, and I'm pretty sure their arms aren't covered in goose bumps like mine are. They all look relatively unfazed.

Except Caroline.

She's grinning ear to ear, and as we take our seats again, she threads her arm through mine and rests her chin on my shoulder. "I knew it," she says. "I was right about you."

As I scan the room, taking in the slips of paper scattered around me, I think I catch Caroline and pixie-cut girl look at each other. "What is this place?" I ask again, hearing the amazement in my own voice.

Pixie Cut answers me. "We call it Poet's Corner."

an overwhelming urge

T he next day, I see them in the places they must have
been all along.

When I walk into U.S. History, Sydney spots me
right away and the two of us exchange knowing glances. Later
that day, as I'm heading to lunch, I pass Pixie Cut and overhear
her friend call her Abigail. I recognize a girl in the student
parking lot and another in the library. Each time I make eye
contact with any of them, I get a hint of a smile, like we're still
separated by an invisible barrier, but now we have something in
common: a secret. By the end of the day, I've seen all but one.

I'm heading to my car when I look up and finally see AJ
heading straight for me, and I feel the corners of my mouth
twitching into a nervous grin. I'm expecting the same reaction
I got from the others. A sly wave. A chin tilt. But instead he

passes right by me, his eyes fixed on the ground in front of him. When I'm a safe distance away, I stop and turn around, watching until he disappears from sight.

I'm trying to decide what to do when Alexis appears out of nowhere, her high heels tapping on the cement and her thumbs tapping on her cell phone.

"There you are!" She stuffs her phone in the back pocket of her jeans. "I was hoping to catch you. I just got the best news!" She pulls me close. "There was a cancellation at the spa. My mom was able to book another appointment."

I look at her sideways.

"Don't you get it?" The words squeak out and she does a little dance in place, shaking my arm around as she bounces and beams and watches me, like she's expecting me to join in. "You can come."

"What about Hailey?"

She purses her lips and looks around, checking to be sure we're alone. "No . . ." she draws the single word out, like it's a musical note. "Not Hailey. You." She pokes my collarbone. And now I know precisely where I reside on her social ladder: second rung from the bottom. Hailey occupies the last one, and as soon as she learns I'm invited to Alexis's birthday and she's not, she'll know it too.

"You have no idea how sad I've been, Samantha. I felt horrible not asking you. Even though our moms weren't friends in preschool, you and I were *best* friends in kindergarten!" I take note of her word choice. I'm not her best friend now, but I was in kindergarten. "I'm glad you're coming. Oh, and plan to spend the night, too."

"Is Hailey spending the night?" I ask. The spa might not be able to accommodate all five of us, but Alexis's enormous bedroom doesn't have any space constraints.

"That would be awkward, don't you think?" I think it would be better than nothing, but I don't say so. "In fact, keep it to yourself, okay? I wouldn't want to hurt Hailey's feelings."

No. Of course you wouldn't.

I unwind my arm from her grasp. "I've got to get to swim practice," I say.

Her face falls, but she quickly recovers, twisting her mouth into a fake grin, raising her voice a full octave. "Yeah, of course. Nine o'clock tomorrow. We'll pick you up."

She takes off in the opposite direction. Part of me still feels guilty about Hailey, but another part of me is excited to spend the day with my friends, getting pampered at a luxurious spa. It will be fun. And it's nice to not be the fifth wheel for once.

I'm on the diving block, staring into lane three, running my thumb across the scratchy surface three times, waiting for the whistle to blow.

When it does, my body responds just like it's supposed to. My knees bend and my arms stretch, and my fingers cut through the water's surface in the seconds before I feel it drench my cheeks. Then the silence.

I kick hard underwater and try to lock in my song, but

nothing comes. As I pop up and start the fly, my strokes feel sloppy, uneven, and by the time I turn and kick off the wall, I'm at least four strokes behind everyone else. I climb out of the pool and get in the back of the line.

Jackson Roth looks over his shoulder at me. "Coach is in a mood today, isn't he?"

"I guess."

We're down to a small group of swimmers now that school's started. The numbers will keep dwindling as fall's extracurricular activities begin, homework picks up, and it becomes harder to squeeze in team workouts at the club. I'm looking forward to that. I prefer to come here at night, swimming under the stars with the adults. They keep to themselves.

I press my fingertips hard into my temples, ignoring everyone around me, while I breathe and try to focus my energy. When it's my turn, I step onto the blocks again, slide my thumb along the surface three times, and dive in, waiting for a song— any song—to come.

And one finally does, but it's not one I expect. Those notes AJ played the other day start running through my head, and as soon as I surface, I know what song will be taking me back and forth across the pool. I speed up the tempo, and my body follows suit until I'm flying through the lane, pushing hard off the wall, throwing my arms over my head, feeling that adrenaline surge every time I lift my chest out of the water.

The tune is clear in my head, but now I want to remember the lyrics and I can't. *Lazy ray* . . . I think he was singing about the sun going down. There was a line about sunlight dancing on your skin and another about a crack in a fence or something.

What was that line?

I'm still trying to piece it together as I step into the shower to rinse off the chlorine. I'm alone in the locker room, so I start humming as I pull on my sweats and pile my hair into a messy bun. On the drive home, I leave the stereo off because I prefer his song over anything I have on a playlist. And I have to remember all the lyrics. It's driving me nuts.

It's easy to stay lost in my thoughts during dinner. Paige got sent to the principal's office today for talking back to a teacher, so she has my parents' undivided attention. My family is arguing over the distinction between "clarifying questions" and "back talk," while I drift off to a better place.

I'm picturing that room and its walls, covered in torn notebook pages and ripped-up napkins, pieces of brown paper lunch sacks and fast-food wrappers, and how all that chaos and disorder gave me such a strange sort of peace. I can visualize the exact spot AJ slapped up those words. But that's all I have. I can't download the song and listen to it on repeat, looking up the lyrics online and deciphering them like I typically would.

I have to get back down to that room.

I'm starting to recognize this for the obsession that it is, but it doesn't bother me. It's innocent, like solving a puzzle. My mind has certainly come up with more dangerous fixations.

"Are you okay, Sam?" Mom asks.

Her voice snaps me back to reality, and when I look up

from my plate, Mom, Dad, and Paige are all staring at me. Dad has a huge grin on his face.

"What?"

"You were singing," he says.

"And humming," Mom adds.

I was?

"Earworm," I say. "This song has been stuck in my head all day."

"It was really pretty," Paige says.

Under the table where no one can see me, I scratch my jeans three times. "Yes, it was."

I'm about to pop a sleeping pill when completely different words start forming in my mind. I feel an overwhelming urge to write them down.

I haven't thought about the notebooks in years, but they're still on the top shelf of my bookcase, and I remember exactly what Shrink-Sue said when she gave them to me. I was to write every day, in the notebook that best matched how I was feeling: the yellow notebook was for happy thoughts. The red notebook was for when I was angry and needed to vent. The blue one was for when I was feeling good. Peaceful. Not happy, not angry. Neutral. Somewhere in the middle.

I open the blue notebook first and see handwriting that belonged to a much younger me. I'd clearly followed Sue's advice for a while, but about a quarter of the way into the book, the entries end.

The red book is filled with thoughts written with a heavier hand. My penmanship is different, but I don't know if that's because I was older or angrier. I read a few lines but stop quickly. It's depressing.

But not as depressing as seeing that the yellow notebook is completely empty.

Tossing the red and yellow ones on the floor, I crawl under the covers with the blue one. Pen in hand, I flip to the first blank page, but nothing's happening.

I don't know what to write about.

I could write about my OCD. Or the number three. Or uncontrollable thought spirals that come out of nowhere, demand my undivided attention, and scare me when they won't stop. Or how I'm terrified about Alexis's birthday tomorrow and it doesn't seem right to be afraid to spend the day with your best friends.

Poets need words. Even when I have the right ones, I can never seem to spit them out. Words only seem to serve me when I'm in the pool.

The pool.

I put pen to paper, and off I go, writing about the one thing that makes me feel healthy and happy and . . . *normal*. Cutting through the surface. Hearing the *whoosh* and the silence. Pushing off that cement wall with both feet, feeling powerful and invincible. Loving how the water feels as it slips over my cheeks.

Two hours later, I'm still going, still writing fast, still turning pages. When I get to the end of the next page I check the clock and realize two things: it's after midnight and I forgot to take my sleep meds.

Normally, that would worry me, but it doesn't tonight. I'm too elated to sleep.

I return to writing, filling my blue notebook, until I finally drift off on my own, somewhere around three a.m.

let me hear

*W*e're all singing along with the music as we pull into the spa entrance, but then Alexis's mom turns the stereo off and we all fall silent, looking around, taking everything in.

The long driveway is lined with lush green trees and pale pink rosebushes, and as the car winds up a steep hill and past a vineyard, I roll down the window and breathe in the scents of freshly cut grass and sweet-smelling lavender.

"Wow," Olivia says from the backseat.

"No kidding," Kaitlyn adds.

"I told you," Alexis says.

I turn to Mrs. Mazeur. "This is incredible. Thank you."

"You're going to love this," she tells me.

Hailey would have loved this, too.

We pull up to a circular driveway with an enormous fountain in the center. It must have a gravitational pull because I start walking toward it, and then I stand there, staring at the water cascading over the edge, listening to the thick droplets land with soothing plinks into the pond below. I close my eyes and let my mouth turn up at the corners the way it wants to.

"Come here, girls!" Mrs. Mazeur is standing at the back of the car, and we all gather around her. "I have a surprise." She pops the trunk, reaches inside, and pulls out a bright green terry cloth bag with Alexis's name embroidered in white. "One for you, birthday girl."

As she reaches into the trunk again, Alexis unzips the bag and sifts through the contents, pulling out body lotion and cuticle cream and facial scrub.

"And one for you," she says, handing Olivia the same personalized bag in red, her favorite color. "Of course purple for you, Kaitlyn," she says.

Mine will be blue.

She closes the trunk and wraps her arm around my shoulders. "I'm sorry, Samantha. I tried to order another one yesterday, but it was too late."

"That's okay." I feel my lower lip start to quiver, so I bite it hard.

"But I have something extra special for you. I want you to pick out anything you want from the gift shop, okay? And I mean *anything.*"

She squeezes my shoulder and takes off, dramatically

gesturing toward the entrance. "Okay, follow me, everyone."

Breathe. Breathe. Breathe.

Inside, the spa smells clean, like cucumbers and mint, and I'm relieved to see another fountain in the corner. I stand next to it and scratch the back of my neck three times, until a woman at the front desk calls us over, gives each of us a fluffy white robe, and assigns us a locker.

I change quickly, text Mom to tell her everything's going well, and join everyone in the waiting area. We're sipping cucumber water and whispering about how incredible this place is, when I hear my name.

Alexis waves at me. "Have fun."

The aesthetician leads me to a room with peaceful, Zen-like music and reclines my chair. "I have you booked for our signature antiaging facial," she says in a soft voice. "All you have to do is relax and close your eyes. Tell me if you need anything."

I'm not sure how to tell her I'm sixteen and don't need an antiaging facial, so I stay quiet, even when she starts chattering about the harmful effects of the sun. Eventually, I stop fixating on the mistake and let my thoughts drift back to one of the poems I wrote last night. I repeat it in my mind, over and over again, until my ninety minutes are up.

As we're all dressing in the locker room, Alexis's mom announces that we're late for lunch and we need to hurry. A few minutes later, we're in the car, winding back down the long driveway and heading into town.

The five of us troop single file along a narrow brick walkway and up a short staircase to the restaurant. "I knew this place was really popular, but this . . ." Mrs. Mazeur looks overwhelmed as she scans the packed café.

While we wait for her to get our table, Olivia reaches into her bag and removes her new lotion and passes it around so we can all try it. Alexis can't stop buzzing about the new convertible she thinks will be waiting in the driveway when we get back to her house.

A few minutes later, the hostess tells us to follow her. She stops at a tiny table with three chairs squeezed around it.

"There are five of us," Alexis's mom says.

"The reservation is for two tables, ma'am."

"And the person I spoke with yesterday assured me the tables would be together." The hostess shifts the stack of menus from one arm to the other, and her eyes dart nervously around the room. "It's okay," Mrs. Mazeur says. "If you could add another chair to this table, I'll sit alone at the other one."

"I'm sorry, ma'am, but I can't do that. Fire code."

No one says anything, but after a few uncomfortable seconds, I feel Mrs. Mazeur thread her arm through mine. "Want to keep me company?"

"Sure." I bite the inside of my lip three times. Alexis doesn't seem to know what to say.

"We're ordering two desserts. Each," she says to the group, and when the hostess steps in front of us, we follow her to the next table.

One. Breathe.
Two. Breathe.
Three. Breathe.

The two of us make small talk for the next twenty minutes while I try not to stare at my friends laughing and chatting and waving sympathetically at me from the other side of the room. When my salad arrives, I awkwardly pick at it. Finally, I excuse myself to go to the restroom and hide behind a potted plant out of view, holding back tears as I text Mom, telling her about my not-so-perfect spa day. She must sense the panic in my words, because after a bunch of texts telling me it's not so bad, she says:

Come home.

Then she follows with back-to-back messages:

We'll be out when you get here.
I love you.
You're in control.
Take deep breaths.

I'm in control.
I take some deep breaths and return to my salad.

The car pulls into my driveway and I can't get out fast enough.
She never wanted me to come.

Alexis tells me she hopes I feel better. Kaitlyn and Olivia echo her words, yelling out the window as they drive away.

"We'll miss you tonight," Kaitlyn says.

No you won't.

"We love you," Olivia adds.

No you don't.

As soon as I close the front door behind me, the tears start falling and the thoughts flood in faster and faster, tumbling over each other, pushing themselves to the front, fighting for my attention.

I shouldn't have gone.

The sun is setting and it's dark and quiet in the entryway. I slide down to the floor and wrap my arms around my knees, letting myself cry, allowing the thoughts to come as fast as they want to. The surrender feels good in a weird way.

The knock on the door makes me jump.

"Just a minute," I yell, dashing into the hall bathroom to check my face. The mascara I carefully applied at the spa is everywhere *but* my eyelashes, and my whole face is bright red and puffy. I clean up as fast as I can and look through the peephole.

Caroline?

"What are you doing here?" I ask as I open the door, and immediately regret my words.

Caroline's face falls and she takes two steps backward. "You invited me over," she says, flustered. "To watch a movie. Remember?"

Oh, no.

"It is Saturday night, isn't it?" The lilt in her voice sounds a little forced. She gives her flannel shirtsleeve a tug and checks the time on that beat-up watch of hers. "You didn't tell me when to come by, so I took a chance." She narrows her eyes, studying my face. "Hey, what's wrong? Are you okay?"

Now that I think about it, I *am* okay. The thoughts are actually gone, and as far as I can tell, they're not quietly waiting in the wings, whispering and preparing to pounce again. They're completely gone.

"Yeah." I pull the door open so she has room to step inside, and I voice the only thought in my head. "I'm really glad you're here."

She obviously knows that I forgot all about our plans, but she doesn't call me on it, so I don't say anything either. To break the tension, I ask her if she wants some water, but she says she's not thirsty. I ask her if she wants some ice cream, but she says she's not hungry. It seems a little too early to start a movie, so I ask her if she wants to come upstairs to hang out in my room and listen to music. She doesn't answer, but I start walking toward the stairs and she follows me.

My room's a mess. I scurry around, scooping up piles of clothes and stuffing them into the laundry hamper.

"I thought people with OCD were supposed to be neat," she says.

"Popular misconception," I say as I kick all the textbooks strewn across the floor into a haphazard pile.

"You don't have to clean up for me, you know. You should see my room. It's a disaster. Stuff everywhere." I ignore her and keep picking things up.

Caroline walks around my room, looking at the pictures on my walls. She stops in front of the collage I made in eighth grade. THE CRAZY 8S is written across the top in hot pink, bubbly letters, and pictures spanning more than a decade are clustered below.

"Wow. You've known your friends for a long time," Caroline says as I'm docking my phone. I start my *In the Deep* playlist. My nerves are still a little rattled.

I walk over and join her. She gestures to the poster. "Do you want to tell me what happened today?" she says, as if she knows my red eyes and puffy face had something to do with my friends.

"How do you know something happened?"

"I have a knack for reading people," she says casually. "Here, look into my eyes and think of a number. Not *three*." I look at her funny but fix my eyes on hers and think about the number nine. Caroline stares back. And then a huge smile forms across her face. "I'm just messing with you. I was only two houses away when your friend's mom pulled into your driveway."

I feel like an idiot. Caroline laughs and takes a couple of steps backward until she reaches my bed. She drops back on my comforter and rests her weight on her hands, legs crossed in front of her. I read her T-shirt: FREE SHRUGS.

"So what happened today?"

She looks like she genuinely wants to hear the story. And I definitely want to talk about it. If Mom were here, we'd be downstairs on the couch eating ice cream straight out of the carton while I spilled every detail. I flop down on the opposite side of the bed, mimicking Caroline's pose.

"Today was Alexis's birthday."

"Alexis? The little Barbie one? Wears high heels, like, every day?" I nod. It's funny to hear how other people see her.

Then I fill her in on the details of the spa day I wasn't originally invited to. I tell her about the drive and the sound of the fountain and the smell of flowers on the breeze, but when I get to the part about the personalized bags, my chest feels tight. I pull at a loose thread on the pant leg of my jeans.

"It's dumb, right? I shouldn't be upset. It was last minute . . ." I let my words hang in the air as I check Caroline's reaction. She doesn't say anything, but her face scrunches up and I can tell she doesn't think I'm dumb at all.

"Her mom obviously felt bad," I continue. "She said I could pick anything I wanted from the gift shop."

"I hope you picked something ridiculously expensive."

I shake my head. "After our appointments were finished, we were running late and she rushed us off to lunch."

Caroline bites her lip.

"But, hey, on the bright side, look at my skin." I lean in a little closer. "Don't I look ten years younger?"

She leans in too. "You're asking me if you look like you're six?" I laugh, and Caroline joins in. "I hope lunch was better."

"Worse."

She stops laughing. "How is that possible?"

"When her mom called the restaurant to change the reservation from four people to five, they told her we had to be at separate tables. I guess she assumed they'd push them together or something."

"No."

"Yep. It was a French restaurant with these tiny café tables—"

"Wait, so you sat with your friend's mom while everyone else sat together at another table?" I'm glad I didn't have to say it out loud. I have a feeling it still wouldn't be funny.

I cross my arms. I faked a headache to come home early, but now I feel a real one coming on with the retelling. "I'm overreacting, right?"

As I wait for her response, I study her eyes. They're narrow and hooded, but I'm no longer trying to figure out how to apply eye shadow to open them up. They're pretty the way they are. Her hair doesn't seem so stringy either, and I'm not dying to cover up her blemishes. I'm just happy she's here.

"You're not overreacting," she says.

"Are you sure? Because you can tell me if I am. I have a tendency to overthink things, especially when it comes to my friends, and I don't know . . . I take things too personally. I mean, it isn't always *them*. Sometimes it's me. I just don't always know when it's them and when it's me, you know?"

I'm not sure if that made sense, but Caroline's looking at

me like she understood it perfectly. It's like I can read her mind right now. She doesn't like that my friends hurt my feelings, intentionally or not. Whether it's them or me, she doesn't understand why I'd choose to hang around with people I'm constantly questioning. And she's sad for me, because my closest friends don't feel all that close anymore, not like they did when we were those kids on that poster hanging on my wall.

I picture the people I saw in Poet's Corner that day. "You don't ever wonder what your friends think about you, do you?"

Caroline doesn't answer, but she doesn't have to. I can tell I'm right by the look on her face.

"You're lucky," I say.

I stare down at my feet, thinking about how I spent last night tucked down in my bed with a flashlight, writing horrible poetry into the early morning hours, waking up feeling drained but euphoric at the same time. I've been thinking about those poems all day. I couldn't wait to get home to write again.

When I look up, I find Caroline staring at me.

"What?" I ask.

A cautious smile spreads across her lips. "Let me hear one."

I look at her like I have no idea what she's talking about, but I'm pretty sure I do. "One what?" I can hear the anxiety in my own voice.

"A poem."

How does she know I've been writing poetry?

"Read me something from the blue notebook."

My head snaps up and my jaw drops.

How does she know about the colors?

She points over at my nightstand, and I twist in place, my eyes following the invisible line that leads from her fingertip to the stack of three notebooks—red, yellow, and blue—piled underneath the lamp.

"You're writing, aren't you?" she asks.

I don't answer her directly, but I don't have to. She can probably tell she's right by the panicked look on my face. I can't read my poetry to her. I can't read it to anyone. Shrink-Sue told me I didn't have to share anything I wrote in those books. I wouldn't have written it if I thought otherwise.

"Is it really dark?" she continues. "It's okay if it is. My stuff can get pretty dark, too."

"No, it's not dark; it's . . . stupid."

"My stuff can get pretty stupid, too. I won't make fun of you, I promise."

"I can't."

"Read me your favorite. Don't think about it, just go. Read."

I laugh. "You're telling me to *not* think. All I do is think. All the time. I think so much, I'm on medication and I see a shrink every Wednesday. I can't *not* think, Caroline."

"Sam."

"What?"

"Go."

I have the perfect one in mind. It's short. I can read it without throwing up. Besides, I kind of like it. And I don't even need my blue notebook because these words have been stuck in my head all day, during my ridiculous facial and in the car after we left the spa and during lunch. They joined the mantras. They kept the destructive thoughts from invading.

I sit up again. My hands are shaking, so I tuck them under my legs as I take a deep breath, close my eyes, and say, "It's called 'The Drop.'"

> Standing on the platform.
> Sun sinking into my skin.
> This water will cover me like a blanket.
> And I'll be safe again.

She doesn't laugh, but the room is completely silent. I open my eyes and look at her, waiting for a reaction.

She hated it.

"We have to get you back downstairs," Caroline finally says, and I can hear the sincerity in her voice, can see it in her face.

She liked it.

I stare at her, wondering if she's too good to be true. Where did she come from? Why is she being so nice to me?

"That'll never happen," I tell her plainly. "That 'keymaster' guy hates me. He won't even look at me."

I picture him on that stool and his song starts playing in my head. I think about the words and where they live on that wall. If I could get back downstairs, I could find his lyrics. I'll commit them to memory next time.

"That's just AJ," she says, giving a dismissive shake of her head. "And he doesn't hate you. But you hurt him, and he doesn't know how to handle that."

"What?" My thoughts stop cold. "*Hurt* him? What are you talking about?"

She looks right at me but doesn't say a word.

"Caroline. How did I hurt him? I don't even *know* him."

"Yes, you do."

I remember how he stood in front of me, blocking my way into Poet's Corner the other day. He looked familiar, but I've never known anyone named AJ, and he's cute enough, especially with that dimple and that adorable guitar-playing thing of his, that I would have remembered him if we'd met before.

"Are you going to tell me?"

She shakes her head. "You'll figure it out."

I stare at her in disbelief. "I don't want to figure it out, Caroline. I want you to tell me." That might have sounded bitchy. I didn't mean it to, but I can't believe she's holding out on me.

She checks her watch. "I have to go." She hops off the bed and starts walking toward the door.

"What about the movie?"

"Maybe another time," she says as she reaches for the doorknob.

My mind is leaping around from thought to thought, like it can't settle on one.

I hurt him. And Caroline's leaving. But she likes my poem. I like talking to her. I don't want her to leave.

"It's okay," I say. "You don't have to tell me. Please . . . stay."

It's killing me not to know what I did, but there are plenty of other things I want to talk to her about. I want to ask her about all the poets. I want to know about that room and how it got there and how it works, and I want her to read me some of *her* poems. I want to be her friend.

She turns around and looks at me. I hurry over to my night-stand, grab the blue notebook from the pile, and hold it up in the air. "I want to get back to Poet's Corner, but I don't know how to. Will you help me?"

we fixed him

Mom's buttering toast for Paige, drinking her coffee, and replying to a message on her cell phone, when she says, "Do you want to talk about what happened yesterday?"

"Nah. I'm good." I down my orange juice. "I talked to my friend Caroline last night."

Mom's typing again. "Who's Caroline?" she asks without looking up.

"Just someone I met at school. She's nice. She came over after I got home from the spa."

Now I have her attention.

"Really?" Her eyes grow wide.

I try to act nonchalant about the whole thing, like this happens all the time, but then I picture Caroline sitting on the floor in my room, helping me with my poetry, and I feel a little bit giddy. "Yeah, I would have introduced you, but she had to leave before you guys got home."

"Have you told Sue about her?"

"Yep." I grab the toast with one hand and punch Paige lightly on the arm with the other. "I'm going to the pool."

The next day, Olivia and I are walking to Trigonometry when I see AJ heading right for us. I almost didn't notice him—I probably wouldn't have if the dark ski hat hadn't caught my eye—because he's looking down at the ground and keeping pace with everyone else. He walks right by me.

Caroline's words have haunted me since Saturday night: "He doesn't hate you, but you hurt him." I can't figure out what I did, and somewhere around two thirty this morning, I decided I was going to find out the first chance I got.

"I left my trig book in my locker," I say to Olivia. "I'll meet you at class."

She waves me off and I do a 180 and start following the ski cap heading in the opposite direction. AJ turns the corner and stops at a locker. Keeping my distance, I watch as he rests his backpack on one knee and swaps out his books.

When he sees me, he tilts his chin in my direction. "Hey." No smile. No wave. Just the chin tilt. He swings his locker door closed.

"Hi." I gesture toward the main corridor. "I saw you in the hall, but . . . I guess you didn't see me."

He shakes his head.

"I wanted to say hello." I dig my fingernails into the back of my neck. *One, two, three. One, two, three. One, two, three.* "And, you know, say thank you . . . for letting me join you guys last week."

AJ checks the area around us and steps in closer. He's a full head taller than me, and when he tucks his chin to his chest and stares down at me, I feel guilty, even though I haven't done anything wrong. His eyebrows lift accusingly. "You haven't told anyone, have you?"

"Of course not. I wouldn't do that."

He's still close. He's still staring at me like he's trying to decide if I'm telling the truth. I square my shoulders and straighten my spine. "I told you I wouldn't, and I haven't."

"Good," he says. Another long pause. "Don't."

"I won't."

He steps out of my personal space and I have a chance to look at him. Really look at him. His dark blond hair is poking out from under the cap, and his eyes are this interesting brownish-green that's almost the same color as the T-shirt he's wearing. He's not clean-cut, like most of my guy friends. He's scruffier, but in a sexy way. I try to read the expression on his face, but I can't, and it bothers me because there's something about the way he's looking at me right now that makes me feel sorry for him. He looks sweet, maybe even shy, and nothing like the confident guy I watched perform on that stage last week.

The questions are spinning in my head, and I want to spit

them out and get it over with. How do I know you? How did I hurt you? How do I tell you I'm sorry if I have no idea what I did? But I push the words down, searching for new, safer ones.

"I really loved your song. It's kind of been stuck in my head."

He takes another step back. "Thanks," he says.

"I've been trying to remember all the lyrics, but . . ."

Invite me back. Please.

I look around again to be sure there's no one within earshot. "That day downstairs, I guess it kind of inspired me. My poems aren't very good or anything." I pause for a moment, waiting for him to say something, but he doesn't, so I keep blabbering.

"I barely slept last weekend." Now he looks at me sideways like he's trying to figure out why this is his problem. "I haven't been . . ." I stop short, realizing I was about to admit that I haven't been taking the prescription sleep meds I've popped every night for the last five years. I keep forgetting. Or maybe I don't forget. Maybe I make a choice to keep writing despite how exhausted I'll be the next day. "I haven't been sleeping. Once I start writing, I kind of *need* to keep going." I let a nervous laugh escape.

The corners of his mouth turn up slightly. Not much, but enough to expose that dimple and catch me off guard.

"You're writing?"

I nod.

"You?" AJ crosses his arms like he doesn't believe me, but at least now I can read the look on his face. He's surprised.

Maybe even intrigued. "You're writing poetry, and not because you have to for a class?"

I shrug. I think he expects me to be offended, but I'm not. I get it. The whole poetry thing shocks me, too.

"Of course, it's total crap," I say, hoping more self-criticism will elicit some kind of reaction, like an invitation to come downstairs and say those words on stage so they can pelt me with paper and, later, glue sticks.

AJ uncrosses his arms and transfers his backpack from one shoulder to the other. "I bet your poems are better than you think they are."

It's not true, but it's a nice thing to say and he looks like he means it. I start to reply, but then I look past him, over his right shoulder, and see Kaitlyn walking in our direction, taking measured steps, hanging back like she's timing her arrival so she doesn't interrupt the two of us.

Invite me back. I want to hear more poetry, more of your songs.

"I've got to get to class," he says. "I'll see ya later, okay?"

And with that, he takes off, leaving Kaitlyn the opening she was waiting for. She lengthens her stride and as soon as she's close enough, she grabs me by the arm with both hands. "Holy shit, was that Andrew Olsen?" she asks.

"Who?"

She lets go of me so she can point at him, and together, we watch AJ open a classroom door and disappear from sight.

"That *was* him! God, we were so brutal to that kid, weren't we?" She shakes her head as I turn his name over in my mind. *Andrew Olsen. Andrew Olsen.*

"Who?" I ask again, and she slaps my arm with the back of her hand.

"Andrew Olsen. Remember? Fourth grade. Mrs. Collins's class?" Kaitlyn must be able to tell by the look on my face that I'm not connecting the dots, because she breaks into this huge grin. She shakes her hips and sings, "A-A-A-Andrew . . ." to the tune of the Chia Pet jingle, and then she starts cracking up.

"How can you not remember Andrew? That kid stuttered so badly he couldn't even say his name. We used to follow him around singing that song. . . . You have to remember this!"

Oh, God. I do. It's all starting to come back to me, and when she sings that horrible song again, I can see Kaitlyn and me in our skirts and ponytails, trailing behind him on the playground while he covered his ears, tears streaming down his face, trying to run away from us. We never let him get far.

"Andrew?" That's all I can get out. I want to throw up. Andrew. That's what Caroline meant.

"Remember? We even made him cry on that field trip to the museum? His mom had to come all the way into the city to pick him up."

I don't want to remember, but I do. I remember everything. How it all started. How it finally ended.

Kaitlyn singled him out early on. Eventually, I joined in. We teased him at every recess, during lunch, after school when he was waiting for the bus. We looked for him—looked forward to finding him. I can even picture his face when he saw us coming, and I remember how it made me feel guilty, but not guilty enough to stop, because it also made me feel powerful in a weird way. And there was always a look of approval on Kaitlyn's face.

When school started the following year, we found out he'd transferred, and Kaitlyn and I were actually disappointed, as if our favorite toy had been permanently taken away from us. I never thought I'd see him again. I'm sure he hoped he'd never see Kaitlyn and me again, but I assume he didn't have a choice since this is the only public high school in the area.

Caroline was wrong. He hates me.

Kaitlyn stops talking, but I guess the horrified look on my face doesn't register with her, because she's still lit up as if this whole thing is hilarious.

"So why were you talking to him?" She pops her hip and plays with her necklace while she waits for me to answer.

It takes me a second to pull it together. When I finally do speak, my voice is shaking and the words come out in fragmented whispers. "We have a class together." Does Poet's Corner count as a class? Probably not.

"He was in my P.E. class last year," she says, "but we didn't have to talk much, so I never got to hear him. Does he still stutter?"

I picture the way he stepped on stage and perched himself on that stool. How he threw his guitar over his shoulder and stated that his song sucked, beaming as he gestured toward his chest, confidently inviting his friends to throw things at him. He sang and his words were beautiful and clear, not broken in any way. Nothing about him was broken.

"No, he doesn't."

He's long gone, but Kaitlyn points in his direction. "See, we fixed him," she says proudly. My cheeks feel hot, and when she elbows me, laughing, my hands ball into fists by my side. "You know what they say, 'That which does not kill us makes us stronger.'"

I'm unable to speak or breathe or move. I can't believe she just said that, and I know I should defend him, but I'm frozen in place, totally stunned. Saying nothing, as usual.

"Besides," she continues, "that was a million years ago. We were little kids. I bet he doesn't even remember us." I feel a huge, uncomfortable lump in my throat. How could I do that do him? To anyone?

"He remembers," I say under my breath as I walk away.

Caroline's at her locker after last bell, and I stall, waiting for everyone to clear out. When the coast is finally clear, I race over to her.

"I know what I did to AJ." My stomach turns over as I say it. "No wonder he doesn't want me downstairs. Caroline, what do I do?"

"You can start by apologizing," she says.

He'll never forgive me. How could he?

"He must think I'm a horrible person."

Maybe he's right. Maybe I am.

"Do you want my help?"

I nod. Caroline turns on her heel and gestures for me to follow her. "Come on," she says. "I know what to do."

She leads me to the first row of the theater and we spend the next three hours working on a single poem. I write. Caroline listens. When I get stuck, she feeds me word after word until we find the perfect one that sums up what I want him to know. When I'm done, we have a poem that doesn't say "I'm sorry" in so many words, but it talks about regret and second chances, a fear of not belonging that runs so deep it changes you into someone you don't want to be. It's about seeing what you've become and wanting—craving—to be someone different. Someone better.

It's me, asking him to let me in. Asking all of them to give me a chance to show them that, deep down, I'm not who they think I am. Or, maybe I'm exactly who they think I am, but I no longer want to be.

that narrow hallway

Fifteen minutes into lunch, I start stuffing empty wrappers back into my lunch bag, collecting my trash, and brushing the grass off my pants. "I have to go to the library and get this book for English," I announce. "Anyone want to come?" I already know they'll pass.

"I'm not allowed in there," Olivia says proudly.

Kaitlyn laughs. "How the hell do you get banned from the school library?"

Olivia rolls her eyes. "Mrs. Rasmussen caught Travis and me making out in the biography section. It's around that corner, you know?" she says, drawing an imaginary curve in the air with her hand. "It's completely out of view. What else are you supposed to do over there?" She giggles.

"Look for biographies," Hailey suggests.

"Nah. Boring." Olivia sits up a little straighter, eyes darting around the circle, enjoying the attention. "Trust me, it was worth getting kicked out. Travis may not be the sharpest tool in the shed, but that boy can *kiss*."

We all laugh.

"I wonder what he's doing this weekend?" Olivia adds as she reaches for her phone.

"I thought you broke up because you two didn't have anything to talk about," Alexis says.

"We don't." She crinkles her nose. "I'm not planning to talk to him," she says, cocking her head to the side and continuing to search for his number.

Kaitlyn pulls a piece of bread from her sandwich and chucks it at Olivia's head.

I mutter a quick "See ya," and head off for the path that leads to the theater. I know exactly where to go—I've pictured those stairs and that narrow hallway in my mind a hundred times now—and soon I'm inside the janitor's closet, pulling the mops and brooms to the side to reveal the concealed seam and the black bolt. Their voices are muffled, like they're far away, and I knock lightly, three times. The sound stops immediately.

I hear the key slip into the lock and the dead bolt click. AJ cracks the door open, just wide enough to see me. "You've got to be kidding."

Ignoring his comment, I come up on my tiptoes, looking

over his shoulder, searching for Caroline. She's part of today's plan. I come downstairs and she tries to convince him to let me in so I can read the poem we wrote.

"I'm looking for—" I start to say her name, but AJ opens the door and steps forward, and I have no choice but to step back inside the janitor's closet. That stupid Chia Pet jingle pops into my head.

What the hell's wrong with me?

He closes the door and uses that key around his neck to lock it behind him. "What, are you on some kind of twisted quest or something? Did your friends put you up to this?" He walks over to the door that connects the janitor's closet to the hallway and peers out, looking for my accomplices.

I was expecting him to be surprised, but not quite so pissed. My hands start shaking and my legs feel like they're going to give out, but I force myself to stand tall and look right into his eyes like Caroline told me to.

"I have something I'd really like to read to you. To all of you." I pull the poem from the pocket of my jeans and open it wide so he can see the proof.

He walks toward me, laughing. "It doesn't work that way, Samantha."

"How does it work?"

He brings his hands to his hips. "It works like this: Members read. Members listen. Non-members do not read or listen, because they aren't allowed inside. Look, I made an exception, but I told you, one time."

"Can't I just—"

He cuts me off. "You need to go."

"Why?"

"Because," he says, "you don't belong here."

My heart sinks. I fold my poem along the creases and stuff it back into my pocket. "Why not?"

His gaze travels around the room, like he's searching for words, but he won't find any on these walls. There's nothing but cleaning supplies in here.

Finally he locks his eyes on mine, and he doesn't say a thing, but I understand completely. He told me the first time I was down here. We're not friends.

I reach into my pocket, removing the folded piece of paper again. I press it into his palm and close his fingers around it. "I didn't remember at first. It was years ago. . . . I don't know, maybe I blocked it out or something. But anyway, I know what I did now, and I am *so* sorry. I'll never be able to tell you how much I regret it. But I'm truly, genuinely sorry. And mortified." Some weird sound escapes, and I cover my mouth. "But I deserve to be, right?"

I turn to leave, hoping he'll stop me. He doesn't.

As I'm about to step into the hallway, I glance over my shoulder. AJ is already back inside Poet's Corner. When I hear the bolt click into place, I return to the door and rest my ear against it.

I can hear their voices on the other side. I feel tears pricking my eyes when I think about Sydney standing on stage, making everyone laugh, and AJ singing, giving everyone chills. I'm curious about Caroline. She said it would be easy to get me inside, as long as we found the right words. She was wrong. Maybe she's up there right now, pleading my case since I can't do it myself. I picture that room. Its tactile walls. All those colorful slips of paper and incredible words I'll never see again.

I climb the stairs, cross the stage, and step out into the sunshine, taking deep deliberate breaths like Shrink-Sue taught me to. By the time I arrive at our tree, I'm under control again.

"Where's your library book?" Hailey asks as I sit down, rejoining the circle.

"It was already checked out," I tell her.

I pluck at the blades of grass—*one, two, three*—and look around at Alexis, Kaitlyn, Olivia, and Hailey, thinking about Sue's advice to make new friends, and realizing that after all those years of saying I couldn't do it, I just tried to. And failed.

can't move on

"Fill me in," Sue says. "How are things with your friends this week?"

I stretch the putty between my fingers, testing to see how far I can pull it before it snaps. "Better in some ways. But different."

"Do you mean they're treating you differently?"

I kind of wish they were. That would be easier. "No. It's more . . . the other way around."

It's been a month since I tried to give AJ my poem. Ever since that day, something's shifted in me. I'm quieter during lunch. Last Saturday night, I skipped a party and went to the movies with my family instead. I've been hanging out with Paige after school, taking her to gymnastics practice, helping her with her homework. I'm having a hard time being around the Eights. I can't even look at Kaitlyn. Every time I do, I think of that smug look on her face when she said we "cured" AJ, and I feel sick.

I kick off my shoes and pull my feet onto the chair, curling myself into a ball. "I don't feel like talking about them today. Can we change the subject?" I ask, resting my chin on my knees.

"Of course. What do you want to talk about?"

I glance over at the clock. I've spent the week obsessing about sitting in this chair, talking to Sue, hearing her advice, playing with my putty. Now I'm here and I have no idea what I want to say.

"I've been swimming every day. I'm feeling good about that. I can tell I'm getting stronger, and it's taking my mind off, well, everything. And I've been writing a lot. It's cathartic, you know? It makes me feel . . ." I search for the right word, something Sue will like, and settle on, "Healthy."

"Hmm. I like that word. Healthy." She says it slowly, letting it linger in the air for a while. I feel a pang of guilt when I picture myself huddled under the covers with a flashlight, writing until late night becomes early morning. This probably isn't the best time to tell her I haven't been taking my sleep meds.

"How are things with Caroline?" she asks. As soon as I hear her name, I feel my shoulders sink a little lower.

"Good. We've been spending a lot of time together. We meet in the theater after school and she helps me with my poetry." God, if the Eights overheard me say that, I'd never hear the end of it, but Sue clearly isn't one of them, because she rests her elbows on the armrest and leans forward to keep me talking.

"I like writing with her. When I can't figure out how to articulate what I want to say, she seems to have the perfect words. And we talk, you know? Really *talk* about things." I shift in my chair, squeeze my putty into a tight ball. "The Eights and I used to talk like that, but we haven't in a long time. It feels kind of . . . strange to have a friend like that again."

"But *good* strange."

"Yeah. Definitely good strange."

My fingers work the putty while Sue settles back in her chair and consults her notes, flipping back to earlier pages, previous sessions.

"We haven't talked about Brandon in a while. Are you still thinking about him?"

Brandon? Wow. Now that I think about it, I haven't given him much thought in the last month. "No. Not really."

She writes it down. "How about Kurt?"

"Kurt? Ew. No." I saw him at lunch today, but *that* didn't even prompt me to think about him in the way Sue's referring to.

"Are you thinking about any other boys?"

"You mean, Am I *obsessing* about any other boys?"

"Not necessarily. Unless that's what it feels like to you."

I grin at her. "Nice spin."

Sue cocks her head to one side, looking smug.

I haven't talked to AJ since I gave him my apology poem and he kicked me out of Poet's Corner, but I think about that day a lot. I think about *him* a lot. I changed the route I take to third period so I'm more likely to cross paths with him. I write about him almost every night before I fall asleep. I was up late last night making a playlist of acoustic guitar songs I could imagine him playing and titled it *Song for You*.

I've figured out where he lives, but I've fought the urge to drive by his house. I know where he eats lunch when he's not downstairs—I've seen him sitting at the round table over by the bathrooms with that other guy and one of the girls from Poet's Corner—but I don't stare at him or intentionally drop objects as I walk by or anything.

I picture his dimple and that sexy, fluid way he throws his guitar over his back. But then I think about the look on his face when he told me I didn't belong in Poet's Corner, and reality hits. I'm not sure I'm obsessed with him, but I'm definitely obsessed with him forgiving me. And I'm curious about him. Caroline knows. Sue would probably want me to tell her, too.

"No, I'm not obsessed with any boys," I say.

She raises her eyebrows, looking at me like she knows me far too well to believe it. I'm not offended. I've been preoccupied with guys since the day she met me.

"But I can't stop thinking about AJ. The boy Kaitlyn and I teased when we were kids." I rest my forehead on my knees, hiding my face.

"You've apologized to him, haven't you?" she asks. I nod without looking at her.

But I can't undo what I did.

I let out a heavy sigh. "When am I going to stop making mistakes, Sue?"

Her laugh catches me off guard, and I look up at her, wide-eyed and confused. "Why on earth would you want to do that?" she asks.

I stare at her.

"Mistakes. Trial and error. Same thing. Mistakes are how we learned to walk and run and that hot things burn when you touch them. You've made mistakes all your life and you're going to keep making them."

"Terrific."

"The trick is to recognize your mistakes, take what you need from them, and move on."

"I can't move on."

"You can't beat yourself up, either."

The room is quiet for a long time. Finally she clears her throat to get my attention. "Why are you scratching?" she asks. I hadn't even realized I was doing it, and when I pull my fingers away, the back of my neck feels sore and raw. I smash my thumb into my putty.

"I *need* him to forgive me," I say.

It's all I think about. It's making me crazy.

"You can't need that, Sam," she says, slowly shaking her

head. "That one's out of your control. You've done your part, and now it's up to him. He'll either forgive you or he won't."

He won't.

I haven't let myself cry over what Kaitlyn and I did to AJ—not when I found out, not when I told Sue a month ago—but I can't hold back the tears anymore, so I let them fall. My chest already feels lighter with the release.

"Hey," Sue says, resting her elbows on her knees. "Look at me. You're a good person who made a mistake." That makes me cry even harder. "Did you learn something?"

I hide my face behind my hand, nodding fast.

"Then this particular mistake has done its job. Forgive yourself and move on, Sam." When Sue hands me a tissue, my eyes meet hers. "Go for it," she says quietly.

I'm not sure how long I sit there wiping my eyes and blowing my nose, but I know even if we go overtime on our session today, there's no way she'll let me leave this chair until I say it. And mean it.

"I forgive myself," I finally say, my voice cracking on each word.

three steps up

As I take my seat in history class, I check the clock on the wall. I still have a few minutes before the bell rings, so I pull out my yellow notebook. I've been thinking about mistakes and forgiveness ever since my session with Sue yesterday, and I'm dying to add a few more lines to my poem on the topic.

"Hey, Sam." I slam my notebook shut and look up. Sydney is hovering over me.

"Hi. Sydney, right?" I ask, as if I don't know her name. But of course I do. I've seen her every day during fourth period for the past month, and each time, I think about her Chicken McNuggets poem and smile to myself.

She rests one hand on my desk and reaches for my silver

S pendant with the other. "Ooh, I love this," she says, lifting it into her fingers. She twists it around a few times, studying it from various angles. She drops it and reaches for her own necklace. "Look. We have excellent taste in letters," she says, holding up a hot pink letter *S*.

"That's really pretty," I tell her, still trying to figure out why she's talking to me.

"So," she whispers, "AJ read your poem to us."

"What? When?" I gave it to him so long ago. I figured if he'd read it, I would have known by now. It's been all I can do to stop thinking about it.

"We've been talking," she says. "We want you to come back."

"Really?"

"Really." She bends down toward my ear. "Some of us wanted you to come back the following week. Some of us took more convincing."

"AJ?" I ask.

"He wasn't alone in his opinion. We all know who you are, Samantha. We remember what you did to him," she says. I hunch my shoulders and tuck my head to my chest, wishing I could disappear. "But I think you meant what you said in that poem. Did you?"

It takes effort, but I sit up straight and look right at her. "Every last word."

"Good. We're meeting at lunch today. Come downstairs

with me after class." She taps my yellow notebook. "Bring this with you," she says. Then she continues down the aisle and takes her seat a few rows behind me.

Holy shit.

My mind is racing and I can't lock on to one thought. I'm still embarrassed, but now elation is starting to take over. I get to see that room again. But then I think about how Sydney tapped on my notebook, and I start to panic.

I'll have to read a poem.

Class starts, but I'm not really paying attention. All I can think about are the poems I've written so far. I swap out my yellow notebook for the blue one and start thumbing through the pages, looking for worthy candidates as I dig my fingernails into the back of my neck three times, again and again.

Horrible. Lame. Ridiculous. Supposed to be funny but isn't. Supposed to rhyme but doesn't. Hmm, this one's kind of poignant—but . . . haiku?

Sweat is forming on my brow, and I keep shifting in my chair, and my neck already feels sore from all the scratching. Maybe I'll have time to ask Caroline for her opinion. She's heard every one of these poems. She helped me write many of them.

Wait. This one's worth considering.

I look up at the whiteboard to check the status of the lesson and pretend to take a few notes, but when the coast is clear I read the poem. Then I turn around and look at Sydney. She's watching me with wide eyes and an encouraging smile, and it reminds me of Caroline's words that very first day: "I'm going to show you something that will change your whole life."

Sydney's chatty, and that's good because I can't breathe, let alone speak. As we weave our way through the doors, down the stairs, and around the tight corners, I listen to her talk about her plans for the upcoming weekend, and I mutter a few "uh-huhs" sprinkled with some "that sounds like funs," but I'm not really hearing a word she's saying. I was feeling so confident once I found a poem to read, but apparently I left that emotion back in the classroom.

Now, it's all hitting me. As soon as I get through that door, they'll all expect me to get on stage and let meaningful words emerge from my mouth. I can't do that. I can't even speak when I'm sitting on a patch of grass next to people I've known my entire life. The air must be thicker down here or maybe the ventilation in the basement doesn't work as well as it should, because I. Can't. Breathe.

Sydney knocks hard on the door that leads inside and we wait. My fingernails find their usual spot and dig in. Hard.

This is a mistake.

The bolt clicks and the door squeaks as it opens, and there's AJ, key in hand. "Hi," he says.

Sydney pulls the door open. Once we're in the room, she spreads her arms wide. "Where do you want to sit?"

I scan the room. The African American girl with the long black braids is resting her knee on one of the couches, talking and waving her arms animatedly, like she's telling a funny story. The girl with the super curly blond hair and the short guy in the artsy glasses are watching her, laughing along.

On the far end of the room, I spot pixie-cut girl, Abigail. She looks different today, eyes thickly lined in a dramatic cat's-eye, and lips painted dark red. She wears it well. Confidently. Her arm is propped against the back of the couch, and she's chatting with that girl with the short dark hair and the small silver nose ring.

I don't see Caroline anywhere.

"Give me a minute, would you?" I say to Sydney as I point at AJ. She gets the message.

He bolts the door and then turns around to face me. He doesn't look angry. He doesn't look upset. He doesn't look *anything*.

"Listen," I say. "I can go if you're uncomfortable with this. I'm . . ." What's the word? Conflicted? Selfish? "I'm wondering if I should be here. I mean, if you don't want me to be."

He doesn't say anything at first. But then he gestures toward the others. "They want to hear what you have to say."

I don't have anything to say.

"I guess I want to hear what you have to say, too," AJ adds.

Now this feels less like an invitation to join the group and more like a test I need to pass. I write shitty poetry. For myself. I don't have anything to say.

"I'm not sure I'm ready for this." The words come out before I can stop them. My breathing becomes shallow again, and my whole body feels like it's on fire. My hands are clammy, my fingers tingly, and the thoughts start rushing in, one after the other.

Everyone's going to laugh at me.

"Are you okay?" AJ asks, and without even thinking about it, I shake my head.

"Where's Car—" My throat goes dry before I can get her name out. I wrap my hand around my neck, and AJ takes my arm, leading me to one of the couches in the back row. "Sit down. I'll get you some water," he says. I rest my elbows on my knees and fix my gaze on the black painted floor.

It's just a thought.

I feel a hand on my back, and I turn my head to the side, expecting to see AJ, but it's Caroline. "Hey, it's okay," she says. As quickly as it began, the thought spiral starts to slow.

"Caroline," I whisper.

"I'm right here," she says. "It's okay."

I can't break down in front of them. I don't want to be someone who breaks down.

"Is everyone looking at us?" I ask.

"Nope. No one's paying any attention. Just breathe."

I listen to her. I do what I'm told.

A few seconds later, AJ returns to my other side with a cup of water. "Here," he says. I take it without looking at him, and drink it with my eyes closed. I imagine him and Caroline silently communicating above my head.

I'm in control. I can do this.

Instead of my own destructive thoughts, I now hear Sue's voice in my head, telling me this is good. That this is something Summer Sam might do. That she's proud of me.

Without letting another negative thought creep in, I bend down, unzip my backpack, and remove my blue notebook.

"I'm ready," I say quietly, and I stand up tall, feigning confidence.

"What are you doing?" AJ asks.

"Reading."

"Sam—"

I cut him off. "No. It's okay."

I'm finally down here, and this is what they do when they're down here. If I'm going to prove I belong, I need to get up on that stage and show them I'm not just one of the Crazy Eights. I'm just *me*.

"Watch for today, Sam." AJ motions toward the rest of the group, sitting, waiting to start. "Please." But I'm already pushing past him, making my way to the stage.

Stepping onto the platform doesn't require any physical effort—it's two feet off the floor at best—but it does call for a heavy dose of forced enthusiasm. I scoot onto the stool and sit up straight. The chatter dies immediately.

I'm sure everyone can see my legs shaking.

"Hi," I say to the group, waving my little blue notebook in the air. "I've been writing a lot of poetry lately, but I'm really new at this." I choose my words carefully. Even if I said my stuff sucked, I doubt they'd actually pelt me with paper balls on my first visit, but I don't really want to test them on it. "So, be nice, okay?"

Sydney opens her mouth like she's about to say something. The others are silently watching me, shifting in place, looking at one another, and I can't help but feel as if I've done something wrong. I find AJ and Caroline at the back of the room. I can't read either one of their expressions.

Keep going.

I open my notebook to the page I dog-eared back in class. "This is called 'Plunge,'" I say.

I take a deep breath.

"Three steps up," I begin. But then I stop, giving myself a second to skim the rest of the poem. It looks different than it did back in U.S. History. Everything's right here. My obsession with threes. My scratching habit. My parking ritual. How I can't sleep.

This poem isn't about the pool at all. It's about the crazy. *My* crazy. All here, spilled in ink. Suddenly, I feel more like a stripper than a poet, two minutes away from exposing myself to these total strangers who may think I'm plastic, but don't currently think I'm nuts.

Shit. Here they come again.

The negative thoughts overpower all the positive ones, and the familiar swirl begins. But this time, the thoughts aren't about standing on stage and reading out loud and wondering if everyone's going to laugh at me. These thoughts are much worse.

They'll know I'm sick.

I wanted to believe that I could get up on this stage and drop my guard like AJ and Sydney did so easily, but now I'm not so sure anymore. They're all watching me, and I look at each of their faces, realizing that I know nothing about them. I don't even know most of their names.

"Three steps up . . ." I repeat, softer this time. My whole body is shaking and my palms are clammy. My stomach cramps into a tight knot and I feel like I'm about to throw up.

I stand, preparing to bolt from the stage, but then something catches my eye at the back of the room. Caroline is on her feet. She brings her fingers to her eyes and mouths the words, "Look at me."

For a second, it helps. I lock my eyes on hers and open my mouth to speak again, but then the walls feel like they're warping and bending, and Caroline's face starts to blur.

Oh, no.

I force myself to bend my knees, like my mom always tells me to do when I have to give an oral report, so I won't lock them and faint.

AJ was right. I don't belong here.

"I'm sorry," I mutter to no one in particular as I roll my notebook into a tube, wishing I could make the whole thing disappear. Then I'm off, heading straight for the door.

The door. I run my finger along the seams, over the dead bolt. I can't get out without the key.

"Hold on." AJ steps in front of me and starts working the

lock. "It's okay," he says. He sounds like he genuinely means it, like he's trying to make me feel better. But I'm not stupid. I can hear a trace of relief in his voice.

I don't know how to write poetry, let alone read it aloud to a group of strangers. Besides, I'm not like the rest of them. I don't *need* to be here. I *have* friends. I feel guilty for thinking it, but it's true. My relationship with the Eights may be superficial, but at least they don't expect me to spill my guts to them on a regular basis.

That's when it hits me: this is all a big joke. Payback for what I did to AJ all those years ago. I bet they'll all have a good laugh about it when AJ finally gets this fucking door open.

My whole face feels hot, and tears are welling up in my eyes as the bolt clicks and the door cracks open. "You proved your point," I whisper to AJ, pushing past him. "Don't worry, I won't be back." As quickly as I can, I slip back into the janitor's closet, past the mops, brooms, and chemicals, and out the door into the hallway.

Caroline will be right on my heels, but I don't want to see her right now. For a second I think she may have set me up; then I remember the way she forced me to look at her. There's no way she would have intentionally hurt me.

I fly up the stairs and into the sun, making a beeline for the student lot. All I can think about is sliding into the driver's seat, starting my *In the Deep* playlist, and shutting out the world. But when I get to the car and reach for my backpack, there's nothing there.

My backpack. It's still on the floor back in Poet's Corner along with everything else that matters. My keys. My phone. My music. My red and yellow notebooks. My secrets. I slump against the car door, hugging my blue notebook to my chest.

a poet wannabe

The asphalt is getting hotter as the early October afternoon wears on, and I've had nothing to do out here in the parking lot but curse the California sun and count the bells.

One: lunch ended. Two: fifth period began. Three: fifth ended. Four: sixth began. That's my cue. I brush the parking lot dust off my butt and head back toward campus, praying I don't see anybody.

I head through the gate and across the grass until I can pick up the cement path that leads to my locker. Maybe Caroline fed a note through one of the vents, telling me where to find my backpack. As soon as I have it, I'll go straight to the office, say I'm sick, and ask if I can call my mom so I can drive home.

The corridors are empty and I reach my locker without

running into anyone. I dial the combination and lift the latch. No note.

To center myself, I look at the inside of my locker door, staring at the three pictures Shrink-Sue told me to tape there, and trying to reconnect with the stronger person I see in the images. I run my finger across the photo of me on the diving block, wearing that willful, determined expression. Confidence. That was the word I said that day.

She wouldn't have run away.

I immediately realize my mistake, and it hits me with absolute certainty: I have to go back. Even if it was all a joke, even if they meant to embarrass me, I have to go back down there and prove I can do it, if not to them, at least to myself. If I can stand on diving blocks and win a medal, I can stand on a stage and read a poem.

I belong in that room.

"Hey." I hear a voice behind me and I turn around. AJ is sitting at one of the round metal tables on the grass between the walking paths. There are two backpacks at his feet. As he stands, he reaches for mine. He crosses the lawn and hands it to me. "Here, Sam."

Sam.

"You should have left it in the office or something," I say, taking it from him. "You're going to get in trouble for missing class."

"And you're not?" he asks, raking his fingers through his hair.

"I thought I'd go home for the day." The brief moment of confidence is gone now that he's standing here. I think about that stage and that stool, how AJ worked the lock to let me out of that room, and my face heats.

He's watching me, not saying a word. My gaze settles on a crack in the cement while I muster up the courage to tell him the truth.

"I panicked," I say. "I thought you guys would laugh at my poem."

"We wouldn't have."

"And then I thought maybe it was all a joke. That you were trying to get me back for what I did to you when we were kids." I force myself to meet his eyes.

"I'd never do that."

I hear Shrink-Sue's voice in my head, talking about mistakes. Reminding me that they serve a purpose.

"I blew it, didn't I?"

"No. We did." His expression is different now. It's softer, almost apologetic. "Look, Sam, we went about that wrong. There's this whole initiation process we sort of . . . skipped over."

I can't tell if he's joking. I hear the words "initiation process" and immediately think of blindfolds and candles and the possibility of water torture.

"Great." I cover my head with both hands and find that crack in the cement again.

"Don't worry," he says. I can hear the laugh in his voice,

and something about it makes me feel more at ease. If he's laughing, maybe he's smiling too. I've seen him smile, that one time he was performing on stage, but I've never seen him smile at *me*. I look up. Sure enough, he is.

"Instead of skipping sixth and going home, can I convince you to skip sixth and come with me?"

"Where?"

"Downstairs."

"Why? Is everyone else there?"

"No. That's kind of the point. You're supposed to get the room all to yourself. I'll show you what I mean." He gestures toward the theater with his chin and takes two steps backward, moving toward the path.

After that first time, all I wanted to do was hang out in Poet's Corner for the rest of the afternoon, reading the walls. I wanted to be alone. I wanted to read every single poem without interruption.

I want to follow him.

I take a tentative step in AJ's direction.

I want to trust him.

He turns around and starts walking, stopping briefly at the table to grab his backpack, and we continue across the grass, straight to the theater. I follow him up to the stage, down the stairs, past the mops and brooms, and into Poet's Corner. He keeps the door open to let light in, and points at the closest lamp. "Hit the light?" he asks.

He bolts the door behind us, and together, the two of us

round the room, turning on lamps as we go. He's faster than I am, but we still meet each other near the front.

"Sit down." He sits on the edge of the short, makeshift stage and I settle in next to him, trying to forget how I made a complete ass of myself in this very spot less than three hours ago.

"So here's how this works." He clears his throat. "The current members have discussed it, and we would like to consider you, Samantha—*Sam*—McAllister, for membership in Poet's Corner."

"Why?"

His brow furrows. "Why what?"

"Why do you want me to join? You guys don't even know me."

"Well, it's not that simple. You'll need to read first. Then we vote."

"So if my poem sucks, I don't get to stay?"

"No. We all write stuff that sucks. We're not judging your poetry."

"What *are* you judging?"

"I don't know. Your . . . sincerity, I guess."

He slaps his palms on his legs, stands quickly, and then holds his hand out to help me up. I take it. I think he's going to let it drop, but he doesn't. He pulls me over to the center of the stage, right next to the stool.

"You should see things from this vantage point first, so you can get used to being up here." He grabs my arms and pivots me around so I'm facing the rows of empty chairs and couches.

"How often?"

"No rules around that." I hear his voice from behind my right shoulder. "You can come up here as often or as little as you like. You have to read once, to put yourself on even ground with the rest of us, but after that, it's up to you."

The idea of reading makes me feel sick again, so I reach for a new topic. "Where did all this furniture come from?" I can't imagine how they got all this stuff in here. It looks impossible, especially when you consider that steep, narrow staircase.

When I turn around again, AJ is perched on the stool with one leg resting on the rung and the other on the floor. His arms are crossed over his chest. From this vantage point, they look kind of muscular. Up until this moment, I thought he was tall and kind of lanky, in a cute way. He's not lanky.

"Prop room," he says.

"What do you mean?"

"When you come down the stairs, you turn to the right to get in here. But if you take a left instead, you wind up in the prop room."

I raise an eyebrow. "The prop room?"

"It's the room directly beneath the stage," he explains. "There's this huge freight elevator they use to bring the furniture up and down for performances. Once the play is done and they no longer need the stage set, those items live in the prop room until they need them again. Or, until they're relocated."

"Relocated?"

He uncrosses his arms and points to the orange couch he

sat in the first time I was here. "That's our newest acquisition. Cameron and I had to take the legs off to get it around that tight corner at the bottom of the stairs. It was wedged in the doorframe for a good ten minutes before we were finally able to jiggle it through." He stands up quickly, takes a bow, and sits down again. "But we pulled it off."

I grin at him. "You got that couch through that door?"

"Barely."

As I scan the room, it dawns on me why everything is mismatched and looks like it came from completely different time periods. An antique bookcase with a modern lamp. A retro '70s chair with a sleek metal end table. "Everything in here came from the prop room?"

"Yep."

"Don't they miss this stuff?"

"Eh. Pieces have been disappearing little by little over the last decade, ever since Poet's Corner began. I'm sure they miss things occasionally, especially the big stuff."

"Like, for instance, a bright orange couch."

"Exactly."

"And even if they did miss it," I say, suppressing a smile, "they'd have no idea where to look."

"Secret room." His mouth curves up on one side. "I should probably feel a little bit guilty, shouldn't I?"

"Maybe a little bit," I say, holding up my hand, thumb and finger nearly touching.

"It's not like they were stolen."

"Of course not. They were simply relocated."

"That couch is really comfortable." He steps past me and jumps down onto the ground with a thud. He falls back into the orange sofa, running his hands back and forth across the cushions. "And inspirational. You know, if you're looking for something to write about, this couch would make a great topic."

I laugh. "Why would I want to write about a piece of furniture?" I have a mental illness and four superficial friends. Surely I have more fodder for a poetic career than to need an ugly orange couch.

When he grins, that dimple on the left side of his mouth catches my eye. "I have no idea." Then he lets his head fall backward and he stares up at the ceiling. "This is good. Keep 'em coming." He motions toward himself with one hand. "What other questions do you have for me, Sam?"

Sam. Again. That makes two.

I walk around the stage, getting a feel for it under my feet. I run my fingertips across the stool, remembering how terrified I was up here. It feels like it's daring me to sit on it again, so I hop up and take a look around. The room looks different now that it's emptier. Safer. At least now I feel like a poet wannabe and not a stripper.

AJ's still reclining into the couch, watching me.

"Tell me more about the rules. You can't criticize anyone's poetry, especially your own, right?"

"True," he says. "And the last time I broke that one, you saw the ramifications firsthand."

I remember how AJ stood up here with his guitar dangling from the strap, inviting his friends to throw paper at him. "Yes, I did." Thinking back on that day reminds me of something else I've been wondering about.

"Why do you always start by saying where you wrote your poem? Why does that matter?"

"Is there a place you like to go when you write? Is there one particular place that inspires you?"

I picture my room, huddled down in my sheets far past my bedtime, writing until my hand hurts. It's fine, but I wouldn't call it inspirational. Then I think about the pool.

"Yeah."

AJ looks right at me. "We think those places matter. We think they're worth sharing, you know? Because when you share them, they become part of the poem."

Goose bumps travel up my arms. "Hmm. I like that."

"Yeah, me too. Which reminds me of another." He hops back onto the stage and stands right in front of me. "The first poem you read in Poet's Corner has to be written here."

"What?"

"Yep."

Crap. Back in history class, Sydney wasn't telling me I had to get up on stage. How could I have been so stupid? "Why did you guys let me start reading today?"

He laughs. "You were going for it. I don't think any of us knew how to stop you."

I hide my face. "Until I stopped myself."

"And I think I speak for all of us when I say we were sorry you did."

"Really?"

They wanted me here.

"Of course. You would've been pummeled with paper when you finished, and I, for one, was especially looking forward to that part."

I roll my eyes at him. "Now, that would have been an interesting initiation."

"Maybe," he says, "but this one's better." He pulls his phone from his pocket. "We meet on Mondays and Thursdays at lunch. Sometimes we call additional meetings for no apparent reason. Is that going to be a problem?"

"No." Actually, maybe.

"If we invite you to join us, I'll need your number." He lifts his phone in the air. I'm not an official member, but he seems to be asking, so I tell him. He types it in, then slips his phone back into his pocket. "Any more questions?" he asks me.

I step off the stage and start walking the perimeter, past hundreds of slips of paper filled with thousands and thousands of words. All these people. Each one so exposed in the most frightening way. I have no idea how I'll ever do anything close to this.

"I think all of you have a gift I don't possess," I say without looking at him.

"What's that?"

I take a few steps forward, watching the walls and the words as I go. "You seem to know how to articulate your feelings and share them with other human beings. I'm afraid my gift is the exact opposite; I'm skilled at holding everything in." My chin starts trembling like it does when I tell Sue something I never intended to admit, but my chest feels a bit lighter now. I doubt this is what AJ meant when he asked if I had any questions, but I have to hear his answer to this one. "How do I learn to do this?"

He gets up from the couch. "I guess you start in a safe place, with safe people, like in this room, with us." He's speaking as he walks toward me. "We trust each other and we don't judge. You're totally free to blurt here."

I laugh too loudly. "Me? Yeah, I don't blurt. Ever. My friend Kaitlyn prides herself on having lots of opinions and always saying exactly what she thinks. She blurts. Sometimes it hurts the people around her."

"That's different," he says.

I feel myself staring at him. "Do you always say exactly what you're thinking?"

He shrugs. "I try to. I like to know where I stand with people, and I figure I owe them the same courtesy. I mean, I'm never rude or hurtful about it, but I don't see any reason to be fake. That's a lot of work."

It is. I would know.

AJ lifts the cord from around his neck and drops it over my head. His fingers graze my shoulders and the key makes a little sound as it bounces against a button on my blouse.

"Is this allowed?" I lift it in my hands, running my finger over the sharp points and grooves.

"Of course. The key belongs to the group. I'm just the one in charge of the door."

I'm feeling a little nervous about being down here alone. What if the power goes out? What if the ventilation fails? Could anyone get to me? "Does anyone else have a key?"

"Mr. Bartlett. He comes in a few times a month to empty the trash, vacuum the joint, that type of thing."

"The janitor? He knows about this place?"

"He's worked here for twenty years. Mr. B knows everyone and everything. But he keeps our secret to himself."

I run my finger along the key again. I don't really want AJ to go, but at the same time, I'm eager to be alone with all these poems. I'm dying to finally find his lyrics.

"I'm going to leave, okay?" he says. I expect him to step away, but he surprises me by stepping toward me. I'm reminded of how tall he is, and I have to tip my chin up to see his eyes. I've thought about him so much over the last month, but now I finally have a chance to really study him.

He's not gorgeous or anything, not like Brandon and the rest of my recent crushes. But none of them ever made me feel the way I do right now.

Everything about AJ is pulling me in. The way he's standing, so confident and in control. The way he's been so relaxed in this room with me today, making me feel like I *do* belong here. The way I remember him playing that one song, how it practically floated out of his body.

"Stay down here as long as you like. Read the walls; they're covered with a decade's worth of words written by more than a hundred people. Meet everyone. Then write something of your own."

"Okay," I whisper. His expression is soft and kind, and his eyes shine when he talks about the room and me becoming part of it.

"Lock the door and turn off all the lamps when you're done. I'll be waiting for you at that table by your locker."

"Okay," I say again.

He starts to step away from me, but he stops. "Oh, and if you want to, practice reading aloud. The stage doesn't feel quite as scary when the room is empty."

He squeezes past me and I press my back against the wall to give him room.

"AJ?" He turns around. I don't want to say it, but I feel like I need to, because I don't want to be uncomfortable down here and I certainly don't want *him* to be. And if they're all gearing up to judge my sincerity, he should understand how much it means for him to forgive me.

"You don't have to do this. If you don't want us to be friends, I get it. It was a long time ago, but the things I said and did when we were kids . . ." I trail off, thinking about the day Kaitlyn and I crank-called his house over and over again, until his mom finally picked up and screamed in our ears, begging us to stop. Or that time we sat behind him on the bus and cleaned out our backpacks, dropping all our gum wrappers, paper scraps, and pieces of lint down the back of his shirt. I shake my head and bite my lower lip hard. "You'll never know how sorry I am."

He doesn't speak right away. "Why are you telling me this?" he finally asks.

"I guess . . . I sort of . . ." I stammer, searching for the perfect words. "I wanted to be sure you knew. Just in case you thought I didn't mean it the first time."

He gives me another smile. That makes three today. This one looks even more genuine than the others. "If I didn't think you meant it the first time, you wouldn't be down here."

I have no idea what to say to that, so I just stand with my thumbs hooked in my front pockets and rock back on my heels.

"But since we're blurting here," he says, "I'll be honest. It wasn't easy for me to let you come down here today. I've accepted your apology, because I think it's genuine and I'm not one to hold a grudge, but let's not push the 'friends' thing, okay?"

As he walks to the door, he raises his finger in the air and circles it above his head. "Read the walls, Sam."

let everything go

I spend the rest of sixth period and all seventh reading the walls of Poet's Corner. The poems here are silly, heart-breaking, hilarious, sad, and many are absolutely incredible. They're about people who don't care enough and people who care too much, people you trust and people who turn on you, hating school, loving your friends, seeing the beauty in the world. Sprinkled among them are heavier ones about depression and addiction, self-mutilation and various forms of self-medication. But most of them are about love. Wanting it. Missing it. Actually being in it. I read some of those twice.

None of the poetry is marked with anything that makes its author identifiable—aside from the fast-food wrappers, which appear to be Sydney's trademark. Hard as I try, I can't figure out which ones Caroline penned, but AJ's proved to be fairly easy; as soon as I found that first song, I had no trouble finding more of his right-slanted, narrow handwriting.

By the time the final bell rings, I've read hundreds of poems. As eager as I am to say I covered every square inch of this place, I've already been alone down here for over an hour. AJ's sitting at the table, waiting for me to return, and I still have a poem of my own to write.

My backpack is still sitting in front by the couch, so I take a seat and thumb through my notebooks. I skip the red one because I'm not angry, and the blue one because I'm not thinking about the pool. The poem that's building inside of me is a yellow one. My head falls back into the cushions, and I let my gaze travel around the walls one more time before I take my pen to the paper. I tap it three times. Then I let everything go.

out of thoughts

I'm perched on the edge of the diving block at the end of lane number three. I adjust my swim cap, press my goggles into my eyes with the heels of my hands, and step into my stance. I scratch the tape three times and dive in.

I spent the whole drive here thinking about my afternoon in Poet's Corner. Sitting on the stage alone. Reading the poems. Writing my own. And AJ, who may not be my friend, but at least he no longer seems to hate me.

But now, everything is so quiet. Not just the pool, but my mind, too. I don't even feel the urge to swim to the beat of a song. I'm mentally spent. Out of words. Out of thoughts. It feels so good to be this empty. It's so peaceful.

Is this what it's like to be normal?

For the next forty minutes, I follow Coach Kevin's instructions, but I wish I were here alone, without him yelling at me to swim faster, push myself harder. When practice is over and the rest of the team heads for the showers, I hang back in the water and keep swimming a slow freestyle, back and forth.

Fifteen minutes later, the club is clearing out. The rest of my teammates are in their sweats and swim parkas, heading for the front gates, so I pull myself out of the pool and reach for my towel. As I'm rinsing off, I start thinking about what's next. If I'm serious about joining Poet's Corner, I'll have to step on that stage and read next Monday. If they let me stay, I'll have to read again. And again. I'll have to come up with an excuse to miss lunch twice a week.

What am I going to tell the Eights?

My heart is racing as I change into my sweats, and my fingers start tingling as I'm heading for the parking lot. I'm almost out the gate when I spot Caroline sitting cross-legged on the grass by my car.

"Hey. What are you doing here?"

She sits up a little straighter and I read her T-shirt: PRO-CRASTINATE NOW!

"I hope you don't mind me dropping by. I figured you'd be here, and I didn't get to see you after, you know . . . what happened at lunch today."

"What happened at lunch today?" I joke. With a dramatic face palm, I fall back onto the grass next to her.

"I'm sorry," she says, laughing.

"Did you tell them about my OCD and my anxiety attacks? Is that why AJ apologized and brought me back downstairs?"

"No," she says matter-of-factly. "I never said a word."

"You swear?"

She draws an *X* across her heart.

Then I remember what Sydney said in history when she invited me to go downstairs with her. I meant to thank Caroline when I first saw her in Poet's Corner, but I never had the chance to. "You know, they let me back in because of the poem you helped me write," I say, coming up on my elbow.

"*You* wrote that."

"Not alone."

She doesn't say anything, but she knows it's true. If she hadn't helped me find the right words to apologize to AJ, he never would have forgiven me.

"Thank you."

She grins. "Anytime."

"I have to get back on that stage on Monday."

"I know. And you'll be fine." She sounds so certain. I wish I felt that confident.

"And let's just say for the sake of argument, I pull it off. Then I'll have to come up with more to read. Which could be problematic since, as you know, most of my stuff is about the . . ." I spin my finger in a circle around my right temple, but I can't bring myself to say the word "crazy."

"They can handle it, you know? The . . ." She mimics my gesture without saying the word either.

I'm sure they can. But it's taken me five years to tell anyone outside my family about my disorder, and even though I let Caroline in on my secret, I'm not ready to share it with the rest of the members of Poet's Corner. Besides, I want their vote, not their sympathy. "I just want to keep it between you and me. At least for now. Okay?"

"You got it." She presses her lips together and turns an imaginary key, locking my secrets inside.

an excellent question

"Where have you been?" Kaitlyn asks as I find a spot in the circle.

"What do you mean?" I start unpacking my lunch bag. "The bell just rang."

"Not today. Yesterday." When I look up, she blows her straw wrapper at me and it bounces off my forehead. "You weren't here at lunch, and Olivia said you missed fifth period."

"I was just worried," Olivia says, playing with her food. "Everything okay?"

"I wasn't feeling well so I went home after fourth." I take a sip of my soda. In my peripheral vision, I can see them all looking at Alexis. "What?" I ask, feeling the familiar adrenaline rush that always kicks off the panic attack. I steel myself for whatever it is Alexis is supposed to report regarding my whereabouts.

She saw me talking with AJ at my locker. Or sneaking into the theater with Sydney.

"I saw your car in the student lot after school." She sounds apologetic, but there's a little accusatory lilt in her voice. An unsaid *Aha. Caught ya.*

I don't want to lie to them, but I can't tell them where I was yesterday. A version of the events I'd been planning when I ran into AJ yesterday pops into my head, so I go with it.

"I went to the office and the nurse took my temperature. Since it was high, she said I wasn't allowed to drive, so my mom had to come down here and get me." I add a dramatic eye roll to punctuate my lie, and give my sandwich my undivided attention, trying not to appear guilty.

They must not have any other evidence against me because Alexis says, "Oh. Well, I'm glad you're feeling better." When I look up again, she's mixing dressing into her salad. Hailey gives me a sheepish grin, like she's relieved to discover that I have a good reason for abandoning them without a word.

It worked for today, but I'm not sure how I'll skip out of lunch on Monday. What am I going to do if I'm invited to join Poet's Corner—fake an illness *every* Monday and Thursday? I'm going to need a better cover story.

Olivia starts telling us about this new band on her dad's label, and how he wants all of us to go to their next show and bring a bunch of friends to help fill the room. While everyone's busy checking the concert dates on their phones, I use the opportunity to disappear into my own world, thinking up ways to get out of lunch.

It's too early for yearbook. I'm not in any other clubs. They'll never believe I'm spending two afternoons a week helping a teacher with some project or preparing for a big science lab or something. Then it hits me. As usual, I'm saved by water. It's perfect. I don't typically swim in the school pool until team practice starts in the spring, but it's open and heated until early December. There's no reason I couldn't start earlier.

When there's a lull in the conversation, I jump in. "I've got a few big meets coming up, so I've decided to start swimming during lunch a few days a week." I offer the information casually as I gesture in the general direction of the school pool. "I'm getting crushed by homework and it's getting harder to get to the club. I'm just mentioning it so, you know, you don't wonder where I am."

"Hey," Olivia says excitedly. "I want to come to one of your meets. I've never seen you race." She glances around the circle. "Have you guys?" They all shake their heads.

No. I can't let them watch me swim. When I'm in the pool, I'm as close to Summer Sam as I get.

"Actually . . . please don't. I know it sounds weird, but it's kind of *my* thing."

Kaitlyn lets out a huff, affronted. "You compete in front of huge groups of people all the time. Why would it bother you if we came to a meet?"

I don't have a good answer at the ready, so I tell them the truth. "I don't know. Complete strangers watching me race is one thing. You guys are different. That would make me totally nervous." I laugh to deflect the impact of their glares, but the sound that comes out of my mouth doesn't sound like a laugh at all.

"We're your best friends," Alexis says. I can't tell from her tone of voice if she's offended or simply pointing out a fact. "Why would you be nervous around *us*?"

It's an excellent question. One I ask myself all the time.

Before I can answer, Hailey jumps in. "It's okay," she says. "We understand."

"We do?" Kaitlyn asks. Her tone isn't hard to gauge at all.

"It's Samantha's thing." I look over at Hailey and silently thank her.

"I still don't get it," Alexis says. "But whatever. Have fun swimming at lunch. Alone."

We go back to eating, and I'm relieved to have that conversation behind me. I start thinking about next Monday, mentally pumping myself up to read my poem in front of the group.

"So, did you guys hear about tomorrow night?" Alexis asks. "Big party."

"Where?" Hailey asks.

"Kurt Frasier's." My head snaps up.

Kaitlyn glares at her. "You have *got* to be kidding. I am *not* going to that asshole's house."

"And I am?" I add.

Kaitlyn reaches over and grabs my hand in solidarity. I pull it away.

"Oh, please. You're not still mad about that, are you?" she asks. "I told you. *He* kissed *me*."

"Kaitlyn, we are not talking about this again." I say it firmly, and she must hear the weight in my voice because she lets out a heavy sigh and drops the subject.

Kurt and I had been together for two months when we went to winter formal last year. He said he was going to get a drink, and twenty minutes later, when I went looking for him, I found him hooking up with Kaitlyn in the coat-check room.

The two of them didn't last long. A few weeks later, he and Olivia got together at a party. It started to look like he intended to work his way through all five of us and was just getting started. I thought we'd collectively agreed that none of us would ever speak to him again. How could Alexis even *suggest* going to his house?

Alexis looks at Kaitlyn, and then at me. "Look, the guy's a douche, but he's a douche with a keg and an empty house, and that's where everyone's going tomorrow night." She turns her attention to Hailey and Olivia. "I'm going. You guys?"

"I'm in," Olivia chirps. When Kaitlyn shoots her a nasty look, she adds, "What? He has a nice house. I bet his parents' liquor cabinet is top shelf."

Hailey seems to want my approval, because she peeks over at me. I shrug and look away. "Yeah, sure," she finally says.

"Okay, fine. I'll go," Kaitlyn says. And then she looks at me. "Samantha?"

"I'm not going." It feels good to say it so definitively. Maybe I'll invite Caroline over.

this it is

The side entrance to the theater is unlocked. I hurry down the center aisle, climb the stairs to the stage, and slide in next to the piano, quietly listening for sounds on the other side of the curtain. When I hear footsteps, I duck inside.

They've already passed by, but Caroline's at the back of the group, and when she sees me, the biggest smile spreads across her face. I smile back as she grabs my arm, pulls me into the pack, and presses her finger to her lips.

Sydney is directly in front of us, walking next to the girl with the super curly hair. They both turn around and wave, but no one says a word as we make our way down the stairs, through the gray hallway labyrinth, and into the janitor's closet.

It's so quiet down here. I'm sure everyone can hear me breathing the way Shrink-Sue taught me to: in through the nose, out through the mouth. Caroline must be able to tell I'm nervous because she squeezes my wrist.

AJ holds the door open and we all file in. Everyone gathers at the back of the room. As soon as they hear the dead bolt click into place, the silence disappears and the energy level shifts completely.

The curly blond one says her name is Chelsea. Next to her, the girl with the dark shoulder-length hair and the tiny silver nose ring says, "I'm glad you're here. I'm Emily."

"Hi," I say. "Thanks." My palms are sweaty and my heart's pounding, but it feels similar to that moment before I dive off the blocks, so I'm pretty sure it's positive adrenaline and not the first sign of a panic attack.

"I'm Jessica." The thin girl with the long black braids raises her hand and whispers, "Welcome."

There's only one other guy. He's short, stocky, and wearing a *North Valley High Wrestling* tee, so I assume that's Cameron, AJ's partner in large-furniture-relocation crime. He adjusts his glasses and waves at me.

I greet Abigail by name and tell her it's nice to see her again, and she surprises me by pulling me into a tight hug. When she lets me go, Sydney throws one arm over my shoulder and shows everyone our matching letter *S* pendants.

Caroline stands there, beaming as if this whole moment is going exactly the way she pictured it, and AJ gives me that casual chin tilt of his and says, "You don't have to read right away today. Listen first, okay?"

"What makes you think I'd just jump up on stage and start reading?" I ask sarcastically, and they laugh.

AJ smiles at me. Then he addresses the group. "We'd better get started." He takes off for the front of the room and plops down on that orange couch he loves so much.

Everyone trails behind him and settles into various spots on the mismatched furniture, but I hang back, giving myself a moment to reacquaint myself with the room.

The walls look a little bit different now. The colors are brighter, the textures richer. Even the penmanship feels personal, almost intimate, like all these words on all these scraps of paper are here especially for me. I've read these poems now. I know these authors. We all share a secret, and it makes me feel small, in a good way, like I'm part of something bigger—something powerful and magical and so special it can't be explained. I breathe it all in, appreciating everything about these walls, especially their chaos.

AJ's standing on the stage now with his arms crossed, and I realize he's watching me, waiting for me to take a seat.

Sydney calls me over, so I sit next to her. I start feeling edgy, but I remind myself that I don't have to read right away. I should listen first. Listen and clap. That's it.

Listen. Clap. And breathe.

I turn around and find Caroline on the couch behind me. She gives me a thumbs-up.

Chelsea takes her seat on the stool. Some of the others are wearing dramatic eye shadow, and a few have visible tattoos and piercings, but not Chelsea. Like Caroline, she's not wearing any makeup at all, and for a moment, I picture what I could do with a little bit of blush and some lip gloss. Maybe some product to shape her curls into well-defined ringlets, and a headband to pull them away from her face.

Then I catch myself.

"I wrote this in my car last week." Everyone's quiet while Chelsea unfolds a slip of paper. "This is called 'Over You.'"

> It only took two hundred and forty days
> > seven hours
> > twenty-six minutes
> > and eighteen seconds
>
> But I can finally say it:
> > I'm over you.
>
> I no longer think about
> > the way your hips move when you walk
> > the way your lips move when you read
> > the way you always took your glove off
> > > before you held my hand so you could
> > > feel me.

I've completely forgotten about
 texts in the middle of the night, saying you
  love me, miss me
 inside jokes no one else thinks are funny
 songs that made you want to pull your car
  over and kiss me immediately.

I can't remember
 how your voice sounds
 how your mouth tastes
 how your bedroom looks when the sun first
  comes up.

I can't recall
 exactly what you said that day
 what I was wearing
 how long it took me to start crying.

It only took two hundred and forty days
 seven hours
 twenty-six minutes
 and eighteen seconds
 to wipe you from my memory.

But if you said you wanted me again
 today
 or tomorrow

or two hundred and forty days

seven hours

twenty-six minutes

and eighteen seconds from now,

I'm sure it would all come back to me.

We're all silent for a minute. No one moves. No one claps.

Only a minute ago I was sitting here, planning Chelsea's makeover, and now I'm staring at her, filled with a strange mix of sadness and jealousy. She had all that? I'm sad for her, but I can't help but feel a little bit sad for myself, too. I want that. She lost it, but at least she *had* it.

"Hello? Glue stick?" The room erupts into applause, and Sydney stands and tosses her the glue. I'm clapping along, but I'm also watching Chelsea, wondering if she's going to cry after that cathartic reading. She doesn't. She throws her shoulders back as she steps proudly off the stage.

"Okay!" I hear the voice at the front of the room and find Abigail bouncing in place, shaking out her arms by her sides. "I still get a little nervous up here," she says, and it surprises me. Abigail doesn't seem like the type to get nervous. Then I remember she told me she was the newest one in the group. She runs her hands over her dark pixie cut and looks down at the paper in her hands. "I wrote this in science class last week."

She holds up a ripped scrap of graph paper, sits on the stool, and takes a couple of deep breaths, like she's readying herself.

"This is called 'As If,'" she says, and she shakes out her

arms again. When she starts to read, I can see the paper trembling in her hands.

Shy, insecure,
afraid to speak up?
"Act as if," they say.
Act as if you're not.

Stand tall when you walk.
Project your voice when you talk.
Raise your hand in class.
Act as if.

Speak your mind. Cut your hair.
Be the part. Look the part.
You can do this.
Just act as if.

If you really knew me,
If you could see inside,
You'd find shy and insecure and afraid.
Acting as if.

Ironic, isn't it?
The only time I'm not
Acting "as if"?
When I'm on a stage.

I'm the first to start clapping. I can't help it. That was totally unexpected.

Sydney hands me a glue stick. "Want to do the honors?" she asks. I take it from her, beaming as I toss it underhand to Abigail.

I glance around, wondering who's next. There doesn't seem to be any assigned order or anything, and I'm waiting for the next person, ready to watch them be brave. Abigail sticks her poem to the back wall, and then returns to the stage as Cameron and Jessica jump up from their seats to join her.

Jessica walks to the edge. She's wearing a tank top, and when she turns, I spot a small tattoo on the back of her right shoulder. When she greeted me at the door, she was so soft-spoken that I assumed she was really shy, but now she's full of energy, and when she opens her mouth to speak, a loud, authoritative voice emerges.

"Okay. I know we've been building this up," she says with her hands on her hips. "You finally get to hear what we've been working on, but we need you to help us out."

She slaps her hands against her legs, starting the beat— *Left-left-left-right, left-left-left-right, left-left-left-right*—and she keeps it going while the rest of us join in. *Left-left-left-right, left-left-left-right.*

Then Jessica looks right at me, the beat still thumping in the background, and says, "We've been working on this for the last month or so, but it's still far from perfect. This is the first time we're performing it down here. So, no judgment."

I'm not sure why she cares what I think, but I'm kind of flattered. Maybe they're as nervous about performing in front of me as I am about performing in front of them.

"This is Edgar Allan Poe's 'The Raven,'" she says, and then steps back in line with the other two. And right on the beat, Cameron takes a step forward and begins speaking in a booming voice.

> Once upon a midnight dreary, while I pondered,
> weak and weary . . .

And he keeps going, reciting the poem from memory. On key lines, the other two join in. He finishes with a bold Only this and nothing more, and Jessica instantly picks up where he left off.

> Ah, distinctly I remember it was in the bleak
> December . . .

Her words are loud and clear and right on the beat, and I feel chills all over when she delivers the last line: Nameless here for evermore.

That's when Abigail jumps in.

> And the silken sad uncertain rustling of each pur-
> ple curtain
> Thrilled me—filled me . . .

She's head-bobbing to the rhythm, singing the verses more than saying them, and the rest of us are still slapping our legs and tapping our feet in unison, keeping the beat, interjecting an encouraging yell now and then.

The three of them say the last line together:

This it is and nothing more.

They stop completely. It takes the rest of us a beat or two to realize it, and we taper off a little more slowly, but then we all stand up, bursting into applause. The three of them hold hands and bow. Abigail curtsies a few more times on her own.

"There's a lot more to that poem," Jessica says when the room is silent again. "Fifteen more stanzas to be exact, but we'll keep working on it."

Abigail pulls a piece of paper off the stool and AJ tosses her the glue stick. She slides it across the paper and the first three stanzas of "The Raven" occupy a previously empty sliver of space on the wall.

"We have time for one more," AJ says from his spot up front, and while he doesn't call me out specifically, I know I'm up.

I don't think I can do this.

Something brushes against my shoulder and I turn around. Caroline's leaning against the back of my couch. "Go," she says, tilting her head toward the stage.

I shake my head at her and mouth, *I can't*, but she raises

her eyebrows and whispers, "Sam. Don't think. Just go."

Before I realize what I'm doing, I hear myself say, "I'll go." It's not loud, but it's loud enough for Sydney to hear, and that's all it takes.

"Sam!" she yells, and suddenly everyone's looking at us. My stomach turns over as I reach down into my pack for my yellow notebook. I take my time finding it.

When I stand, all eyes are on me, and my first instinct is to sit back down, but I force myself to step into the aisle instead. The room is so silent, I can hear my sandals slapping against my heels. I step onto the stage and turn around, giving myself a moment to take in the room. I feel my shoulders relax.

I can do this.

"I wrote this here in Poet's Corner," I say, perching myself on the stool. Everyone claps and cheers. The notebook quivers in my hands.

"I have this thing for the number three. I know it's weird." I'm expecting a few confused looks, but their expressions don't change at all.

Okay. The hardest part is over. They know about the threes. Read.

"This poem is called . . ." I stop. I look at them, one at a time, saying their names in my head to remind myself that they're no longer strangers.

Sydney, Caroline, AJ, Abigail, Cameron, Jessica.

The next girl takes me a second.

Emily.

But then I look at the girl with the blond curly hair and my mind goes blank. She read first today. Her poem was incredible. Her name starts with a C. When she raises her hand and waves, I realize I'm staring at her, and I feel the adrenaline surge kick in as heat radiates from my chest to the tips of my ears.

Shit.

Now, my breathing feels shallow and uneven again, and I rest my hand on my stomach. I think I'm going to be sick. I fix my gaze on the poem I wrote down here last week, and the words blur and spin. I blink fast and try to focus again. But I can't.

I can't do this.

I'm about to make an excuse and step down, when I feel a hand on my left shoulder. I turn my head and see Caroline standing there. I want to say something, but the inside of my mouth feels like I've been chewing on a piece of chalk.

"Close your eyes," she whispers. "Don't look at anyone. Don't even look at the paper. Close your eyes and speak." I start to object, but she cuts me off before I can say anything. "You don't need to read it. You know this poem cold. Just close your eyes. Don't think. Go."

I close my eyes. Take a deep breath. And begin.

"It's titled 'Building Better Walls,'" I say.

> All these words
> On these walls.
> Beautiful, inspired, funny,
> Because they're yours.

Words terrify me.
  To hear, speak,
To think about.
  Wish they didn't.

I stay quiet.
  Keeping words in
Where they fester
  and control me.

I'm here now.
  Letting them out.
Freeing my words
  Building better walls.

I didn't feel Caroline's hand leave my shoulder, but when I open my eyes I spot her in the back of the room again. She's clapping and screaming along with everyone else, and although I'm still shaky, it feels different now, more like euphoria than fear.

Chelsea. Her name comes to me the second I see her smiling.

And suddenly there are glue sticks flying at me from all directions, and I'm laughing as I deflect them. Finally, I catch one in midair.

AJ steps onto the stage and comes in close. "Congratulations," he says.

I lean in even closer. "I thought you needed to vote?" I whisper.

He nudges me with his elbow. "We just did," he says, gesturing toward the glue sticks scattered all over the stage. Then AJ points to the one in my hand. "Go ahead. Make it official."

I run the glue across the back of my poem, and then I step off the stage and walk toward the back of the room, past all of them. I stop right next to Caroline, find an empty spot on the wall, and slap my words against it.

melt with you

Three weeks later, I'm beaming as I open my locker after lunch.

Today, I read a simple, six-word poem I wrote on a hot pink, happy-looking Post-it. On one side, it said: *What you see . . .* And on the other side: *It isn't me.*

I wondered if the Poets might consider a six-word poem to be a cop-out, but I forced myself not to question it, and when I read, I stood tall and didn't even break a sweat. When I finished, they were up on their feet, cheering loudly like they always do. As I mounted my poem to the wall, I bent the paper so it stuck straight out, making both sides visible.

Four times on stage. Four poems on the wall. I don't quite feel like one of them yet, but at least I'm contributing.

I grab the block of pink Post-its out of my backpack and carefully write out the same poem, and then I stand back and stare at my locker door, looking for the perfect home for it. I move a few things around until those three photos Shrink-Sue asked me to print slightly overlap the ones of the Eights and me. The noise ordinance looks out of place, so I crumple it into a ball and stuff it into my backpack. I move the picture of me standing on the blocks right next to the small mirror, and let the words "What you see . . ." bridge the gap between the two.

I'm leaving campus that afternoon as the Indian summer sun beats down. It's late October, but it's got to be almost ninety degrees out here. After I open my car door, I let my head fall back, face toward the sky, and close my eyes, feeling the rays heat my cheeks. It feels calming. But the water will feel even better. I can't wait to get to the pool.

Throwing my backpack on the passenger seat, I turn the key in the ignition, but before I back out, I thumb through my playlists, trying to find something that matches my mood. I settle on *Make it Bounce*.

The student lot is almost empty, so it doesn't take long to get out through the gates and onto the street. I'm humming along while I wait for the light to change, and when it does, I take a left onto the main road that leads through town and toward the swim club. I've only made it a block when I hit another red light. I turn the volume up another notch. As I'm waiting, I look out the passenger window. My breath catches in my throat.

AJ is sitting at the bus stop with his arm around a girl, and I squint to get a better look. Her head is down, so I can't see her face, but I recognize her by her build and the way her dark hair flips up at her shoulders. It has to be Emily. Out of all of them, I know her the least. She always sits in the back with Chelsea, and I've never heard her read on stage, but I often think about her warm greeting the day I joined.

She slides her fingertips under her eyes and I realize she's crying. I glance over at AJ. He's staring right at me.

I turn away quickly, but when I look back again, he's signaling me to pull over. As I approach, I cut the music and roll the window down. AJ leans in.

"Hey, can I ask a favor? Em needs a ride." He looks back over at her and I follow his gaze in my rearview mirror. "Her mom is really sick, and her dad sent this text telling her to come straight home, which . . . can't be good."

I look at the odometer.

I'm not supposed to have passengers.

I glance into the rearview mirror again and see Emily typing away on her phone and brushing away tears at the same time. "Sure. Of course."

When AJ returns with Emily, he climbs in back.

Wait. He's coming too?

"Hi. Are you okay?" I ask, and she gives me a weak, "Yeah. Thanks."

From the backseat, AJ feeds his arm over her shoulder

156

and she wraps her fingers through his. I look at their hands, intertwined.

Of course he has a girlfriend. How could I have missed that?

I feel a pang of sadness, but I push the thought away, forcing myself to think of Emily and whatever's going on in her life so I don't fixate on anything else. It works.

AJ navigates. *Left here, right here, straight for about a mile, and stop, it's this house, the white one on the left.* I look at the odometer, resting on zero.

I overshoot the driveway on purpose. I pass two more houses, turn around in a court, and double-back. Three. Perfect.

Emily's house is small but cute, cottagey-looking, complete with a white picket fence, a big oak tree smack in the middle of the lawn, and a tire swing hanging from the thickest branch. It's painted white with bright blue trim and bright blue shutters, and it looks so cheery, it strikes me as odd that anyone could be sick or sad on the other side of that bright blue door.

"Thanks, Sam," Emily mumbles as she climbs out of the car. AJ steps out onto her driveway, and when he hugs her, she buries her face in his chest. He says something I can't hear, and she comes up on her tiptoes to kiss him on the cheek.

He climbs into the front seat next to me, and together, we watch Emily open the door and step inside. "Thanks," he says. "That was really cool of you."

"Of course."

Wait. He's not staying with Emily? I have to do the odometer thing all over again?

"Is she okay?" I ask as I back out of the driveway.

"I don't know." He's quiet for a long time, staring out the window. "Her mom has stage four lung cancer," he finally adds.

Now I really don't know what to say. I'm curious to know more about Emily's mom, but I don't want to ask, and AJ doesn't seem to be planning on sharing any more information, so we're both silent for the next few blocks as I snake through the residential neighborhood, back the way I came, heading toward the main road. He tells me to take a right—I assume to get to his house—and then goes back to staring out the window.

I'm sad he has a girlfriend, but watching him right now reinforces what I already suspected about him: he's a good guy.

"How long have you been together?" I ask.

"We're not together." He doesn't look at me. "We're just friends. We've been good friends for a long time."

They're friends.

It reminds me of what he said in Poet's Corner that day, warning me not to push the friends thing with him.

Out of nowhere, he shakes his head hard and sits straight up. "Sorry. I'm worried about her. I'll snap out of it." He twists in his seat to face me. "Subject change. I liked the poem you read this afternoon."

"Thanks." I picture the Post-it in its new home on my locker door, and smile to myself. "Sometimes there's a whole side of your personality you don't always show everyone, you know?" I glance down at the odometer. It's on seven. "I've been thinking about that a lot lately."

He leans back in his seat and I steal a glance at him. He's watching me with an inquisitive look in his eye. "It's interesting. Usually, after people read a few times, they start to make more sense to me, but every time you read, I find myself . . ." He pauses, searching for the right words. "More curious about you."

"Good. Then we're even," I say.

"Are we?" he asks.

"I've been curious about you for a while now." I'm not sure where this boldness is coming from, but it feels pretty natural. I look over at him. "Sorry. That was all your fault."

"Mine?" He laughs. "How so?"

"Blurting." I take a left at the light and merge into traffic, picking up a little speed. "I've been practicing."

"And how's that going for you?"

"Not so great. I probably took it too far today."

He raises his eyebrows. "How so?"

"Kaitlyn isn't speaking to me because she told me my hair looked ridiculous like this." I point at the braided, twisty thing I did this morning. I wanted to try something new. "And instead of heading off to the bathroom to change it like I normally would, I told her that her blush was too heavy and she looked like a mime."

"Well, if she looked like a mime, it makes perfect sense that she's not speaking to you," he says.

That cracks me up.

"I shouldn't have said that to her," I say, grimacing. "It was probably more bitchy than blurty, wasn't it?"

"Maybe. Don't worry, you'll get the hang of it." He grabs my phone from the cup holder. "Want me to put on some music to kill this awkward silence?" he asks with a grin.

Normally I'd be irritated by the idea of someone poking around in my music—it seems personal, like rifling through my underwear drawer—so I'm surprised when I hear myself say, "Sure" and then tell him my password, like I do that all the time. Out of the corner of my eye I can see him sliding his finger across the screen. I don't even feel the urge to grab the phone out of his hand.

"Hmm," he says.

"What?"

"Oblivious to Yourself. A Cryptic Word. It's a Reinvention. Are these playlist titles, or a creative way to study for the SATs?"

I've never let anyone see my playlists, and I've never told anyone how I name them, but he's looking at me like he's genuinely curious.

"You'll think it's weird."

"Try me."

I can tell from the expression on his face that he's not going to let me off the hook.

"Fine. When I was in fifth grade, my mom and I went to see this linguist speak at the public library. I fought with her about going, but once I got there, I was completely fascinated.

"He talked about words—where they come from, how new ones evolve, how politicians and advertising executives and even journalists use them to subtly manipulate people's opinions. I've had this thing for words ever since. Especially lyrics. I don't just listen to songs, I study them. It's kind of a hobby."

Shrink-Sue doesn't call it a hobby. She calls it an obsession. A ritual. Whatever.

AJ looks like he approves. He still seems interested. So I keep talking.

"I've mentioned that I have this thing for the number three, right? Well, when I'm done making a new playlist, I pick one song that, sort of, captures the mood, you know? And then I find three words I like within those lyrics, and that becomes the title.

"Like the playlist *Melt with You*. It's a bunch of upbeat eighties dance tunes, and kicks off with the song *Melt with You*. And I love the word 'melt'. . . it's so visual, right? And the songs are kind of cheesy, so it fits. *Mellllt*." I say the word slowly, drawing it out, and I feel my mouth turn up into a satisfied smile. "See. It makes me happy every time I say it."

I look over my right shoulder, wondering if he's considering asking me to pull over and let him out of the crazy girl's car. Instead I find him sliding his thumb up and down the screen again. "Okay, I've got to know about *Grab the Yoke*." He glances at me. "Yoke. Great word. Limited uses."

Hmm. I'm not sure how to explain this playlist without admitting more than I'm ready to. I go for it anyway. "Track four, 'Young Pilgrims' by the Shins."

"Excellent song." I catch his head bouncing lightly, in time with the beat, and I can tell he's thinking through the lyrics, hunting for the word "yoke."

I spare him the effort and feed him the line. *"I know I've got this side of me that wants to grab the yoke from the pilot and just fly the whole mess into the sea."* I pull up to a red light. "I love that line. I don't often want to grab the yoke and crash into the sea, but sometimes I do."

Great. Now he's staring at me like he's worried about my safety or something. "That one's kind of a depressing playlist. I listen to it when I need a good cry. But don't worry, I'm not about to off myself or anything."

"What's *Song for You*?" he asks, and I feel the blush heat my cheeks when I think about the playlist filled with acoustic guitar songs I selected because I could see him on stage, playing them, singing them. At night, I sometimes pop in my earbuds, close my eyes, and imagine him playing them and singing them to me.

"Nothing. Just a playlist," I say, hoping he won't open it up to check its contents.

He doesn't respond right away. There still isn't any music on, and now he's telling me to turn onto his street.

"So your fascination with words isn't a new thing?"

"No. Just the poetry part."

I can tell we're getting close to his house, but I'm not ready for him to get out of my car. I try to think of a question that will keep him talking even after we reach his driveway.

"When did you start playing guitar?" I ask.

"Seventh grade," he says.

Keep him talking. Keep him talking.

"What made you choose guitar?"

"You." He's still running his fingertip along my phone, and he doesn't take his eyes off the screen after he says it.

"Me? What do you mean 'me'?"

"Do you really want to know?"

I look at him out of the corner of my eye. "I think so."

"It's this one here," he says, pointing up at a long, steep driveway. I check the odometer. It's almost on three. I turn left, step on the gas, and stop in front of his garage door. When I pull the parking brake, the odometer hasn't moved much, but it's close enough.

Three. Yes!

I cut the engine and twist in my seat so I can see him better. "So, what do I have to do with you playing guitar?" I ask. I was bursting with curiosity, but now that I study his face, I'm not sure I should be.

"Well, not *you*, per se. But a bunch of people like you were when we were kids."

Uh-oh. My stomach drops.

He tosses my phone into the cup holder. "I transferred to a new school in fifth grade, but as you can probably imagine,

I was a big target there, too." He laughs a little, even though it's not funny at all. "My mom finally took me to see a speech therapist. I went every week, but I didn't make much progress. Eventually, it seemed easier to just stop talking."

I suck in a breath and press my lips together.

"But then, in seventh grade, I had this incredible music teacher. She handed me a guitar. She worked with me after school, every day, all year long, teaching me how to play. It gave me something I didn't have before, you know? It kind of . . . gave me a voice, I guess."

"Yeah," I say, hanging on every word he says.

"Then, one day, I started singing. And when I did, the stutter disappeared completely."

"Really?"

"It was like I needed to trick my brain, to distract it with something else. After that, my speech therapist starting working music into our sessions, and ever since then, it's gotten better. Now it only hits me when I get really nervous. Like, when I'm sitting in my driveway in a girl's car." He peeks up at me from behind his thick lashes. "Then I trick my brain by doing this."

He looks down at his hands and I follow his gaze. He's got his finger and thumb pressed together, brushing them against the seam on his jeans. "No one realizes it, but when I have to talk in class, I'm always playing invisible guitar strings under my desk."

"AJ . . ." I begin, but I don't know how to finish. I have no idea what to say.

He reaches behind him, feeling for his backpack. "Do you want to come in?"

I look up at the house for the first time. It's a small single-story nestled into the trees, like one of the original cabins built in our Northern California town back in the 1940s. There are lots of houses like this around here, but most have been added on to, remodeled, or knocked down completely. This one doesn't appear to have had any work done to it.

"Do you want me to?"

"Yeah." He opens the car door and looks at me, smiling. God, I really like it when he does that.

"I don't know." I smile back at him. "That might make it seem like we're becoming friends."

"Hmm," he murmurs. "Maybe we are."

three little chords

Inside, AJ's house is pretty and well decorated, but just as dated as the outside. The carpet is dark brown shag, and I don't even want to venture to guess how long the wallpaper has been there, but the furniture is nice, and even though it's a mishmash of styles, it all kind of works together. It's cute.

AJ sets his keys on the table in the entryway and drops his backpack on the floor.

"Is your mom home?" I ask.

"She's at work. She gets home around six." He gestures toward what I assume is the kitchen and says, "Do you want anything to eat? Something to drink?"

I shake my head and set my keys on the table next to his. "Is anyone else home?"

He looks down the hallway. "My brother, Kyle, might be here, but I doubt it. He plays soccer so he's never around."

Of course. Why hadn't I put the two together before? "Kyle's your brother?"

Kyle Olsen was the first freshman in years to make it onto the varsity soccer team. He's really good. He's also incredibly good looking. Because of his age, Olivia was worried about what the rest of us would think after she hooked up with him at a party last year, but over dinner the next night, we collectively listed his attributes on a napkin and unanimously approved him as the only freshman acceptable to date. Armed with the Crazy Eights' stamp of approval, Olivia jumped in with both feet. But she was mortified when, in the days that followed, Kyle didn't go out of his way to see her again and gave single-word replies to her many, many texts.

AJ steps into the living room and I follow him. The walls are covered with framed photos of both of them, but Kyle's definitely stand out, his action shots on the field dominating AJ's formal school pictures. I note the photos of his mom with the two of them, and I wonder what happened to his dad, but I don't ask. I'm going with divorce. Kaitlyn's dad died when we were in third grade, and there are still pictures of him all over their house.

"In case you're wondering, yes, I'm well aware of the fact that my little brother's a lot cooler and much better looking than I am." He points at a close-up of his brother in a case-in-point sort of way and then grins at me. There's that dimple again. I look at a photo of Kyle. He doesn't have one of those. "I'll probably need therapy someday."

I try not to take his therapy comment personally. "Hey, don't knock it. You might enjoy paying someone to listen to you talk about your problems."

"I wasn't knocking it at all."

I roll my eyes. "Besides, I doubt you'd need it. You seem pretty well adjusted."

He steps closer and leans in, like he's telling me a secret, and the sudden gesture of familiarity takes me aback. He seems even taller now that he's this close. He looks cute in his button-down shirt. And he smells good, like boy deodorant. "Everyone's got something," he says.

"Do they?"

"Of course they do. Some people are just better actors than others." His words remind me of Abigail's poem about acting "as if."

He's still close, nearly touching me, and I feel an overwhelming impulse to tell him my "something." If I stood here in his living room and told him about Shrink-Sue and my OCD and my sleep issues and my severe *lack* of adjustment—how, over the years, I've become an Oscar-worthy actress, so skilled you'd think I'd tricked myself into actually *being* one of the normal ones—would he understand? I bet he would.

My mouth drops open and the single syllable "I" falls right out, as if my body's ready to spill everything, even though my brain is telling me in no uncertain terms to zip it. He's watching me, waiting for me to say more. "Can I get a glass of water?" I ask.

Chicken.

He raises his eyebrows. If he asks, I'll tell him everything. The words are right there. They just need a little nudge, the tiniest bit of permission. But AJ says, "Sure," and steps backward, breaking our invisible connection.

I watch him leave the room, and as soon as he's out of sight, I blow out a breath, shut my eyes tight, and dig my fingernails into the back of my neck three times. He just told me all about his stuttering, and that couldn't have been easy for him. I should tell him about me. He'd understand. I'm sure he would.

The water is running in the other room, and when I hear it stop, I use that as my cue to pull myself together. I open my eyes and quiet my fingers before he returns.

"Here you go." He hands me the glass.

"Thanks." His lips are full and they look like they'd be really soft. I wonder what it would be like to kiss him.

"Follow me," he says, and so I do, down the hallway, past two other bedrooms, and into his. He closes the door behind us.

I've seen plenty of boys' bedrooms, mostly at parties, but stepping into AJ's room feels different, like I'm doing something scandalous. Kurt was the most serious boyfriend I've ever had, but his mom had a strict rule that girls weren't allowed beyond the kitchen. One time, we snuck into his room anyway. I don't remember feeling like this.

I recognize some of the bands in the posters on his walls, like Arctic Monkeys and Coldplay, and I'm pretty sure the guy with the guitar is Jimmy Page. His desk is cluttered with mountains of loose papers, notebooks, gum wrappers, and empty soda cans. I can barely see the computer monitor and its matching keyboard.

His bed is just a mattress and box spring sitting directly on the floor and pushed into a corner under the window. It's neatly made with a navy blue comforter and white pillows, and I try not to stare at it.

"So this is where you write?" Every time he steps on stage to play a song, he begins by saying, "I wrote this in my room," and it always makes me wonder what it looks like. In my head, I have this picture of him sitting at a desk with his guitar on his lap and his notebook in front of him. But there's no room on that desk for even the smallest pad of paper.

He holds his arms out to his sides and says, "Not much to see, but yeah. This is it." He struts over to the corner of the room and lifts his guitar off the stand, and it sort of floats along with him, as if it's part of his body. He sits on the edge of the bed and starts playing. I'm not familiar with the song, but it's soft and melodic, like a tune I'd put on my *In the Deep* playlist.

I'm not sure where to go. I'm dying to sit next to him, but that feels too awkward, so I finally settle on leaning against his desk. On top of a stack of papers, I spot a tortoiseshell guitar pick. I start fiddling with it to distract myself.

Actually, I like this spot. From here, I have a perfect view of his hands. I stare at his fingers, mesmerized by the way they slide up and down each string, and I begin to picture them sliding up and down my body instead, tracing the curve of my hip and slipping over the small of my back. I watch his mouth move, too, enjoying the way he unconsciously smiles and licks his lips as he plays. He glances over at me. I suck in a breath. And before I know it, I'm taking slow, cautious steps, moving in his direction.

When I'm standing right in front of him, I wrap my hands around the back of his neck. "Don't stop playing," I say as I rest my elbows on the edge of his guitar and bring my mouth to his. His fingers continue to glide along the strings, his notes still filling the room as his tongue slips slowly over mine in perfect synchronization with his song. My fingers move through his hair. I ease him closer. Then the music stops.

"This is all the stuff I'm working on," he says.

His words jolt me back to the room and I realize he's holding up a clipboard bursting with paper, and I'm still standing next to his desk, at least six feet away from him. I cover my mouth and catch my breath, as AJ drags his thumb through the pages. "There's a lot of crap in here, but the ones on top might actually have potential."

It sounds like an invitation to join him, so I slip his guitar pick into the front pocket of my jeans, and with shaky legs, I walk toward his bed and sit. I'm still trying to breathe normally and block out that kiss that didn't actually happen, but it's even harder now that he's this close. And when his lips still look so insanely soft.

"May I?" I ask, pointing toward the clipboard. He gives me a single nod as he hands it to me. I can't imagine offering up my three notebooks and letting someone have their way with them, but he doesn't seem to mind. He goes back to playing.

AJ plucks and strums next to me while I read page after page. Some of his songs are funny—humorous observations on mundane things like microwave burritos and car washes—and some are much deeper, far more intense, and not funny at all. I go from laughing to chills and goose bumps and back to laughing again.

"Stop it," AJ says. He looks amused as he watches his fingers pick at the strings. He's still filling the room with notes.

"Stop what?"

"You're being too nice to me. They're not that good."

"They are," I say, flipping to another one.

AJ stops playing. He holds his hand out. I give him the clipboard and he drops it on top of the comforter, slightly out of my reach.

I expect him to start playing again, but instead he shifts position and lifts his guitar over his head. "Here," he says as he loops the strap around my neck.

I try to push the guitar away. "No way. I don't have a clue how to play this thing. I liked listening to you." I reach behind us, feeling for the clipboard. "Play something you're working on," I say, but he stands up and grabs my arms, and I freeze in place. I hold my breath. I look at him. I don't move because if I do, he might move his hands.

"Right now I'm working on teaching you to play guitar," he says.

He adjusts it in place and shows me where to put my fingers, saying things like, *That string. Good. Now index finger on that one. Not so flat. Bend your fingers more. Use the tips, not the pads. Better.*

"That feels weird."

"Then you're doing it right."

It feels like my hands can't stretch far enough.

"Now strum."

A sound comes out. It actually resembles a chord.

"Good, now move this finger here." He lifts my finger off one string and moves it to another. "Now strum again."

Again, that sounds like a chord. It even sounds like those two chords work well together.

"That's good," he says. "Now play both of them." I move my finger back to the first string, play the chord, move it again, and play the next one. And then he shows me how to play another, and I put the three together, over and over again. AJ returns to his spot on the bed, watching me.

"See?" he says. "Told you. Piece of cake."

"I'm not bad." I play my three little chords again, this time with a little more shoulder and a bit of attitude.

"Okay, this next one is trickier." He climbs onto the bed, and now he's on his knees, right behind me. I feel his thighs brush against my hips. "Scoot back a bit," he says, and I do.

Oh, please let this be real.

He moves in even closer, resting his chest against my back and reaching around me, looking over my shoulder, repositioning my hands.

"There, that's easier." He says it like he's a teacher and I'm his student and this is totally normal, just part of the job. His voice is low, but he's so close to my ear, I can hear him breathing. "Pinkie here. Okay, try that," he whispers. I strum, and when I do, it sounds like a real note.

"Now play the other three and add this one."

I'm not sure I can do this when I can feel his chest rise and fall against my back, but I go for it. The last note feels awkward, and it takes me a few tries to get it right, but eventually I get all four chords to work together, and it sounds a lot like music. "That's really good," he says. "How does it feel?"

His breath is warm on my neck. "It feels incredible."

"Want to play it one more time?" he whispers in my ear. My fingers are glued to the strings and I can't move them. I shake my head, because I don't want to play it one more time. I want to bring my hand to his cheek because it's right *there*, and I want to turn my head a little more to the left and kiss his lips because they're right there too. He's quiet. I wonder if he's thinking the same thing I am.

He's not. Teaching moment complete, he scoots out from

behind me and sits by my side again, this time leaving slightly more space between us. I miss him instantly.

"Thanks." I give him his guitar, and he takes it without putting up a fight this time.

"That wasn't so horrible, was it, Sam?" he asks, as he feeds his head through the strap.

Sam. I'm still not used to hearing him say my name.

"No. It wasn't." I'm all buzzy. To clear my head, I stand and walk around the room, shaking out my hands, giving all my attention to the posters on the wall. On his desk, behind a big stack of papers, I see the top half of a silver picture frame. I pick it up.

It's AJ and a girl I've never seen before. She's sitting between his legs, leaning back against his chest. Both of his arms are wrapped tightly around her waist and his chin is on her shoulder. She's pretty. Not in a glamorous way or anything, but in that natural, sporty kind of way.

I hold up the frame and ask, "Who's this?"

AJ gives a quick glance in my direction, fingers still on the strings, but when he sees what I'm holding, he stops playing. "Um . . . that's Devon."

He sets his guitar on the bed and stands, combing his fingers through his hair as he approaches me. "We broke up last summer. I didn't even remember that was still on my desk." He waves his hand toward the stack of papers it was hiding behind as proof.

I stare at the photo again. "Do I know her?"

"No. We met at one of Kyle's tournaments. She went to Carlton." Our rival high school, one town away. "She would have been a senior there, but her dad's company transferred him to Boston last July." He crinkles his nose. "That was kind of the end of us."

She's a year older than him. Interesting. They've been broken up for more than three months and her picture is still on his desk. That's interesting, too.

"We stayed in touch until school started, but then, I guess we got busy with other things. I haven't talked to her in a while."

"She's pretty." I say, running my finger along the silver frame, wondering if blurting is allowed or frowned upon in situations like this. I want to know about Devon. I *need* to know about Devon.

I feel that familiar swirling in my mind, starting like a whirlpool, spinning slowly, steadily, but preparing to build and speed, fed by information and the need for more information, until it's a full-on maelstrom.

"How long were you together?" I ask, against my better judgment.

"Almost a year."

"That's a long time."

"Yeah."

I study the picture again. Her blond hair hangs down past her shoulders, her bangs swept to the side. There's something about the way she's squinting her eyes, like they're doing more than smiling, and I wonder if AJ said something that made her laugh right before the shutter snapped.

The questions keep coming. I can't stop staring at the two of them. They look so comfortable together, so happy, and I can't help but wonder if I'll ever feel that relaxed with another person. Will a guy ever look at me the way he's looking at her in this photo? Kurt never did. Brandon never even thought to. AJ and Devon were a real couple. You can tell.

I look up at him. "Did you love her?"

He studies the photo in my hands. Then his eyes fix on mine. "Yeah."

"Do you still?" The corners of his mouth turn down, and I can't tell if I crossed the line or if he's simply giving his response some serious consideration.

"I don't know."

It's honest. I'm not upset by his answer. It's sweet, actually, and the information is satisfying in the way I need it to be.

I glance over at his bed, trying not to think about my next question. It's right on the tip of my tongue, but I can't bring myself to ask it, even though AJ's standing there, patiently waiting for me to speak.

"Did you bring her to winter formal last year?" I ask instead, and he gives me a funny look.

"Yeah." After a brief pause, he asks, "Who did you go with?"

"Kurt Frasier."

"He seems nice."

"He's a dick."

"Oh."

"Worst school dance story ever."

"Tell me."

"You're just trying to change the subject."

"Yes. Desperately."

That makes me laugh.

I drop the picture frame back behind the papers where I found it, but it barely leaves my grasp before AJ reaches for it and stuffs it into a drawer.

"Actually," he says, "don't tell me. It's a really bad idea for wimpy musician guys like me to want to physically harm jock football players. You'll tell me he was mean to you, and because I'm your friend"—he brushes his elbow against my arm—"I'll see him at school and feel the need to defend your honor, and an hour later I'll be in the ER getting stitches in my eyebrow or something."

I smile. "We're friends, huh?"

He takes a tiny step toward me. Close but not too close. *Friends*-close. "Can we be?" he asks.

Two weeks ago, I was okay with being his friend, but that's not what I want anymore. I like him. I like everything about him. The way he plays. The songs he writes. The things he says. The way he makes me want to speak out, not hold my words inside. That dimple. Those lips. I have to know what they feel like. Maybe this is like blurting? Maybe I'm not supposed to think about it; I'm just supposed to do it. But I want him to make the first move.

Please kiss me.

"Sure," I say.

"Good," he replies. "Friends."

But I want more. I picture Devon again. She had more. Then again, she probably never teased him for a stutter he couldn't help and harassed him until he switched schools.

"I should go," I say. I'm still standing close enough for him to touch me again, and for a moment, I wonder if he's going to. He doesn't move, but his eyes are locked on mine like he's trying to read my thoughts. If he could, he'd understand how much I want him to wrap his arms around my waist and rest his chin on my shoulder, looking as relaxed and happy as he did in that picture.

He takes a deep breath and blows it out slowly. "Okay," he finally says, and then he walks over to the door and turns the knob, and I reluctantly follow him down the hall.

He grabs my car keys off the table in the entryway and dangles them in front of me. "Thanks again for helping Em," he says.

"Of course."

"I'll see you tomorrow."

"See you tomorrow."

I don't want to leave. I'm not entirely sure he wants me to.

AJ stands on the porch, leaning against a post with his arms crossed, watching me climb into my car. I back out of the driveway, wondering what would have happened if I'd been brave enough to tell him what I was really thinking.

this white rabbit

Somewhere around midnight, I thought about taking my sleep meds and calling it a night. But I couldn't stop researching, and so by four a.m., I've learned a lot about Devon Rossiter.

I've been manically opening window after window, clicking on link after link, scanning site after site, but I'm still following this white rabbit down the hole, trying to feed my brain enough information to reach my own personal wonderland.

Like Kyle, Devon's an impressive athlete, well ranked on the varsity team. Carlton High posts everything from team to individual player stats, so not only can I see her official photo (again, pretty, very little makeup) I can see every point, goal, shot, assist, and steal for every game she played last season.

There are lots of team photos, and in each one, she's wearing her long blond hair in a ponytail with her bangs pulled back in a sporty-looking headband. There are a few videos, but she's not in many of them.

Across the Internet, I've uncovered a few articles about her. I can't figure out where she lived, but that would be easy if I really wanted to find out. Even if my mom didn't represent either side of the sale, I bet her laptop has all the details. I can't tell where they live now, but I've located her dad's new office in Boston on Google Maps.

Devon seems to be settling in well at her new school, making friends both on and off the team. Her Facebook page is open, so I can see everything, including a long and photographically detailed history of her "almost a year" relationship with AJ. There are pictures from our winter formal—I recognize the background—and I notice that she's wearing more makeup in these shots, but still not as much as I wear every day. There are photos of the two of them at the beach and the two of them at her niece's third birthday party and the two of them at various soccer tournaments, including one of her standing in between AJ and Kyle, her arms draped over their shoulders. She checked in at a few movies and tagged AJ, too.

Of course, that leads me to AJ's Facebook page, but I find his almost completely untouched, save the times she's tagged him. There's nothing about him here. Nothing about music. Nothing about poetry. Nothing about his brother or his mom, and nothing that connects him to the people in Poet's Corner.

With every click, I feel the tightening in my stomach, the adrenaline rush, the *need* to learn more—not about her, about *them*. I have to understand this relationship and what's at the root of that expression on AJ's face when he's looking at Devon and not at the camera, which he's often doing.

It's not jealousy. It's my OCD, this inexplicable, uncontrollable *need* to know one thing, and then one more thing, and then yet another thing, until my brain is exhausted. And tonight, I'm having a hard time reaching that level, because it's been hours and I still don't know what it feels like to be in a relationship like this one—to be that close, that connected to someone else—and I need to figure it out in a way no one but Sue would ever understand.

Sue. If she saw what I was doing right now, she'd lose it.

I shut my laptop and let it drop to the floor next to my nightstand. I shouldn't be doing this. Devon doesn't live here, and she and AJ aren't together. And even if she did and they were, he's not my boyfriend. We're barely even friends.

My logical mind knows these things are true, but still, when I close my eyes, there's this image of AJ and Devon twisted up in the sheets together. His mom isn't home until six o'clock on weeknights. His brother's never home either. He loved her and he still might. How often did they meet at his house after school? Did they cut classes, spending full days together in his bed? They must have, at least once. Serious relationship, empty house, that's what you do.

I don't want to think about the two of them, arms and legs intertwined under his blue comforter, but I can't fall asleep because I can't get the image out of my head.

grip the bat

Caroline and I are sitting in the front row of the theater in our usual seats. I'm jittery from my lack of sleep and the three Cokes I've had since lunch. This morning, I found AJ's guitar pick in the pocket of my jeans, and I've been fiddling with it ever since, like it's my thinking putty. I've already decided I'm going to tape it up on the inside of my locker door.

"You're freaking out about a girl he hasn't spoken to in months," Caroline says.

We've been trying to write a new poem, but I'm having a hard time concentrating. I keep picturing the way AJ folded his arms around me, his chest pressed against my back, his warm breath on my neck. I can't stop reliving that fantasy when I crossed the room and kissed him. I'm trying to think about the good parts of being alone with AJ in his room yesterday—because there were many of them—but no matter what I do, that photograph pops into my mind every time.

"They were together for almost a year. It was serious, Caroline."

"So? It's not serious now."

I close my notebook, leaving the pencil in the binding to mark our place, and lean back in the crushed red velvet theater seat. "See, this is good. Keep going," I say, curling my finger toward me. "This is why I told you. I knew you'd talk some sense into me. Did I tell you she's a senior?"

"Three times now." Caroline shifts in her chair and folds her arms across her chest. "Do you really want to hear what I think, Sam?"

"Of course I do." I throw my head back and stare up at the ceiling. She doesn't say anything. I look at her, so she knows I mean it. "Please. I want to know what you think."

"Fine," Caroline says. "I think he likes you."

"You do?"

She doesn't answer my question; she just keeps talking.

"I also think you're overcomplicating this whole thing. I think that even when good, totally normal, completely healthy things happen in your life, like"—she starts articulating her points on her fingers—"your new car, writing poetry, spending an afternoon at AJ's house, meeting me . . ." She sits up straighter wearing a big fake grin, then returns to her serious tone. "You seem determined to find a way to make them *unhealthy*."

"You? I haven't turned you into anything unhealthy."

"Maybe not yet."

"What's that supposed to mean?"

She laughs. "You're missing the point, Sam. These are all good things, all *normal* things. And rather than enjoying them, you find a way to twist them into something toxic."

I roll my eyes and let out a sigh. "Trust me, I want to stop thinking. I wish I could."

Caroline kicks her feet out in front of her and leans way back in the chair, crossing her arms behind her head and staring off into the distance. "You should hit baseballs."

"Baseballs," I say flatly.

"My dad and I used to go to the batting cages at the park. Have you ever been?"

"I think I went when I was a little kid. It was ages ago. I don't really remember it. Why?"

"You get in the cage all alone." Caroline sits up straight and begins talking louder and faster, using her hands for emphasis. "Then you grab your bat and take your stance, and even though you're expecting it, there's a sense of surprise when this ball comes flying out of the machine right at you." She points to her head. "So you grip the bat tighter and bring it to your shoulder. You watch the ball. Then you step into it and swing."

"Okay," I say, wondering where she's going with this.

"You hear this *crack* when the bat connects, and then the ball's gone, soaring off into the distance. But you can't relax, because now there's another ball speeding your way. So you tighten your grip, take your stance, and swing again. And you keep going until your time runs out. By then, your shoulder is throbbing and you're totally out of breath, but you feel pretty damn good."

"You're saying my thoughts are like baseballs."

Her lips curl into a satisfied grin. "Exactly. And you, my friend, stand there in the batting cage and let those balls smack you in the head, over and over again. But you don't have to." She taps her finger against her temple. "You have a perfectly good bat."

"I have a broken bat."

"Eh. It'll do," she says. Then she leans back in the chair again and crosses her arms, looking proud to have said her piece. "Are you still glad you asked me what I thought?"

"Actually, I am."

"Good. Can you be happy, please? Things are going well, aren't they?"

They are. I can't wait to get downstairs on Mondays and Thursdays. I'm even starting to look forward to stepping up on that stage. I haven't had an Eights-induced thought spiral in weeks.

"Yes."

"You can trust them, Sam," she says. "Let your guard down with AJ and everyone else. And please, stop thinking so much. You're exhausting."

I give her foot a kick. She kicks me back. And we return to writing.

he reaches out

Over the next week, I see AJ everywhere.

I pass by him between classes, and not only after second period the way I've intentionally scheduled. At lunch each day, I see him sitting with Emily and Cameron, and when I catch him stealing glances at me, he quickly looks away and pretends to be deep in conversation. I've seen him in the student lot twice now, climbing into Sydney's car. Both times I drove away wishing he'd climbed into mine.

On Monday, I tried to talk with him after Poet's Corner, but he said he had somewhere he needed to be and sped up the stairs so fast, Caroline even looked at me and said, "Well, that was awkward."

I'm starting to wonder if I imagined the whole thing last week, because it's as if the two of us never chatted over linguistics and playlists, I never saw his room or his clipboard filled with music, and that an incredibly sexy acoustic guitar lesson—the one I'm still obsessing about and not even *trying* to block from my mind—didn't happen at all.

As I'm walking to third period on Wednesday, I see him heading right toward me. I'm expecting one of his usual nonchalant chin lifts, and preparing to return it with one of my own, but instead, he slows his steps and actually makes eye contact with me.

"Hey," he says under his breath as he comes to a stop. "Do you have a second?"

I nod and he waves me over to the side of the corridor and out of traffic. He dips his head toward mine. "How are you?" he asks.

He's not wearing a cap today, and when his hair falls forward, I have to fight the urge to push it away from his face. "I'm good. How are you?"

"Fine." He looks so nervous, shifting his weight, like maybe this isn't going the way he'd planned. Then I realize he's picking at his imaginary guitar strings against his jeans. I wonder if I'm fidgeting too, so I check myself and find my hand at the back of my neck, my nails all set to dig in. I wrap my backpack strap around my finger instead.

"I just wanted to . . . to see how you were doing."

I try to think of something interesting to say—something open-ended that we will have to continue talking about when we have more time. But before I can speak, he reaches out and brushes his thumb against my arm. It's not a mistake. It's deliberate.

"I'd better get to class," he says.

"Yeah," I say. "Me too."

He drops his hand and slips back into the crowd, and I look around the corner, watching him walk away. It's all I can do to not follow after him. I want to talk to him longer. I want him to touch me like that again.

I bite the inside of my cheek three times and head off in the opposite direction.

safe with them

"It must be Wednesday!" Colleen chirps when I open the door. She walks around to my side of the counter and gives me a bottle of water. "It's been a crazy day around here. Sue had an emergency at the hospital this morning, and we've been running behind schedule ever since."

It's funny. Sometimes I forget that Shrink-Sue has other patients, let alone patients who require her to drop everything and come to a hospital for them. I'm glad I don't need her *that* much.

"Get comfortable," Colleen says.

I stick in my earbuds, and instead of choosing my usual waiting room playlist, I turn on *Song for You*. Leaning against the wall, I mentally bring myself back to the school corridor, happy to have a few quiet moments to think about what happened with AJ this afternoon. He was so nervous, and so cute, and so close to me. As music fills my ears, chills travel through my body, and I realize I'm brushing my thumb back and forth across my arm, exactly the way he did.

Something catches my eye, and I see Colleen waving from behind her desk. I give a tug on the cord, and my earbuds fall into my lap. "She's ready for you."

I shuffle into Sue's office. She doesn't waste any time getting down to business. "So, fill me in on your week."

As I stretch my putty, I give her the basics. Everything with my family is good. School's fine. The poetry's going well, getting better, still therapeutic. We get to the inevitable conversation about the Crazy Eights, but surprisingly, there isn't much to tell. Things have been fairly drama free.

"How are things with Caroline?" she asks, and today, I don't smile like I normally do. Instead, I feel my blood pressure spike.

"I've been thinking about her a lot this week. I'm feeling really guilty, you know?" I picture her the way the Eights would see her: frayed flannels and weird T-shirts, blemished skin and stringy hair. "She's my friend. I shouldn't be keeping her a secret."

"Does she mind that you haven't introduced her to the Eights?"

I shake my head. "No. I asked her earlier this week. She told me she has no interest in meeting them."

"What would they say if you told them about her?"

I squeeze my putty hard. "They'd feel threatened. You know how they are about other girls. It's a loyalty thing."

Sue writes something down in her portfolio. "Then maybe you shouldn't tell them?"

"Is that okay?"

"It sounds like it's okay with Caroline. Is it okay with you?"

"I guess so." My heart starts racing again. "Actually, I don't feel like talking about this today."

She considers me for a moment, and then returns to her portfolio, flipping pages back to review her notes from earlier sessions. "How's your swimming going?"

"I've been going to the pool six days a week since school started. I'm still swimming with the team, but I'm also starting to swim by myself at night. It feels great. *I* feel great."

This is going to be an easy session. Sue's had a busy day. She's behind schedule. Let's wrap it up so I can get to the pool.

I'm trying to decide what to say next, when Sue closes her portfolio, rests her elbows on her knees, and locks her eyes on mine. "Why do you look so tired?" she asks.

"What?"

"How have you been sleeping?"

Sue doesn't move. I'm pretty sure she's not even blinking. I consider cracking a joke, or coming up with an excuse, but after a long pause, I decide to tell her the truth. "I stopped taking my sleep meds," I whisper.

"When?"

I blow out a breath. I know the exact date. It was the week

Caroline first introduced me to Poet's Corner. I couldn't get AJ's song out of my head, and at some point, an obsession with his words turned into an obsession with my own. "Over two months ago."

She lets out a heavy sigh. I can't see what she's writing, but knowing she's documenting my failure makes me feel even worse.

"You can't get by with four to five hours of sleep each night, Sam."

I've been doing exactly that for the last couple of months, and I'm fine. I'm not failing my classes or anything. Well, I might be failing Trigonometry, but that doesn't have anything to do with the amount of sleep I've been getting. That's entirely about me sucking at trigonometry.

"What are you working on that late at night?"

I tuck my feet underneath me and recline into the chair, staring up at the ceiling. "Poetry," I say, which is true, but not entirely. Sometimes I'm writing. Sometimes I'm reading other people's poems on the Internet. Sometimes I'm listening to music and looking up lyrics, but that counts as a form of poetry, doesn't it?

"Can't you do that during the day?"

I shake my head hard. "No time." But it's more than that. It's not that I don't have the time, it's that the time's not right. Even when I'm writing during my swim, or in the theater with Caroline, it's dark and quiet. I need it dark and quiet. I need to write at night, where no one can see me.

"Sam," she says strictly, and I smash my putty between my fingers. "Have you stopped taking your other medication?"

"No. I wouldn't do that, Sue."

I remember how I used to be before we found the right meds. I used to fixate on something—it could be anything—something one of my teachers said, or something one of the Eights said, or something I heard on the news. I knew the thoughts were irrational, but one thought led to another, and to another, and once the spiral started, I couldn't control it.

It was horrible. I'd yell at my parents. Throw tantrums like a six-year-old. I was tired all the time, because trying to function while you're trying to ignore all those swirling thoughts is physically and mentally draining. I'm still myself on the meds, but they help me control the thought spirals. I wouldn't go back to a life without them.

"This matters to you, doesn't it?" I must look confused, because Sue adds, "The poetry."

"Yeah. More than I expected it to."

It's not only the writing I crave; it's everything that goes along with it. It's the look of anticipation on people's faces when I step up on that stage. It's the way Caroline tells me I'm getting better with every new poem, that I'm finding my voice. It's the way I can construct verses during a one-hundred-meter fly.

It's everyone downstairs, too. How invested I now feel in their lives. How my heart aches when Emily tells us that her mom is getting worse, not better. How Sydney's poems always put me in a good mood. How Chelsea hits me right in the feels with her pieces about her ex-boyfriend. It's the way Poet's Corner is changing my life, exactly like Caroline said it would.

More than ever before, I feel compelled to tell Sue about that room. I feel guilty about not telling her. And, aside from Mom, she's the only one who would truly understand how walking into that room feels like diving into the pool; how the paper on the walls gives me such an overwhelming sense of peace.

But I can't break my promise.

Sue must see something in my expression, because hers softens and she starts tapping her mechanical pencil against her knee like she does when she's thinking.

"What if we compromise?" she asks. "I have another sleep medication I'd like you to try. It's fairly new. It's fast-acting and has a short half-life, so it'll be out of your system quickly. You could write until midnight, then take it, and you'll get at least seven hours of sleep. You can write, and also give your brain and body the rest they need. What do you think?"

I like the idea of writing when I need to. Mostly, I like doing it with Sue's permission. "Sure," I say.

She hunches over and scratches out a prescription. "Take this every night at midnight or earlier." She hands it to me. "Now, I have something important to say."

Uh-oh. Here it comes.

"Things are going really well for you right now, Sam. That's because you're making some positive changes in your life, but it's also because we've found a treatment plan that's working. Weekly talk therapy, medication to help you sleep, and medication to keep invasive thoughts from turning into anxiety attacks. You are not allowed to modify this combination on your own."

"Okay."

"In the future, you talk to me *before* you stop taking any of your meds. Are we clear?"

"Yes."

"Good." She sits up straight and crosses her legs. "Now, is there anything else you'd like to tell me?" She folds her hands in her lap and waits. I sneak another peek at the clock. Crap. How could I still have thirty minutes left in this session?

I fall back against the chair and close my eyes. "AJ," I say matter-of-factly.

"The one you and Kaitlyn used to tease."

I nod.

"How long has this been going on?"

I do the math in my head. It's been more than two months since Caroline first led me down those stairs and introduced me to him. A month since he let me back into Poet's Corner. A week since he invited me to his house and declared us "friends."

"For me? A couple of months. For him . . . there's nothing 'going on' because, as with all my other crushes, this one's completely one-sided."

"Why do you say that?" she asks.

"We're friends." I think about the way he touched my arm in the hallway today, and I feel the corners of my mouth turn up against my will. "But I like him. He's nice to me. The whole thing feels . . . normal."

"How does it feel normal?" she asks softly, using the tone of her voice to get me to tell her more.

I want to tell her everything.

I stretch my putty in my hands, trying to decide where to begin. Finally, I stop searching for the right thing to say—the thing I think Sue *wants* to hear—and instead I just start talking in that scary, filterless way. "I don't think I'm obsessed with him. I mean, okay . . . I might be kind of fixated on his ex-girlfriend, Devon. I started looking her up last week, and it was pretty bad at first. But I'm starting to get it under control." I tell Sue about Caroline's baseball trick. Sue writes it down.

"But so many things feel better lately. I'm not spending half my evening wondering if I'm going to pick the wrong thing to wear the next day. During class, I'm not worrying that I might say something at lunch that will piss off one of my friends so they all gang up against me and ignore me for three days straight. For the first time in a long time, *I don't care* what they think. And it's not because of this guy or the writing or Caroline, or, I don't know, maybe it is. Maybe it's about all those things."

I'm getting all fired up now and I can't sit still, so I leave my chair and walk over to the window overlooking the parking lot.

"All I know is that I feel good about myself for the first time in ages. I might still be obsessing, but I'm *obsessing* about poetry and words. I'm swimming almost every day, and my body feels strong and my mind is so clear. And I like this really nice guy who might not think of me as more than a friend, but at least he's not a jerk like Kurt, or completely unattainable like Brandon."

She drops her portfolio on her seat and walks over to join me at the window.

"I'm not obsessing about my friends turning on me or kicking me out of their little club. I no longer care if they do."

It feels freeing to say the words out loud, and as I do, it occurs to me how true they are: I care more about what AJ and Caroline and the rest of the people in Poet's Corner think of me. If *they* kicked me out or stopped talking to me, I'd be devastated, but, of course, they'd never do that in the first place. I feel safe with them.

"And maybe it's obsession. Maybe it's not 'normal' at all. But I feel good when I'm with them."

"I can tell."

And without revealing the secret room underneath the school theater, I spend the rest of the session telling her about AJ, Caroline, Sydney, Cameron, Abigail, Jessica, Emily, and Chelsea. My eight new friends.

not a date

The parking lot is practically empty. I swipe my card key across the panel, the gate clicks open, and I step inside, looking around and wondering why there's no one here. Team practices ended hours ago, but even though it's after eight o'clock, there are usually a few adults swimming laps when I arrive. Tonight, there's one person in the pool. I'm relieved she isn't in lane three.

I drop my swim bag on a chair near the edge and unzip the side pocket that holds my cap and goggles. From the main compartment, I grab my towel, and when I do, I spot my blue notebook. It's such a nice night, so I stuffed it in here at the last minute, thinking I might sit on the lawn and write for a while after my workout.

I've never actually *written* at the pool before. My poems come to me as I'm swimming, and I put them on paper when I get home, but they never sound quite as good as they did in my head. This way, I figure I won't lose my groove.

I'm only halfway through my workout when the other swimmer leaves the pool and heads for the outdoor shower. A few laps later, I see her unlatching the gate and disappearing into the parking lot.

I'm alone. I hop out of the pool and walk over to the chair, grab my blue notebook and a pen, and set them on the edge of the pool under the diving block.

By the end of my workout, the paper is soaked through at one corner and some of the ink is smudged, but I can still read my latest poem clearly. I add the final line and read the whole thing through, top to bottom, crossing out a word here and another there, swapping them out for better ones as I go. When I'm done, my toes are sore from sliding them back and forth against the wall, but I don't care. This poem is actually pretty good.

I wrap myself up in my towel, jam my notebook back into my bag, rinse off in the shower, and head into the locker room to change into my sweats. I'm piling my hair into a ponytail when my phone chirps. I grab it off the counter and read the text:

you were really good today

It's from a number that's local but unknown. I type:

who is this?

I rest the phone on the counter next to the sink and gather the rest of my things together. I'm throwing my bag over my shoulder when the phone chirps again.

AJ

My bag slips to the floor and lands with a *thud*. I check the string. This isn't a message to the whole group; it's a message for me. My eyebrows pinch together as I reply.

hey

It's been two weeks since that day at his house, when he taught me how to play guitar, told me about his ex-girlfriend, and we became friends and nothing more. I'm not sure what to say, so I stand there, leaning against the bathroom sink, holding the phone with both hands, and waiting for his reply. Finally one comes.

what are you up to?

I can't really tell him that I'm standing in a semipublic bathroom, my hair still wet from the shower, wearing sweats and no makeup, so I fall back on what I was doing fifteen minutes earlier.

not much. just writing

sorry. didn't mean to interrupt

you didn't

I'll let you get back, just had to tell you I
really liked your poem

Yesterday, when I took the stage for the sixth time, I read a poem about unreliable friends, people you love and feel bonded to but can never truly trust. It was about feeling alone and vulnerable, and never being able to fully let your guard down. When I read it, my voice was clear and loud and direct, and I've never felt more confident on that stage, but I've never felt more exposed either. Everyone clapped and I slapped the paper on the wall, officially giving myself another contribution to Poet's Corner. And it felt good. Really good.

thanks

I'm not sure what to say next, but I don't want the conversation to end, so I decide to keep it going, being mysterious, or flirtatious, or maybe a little of both.

remember when you asked me if I
had a favorite place to write

yeah

that's where I am

As I type the words, I'm thinking about what AJ said that day I was alone in Poet's Corner with him. When I asked him why everyone starts by saying where they wrote their piece, he said that the places matter, and by voicing them, they become part of the poem. I liked that idea.

I'm intrigued . . .

I bite my lip. Is this still friendly chatter? Or are we flirting now? He might be flirting. I'm not sure.

Just in case we are flirting, I wait for a minute before I reply, letting his words hang in the air a bit longer, keeping him "intrigued."

are you going to tell me?

I stare at the screen for a long time, gathering my nerve to reply with the first thing that pops into my head, which is definitely flirtatious, no way around it. I leave the locker room, throw my bag down on the grass, and then sit, legs folded underneath me, thumbs hovering over the keyboard. He's the one who keeps telling me to blurt. And blurting in a text is way easier than blurting face-to-face. Feeling shaky all over, I type:

want me to tell you or show you?

Before I can chicken out, I press SEND, and my heart starts beating faster and harder than it had been when I was swimming laps. I drop the phone on the grass and shake out my arms, wishing I could un-send that text. But I can't. It's out there. I can't take it back now. Crap.

I can see the screen. There's no response. He doesn't know what to say. I pushed it too far. I wind my wet ponytail around my finger, feeling stupid and starting to wonder if he's ever going to reply, when the words appear in a speech bubble on my screen:

show me.

I fall back on the grass and reach for the phone, covering my mouth with my hand to hide the stupid grin that just appeared out of nowhere. Play it cool. Play. It. Cool.

tomorrow night?

pick you up at 8

He'll be in my car again. I start to panic about the odometer, but then I force the thought away with a nice memory of the day he sat in my passenger seat, listening to me talk about my playlists and how I named them. Telling me how he learned to play guitar, even though it was painful to hear. My parents would kill me if they knew I was driving around with passengers. So would Sue. But I can't pass up this chance. I want him to sit in that seat again, to talk to me like he did that day.

see ya then

I stare at the screen for what feels like a long time, wondering what this whole thing means. Wondering if it means *anything*.

It's not a date. It's me showing a fellow poet where I like to write. That's it. But the thought of bringing AJ here makes me feel giddy and light-headed. I look around the empty club, hoping it will be this quiet tomorrow night.

bring your swimsuit

I press SEND and wait until the ellipses finally appear on the screen, telling me he's typing his reply.

I'm not sure I'm intrigued anymore

I laugh. I'm not ready for this conversation to end, so I read back through the string as if that will keep it alive, and to double-check to be sure I didn't misread anything. I don't think I did. He started it. I kept it going and turned a friendly check-in into something else. "It's not a date," I say aloud as I run my finger along the glass. "We're friends."

Even if that's all we are, it's okay. This is already more than I ever expected from AJ Olsen.

the bottom rung

Last night, I took the sleep meds that knock me out for eight solid hours, and set my alarm to wake me up fifteen minutes earlier than usual. This morning, I showered quickly and rushed through breakfast with Mom and Paige, all so I could get to school early and talk to Caroline before first bell. I can't wait to tell her about my non-date tonight with my friend-and-nothing-more AJ.

I'm ten minutes ahead of schedule, buckling my seatbelt and about to pull out of the driveway, when I get an all-caps text from Kaitlyn, telling me she hates Hailey. I let out an annoyed sigh as I put the car back in park. I should have known the drama-free state of existence wouldn't last long.

I'm replying when I get a text from Hailey, telling me that Kaitlyn is going to kill her. The text contains a link and I click it.

It leads me to a photo of the eight of us, taken in Sarah's backyard the summer before third grade. We're all in our swimsuits, but Kaitlyn is wearing her bottoms and nothing else. It already has more than thirty likes.

I separately tell them both I'm on my way.

By the time I arrive at Hailey's locker, Kaitlyn and Alexis are already there, screaming at her about practicing proper judgment and considering the feelings of others. My palms feel sweaty as I near the scene, and a horrible chill travels up my spine when I get close enough to hear Hailey's voice crack as she tries to defend herself without breaking down into tears. I get it. I've been in her position before, too many times to count.

Without even thinking about what I'm doing, I step in front of Hailey and push Kaitlyn away, holding her at arm's length. "Calm down, you guys."

"Do you even know what she did?" Kaitlyn yells at me. Then she returns her attention to Hailey. "What were you thinking?" she screams over my shoulder.

"I thought it was funny. I thought *you'd* think it was funny." Hailey's voice is low and unsteady. "I'm sorry. I took the picture down."

"After it got more than fifty likes!" Alexis says, jumping in to support Kaitlyn like she always does.

"You looked pretty," Hailey tries, but that makes Kaitlyn even more infuriated.

"No one's looking at my face, Hailey!"

"Oh, come on. We were little kids."

"Kaitlyn." We make eye contact and I don't let her go. It feels weird. I don't think I've ever looked her in the eye with such conviction before. "You have every right to be angry, but you have to calm down, okay? Let's talk about this at lunch."

"No, Samantha!" she yells in my face. "We'll talk about it now."

"No, Kaitlyn. We won't." I don't even blink.

I grab Hailey's hand and pull her away before either one of them has a chance to respond, and steer her around the corner, down the hallway, and over to the bathroom in the next building. Hopefully they won't think to look for us there. Once we're inside, Hailey slams her hand against the bathroom door as tears start streaming down her face.

"You know what sucks?" Hailey yells. "She would have done that to me. Or to you. And if we got upset or embarrassed she would have called us 'oversensitive' and told us 'not take everything so personally.'" She mimics Kaitlyn's voice on that last part and nails it.

Black streaks of mascara slide down Hailey's bright red cheeks, and I grab a paper towel from the dispenser and run it under the cold water. I hand her the towel. "Still. You had to know Kaitlyn would be upset. That was kind of messed up."

She takes the towel from me and sets it straight on the counter. She hugs me hard.

"It was. I don't know why I did it, Samantha," she says, but

211

I'm pretty sure I do. Whether it's conscious or not, I'm guessing it has something to do with being on the bottom rung. "Thanks for stepping in. I didn't expect you to do that."

My chest tightens. Hailey *should* expect her friend to step in and defend her. Is this the first time I have?

I hug her back and tell her it'll be okay, because it always is. "They'll punish you for a couple of days, but then they'll find something else to move on to."

"You think?"

"I'm positive. By this time next week, we'll all be referring to it as 'Itty-bitty-titty-gate' and laughing our asses off." That makes Hailey crack up. She hugs me even harder.

There's still time to chat with Caroline, so I grab the wet paper towel off the counter and press it into Hailey's hands. "I have to run. Clean up and go to class, okay? Try not to think about it." They're empty words. Of course she'll think about it. "I'll see you at lunch."

"Will you?" she asks.

"Will I what?"

"Be there at lunch?" She stares at me. "You've missed a lot of them lately."

"Have I?" Hailey raises her eyebrows like she's wondering how I could ask such a ridiculous question.

Over the last few weeks, two missing lunches turned into three and sometimes four. If I'm not in Poet's Corner, I'm hiding in the first row of the theater, writing with Caroline.

"Déjà vu," she says as she starts wiping her makeup off.

"What do you mean?"

"It's Sarah all over again. She disappeared a little bit at a time, remember? Gone a few days here. Then a few days there. And then she was gone for good."

"Hailey—"

She doesn't let me finish. "Sam. I don't want you to disappear, too. If you were gone, I don't . . ." She wrings the paper towel in her hands.

"I'll be there today. I promise." Of course I'll be there today. It's Wednesday. But if it were Monday or Thursday, I'd skip Poet's Corner to be sure Hailey was okay. "I'll see you at lunch," I repeat.

I race to my locker and take my time gathering my books, hanging back as long as I can. But Caroline never shows up.

here you are

I'm relieved to find the swim club parking lot completely empty, and I pull into a spot near the front gate. The odometer wasn't a problem. I've driven here so many times, I know all the back roads and cheats that help me park correctly.

"North Valley Swim and Tennis Club," A.J. says, reading the sign as I pull into a spot. Then he turns to me. "A pool?"

"I'm a swimmer," I say.

"Really? I didn't know that."

I shrug. "I currently hold the county record in butterfly."

"No shit?"

"No shit."

I'm feeling pretty confident as I walk to the back of the car and pop the trunk. Throwing my swim bag over my shoulder, I slam the trunk closed, head for the gate, and swipe the

214

card key against the panel. The gate clicks open, and once we're inside, I point out the men's locker room and tell him I'll meet him at the pool.

Two minutes later, I've washed my face, changed into my suit, and I'm back outside again, throwing my towel on the banister next to the showers like I always do. I've walked around crowded meets in a swimsuit since I was six years old, and I can't remember the last time I felt self-conscious about it, but tonight I do. I slip into the shallow end before AJ gets outside.

The water is warm and I dunk under, wetting my hair, smoothing it back off my face. While I wait for him, I think about Hailey. People made comments about that photo all day, and by the time the final bell rang, Kaitlyn was even more pissed at her. I make a mental note to text her when I get home.

AJ emerges from the locker room and stands there, shifting his weight back and forth, looking adorable and awkward. I call his name and wave him over.

"It's freezing out here," he says.

"The pool's a lot warmer."

"You want me to get in?"

"You *are* wearing a swimsuit." I look up at the sky. "And it is a nice night." The evenings have turned a little colder over the last couple of weeks, but still . . . it's California. The air has a bit of a bite, but the sky is clear and there are plenty of stars.

AJ nods and I watch him walk to the opposite side of the pool, past all the lane lines, and climb the ladder to the diving board. Without hesitating, he struts to the end of the platform and does a pencil dive. Feet first. Stick straight. Right in. He pops up to the surface and swims toward me, doing some kind of weird-looking hybrid stroke I've never seen before. "Let me guess," I say when he's close enough to hear me. "You never took swim lessons?"

He reaches a point where he can stand and he starts walking toward me, speaking while he tries to catch his breath. "Not a single one. I'm a natural, right?"

I laugh. "Exactly what I was thinking."

He leans back, resting his arms on the edge of the pool. "*This* is your favorite place to write? A pool."

Now that he says it that way, I realize how strange it sounds. "Yeah. I used to recite song lyrics while I swam, but ever since that first time in Poet's Corner, I've been writing poetry while I swim laps instead." I fall forward into the water and with one big stroke I'm standing right next to him. I press my palms into the concrete and lift myself out of the pool. I can feel him watching me as I walk to the opposite end.

I step up on the block of lane number three. As I take my stance, I run my finger along the scratchy surface three times, and then I dive in, pushing off with my legs as I squeeze my arms tight against my ears. Palm over hand, I pierce the surface and dolphin kick hard under the water—one, two—and on three I pop up, throwing my arms over my head. I find my rhythm: One, two, three. One, two, three. Once I have a beat, I start thinking about words.

When AJ's legs are visible under the water, I head right for

216

them. I come in close, touch the wall with both hands and push off again, swimming back to the blocks, keeping the rhythm, and making up a poem as I go. On the other side, I do one last turn and head back to the shallow end. Back to AJ.

I stop a few feet short of him and stand up, panting and trying to catch my breath. I dunk underwater and slick my hair back off my face, feeling myself flush as I think about what I just wrote.

AJ is taking big strides toward me, pumping his arms exaggeratedly as he goes. When he's close enough, he brings his hands to my shoulders and fixes his eyes on me. "Sam McAllister! What was that? And these shoulders!" He gives both of them a squeeze, and I wish I could sink back under the water and die.

"I know. They're horrible and manly. My friends make fun of them all the time."

He looks at me sideways. "Why would they do that?"

I'd shrug, but I don't want to draw any more attention to my shoulders. "Because they get off on the misery of others?"

"No, I mean why would they do that? You could knock them into next week with these." As he steps closer, his hands slide down my arms. I wanted to escape his grip, but now I'm hoping he'll stay right where he is. "Do you swim every day?"

"I do all summer, but once school starts and I get busy with other stuff, I tend to let it slip until the school team season begins in the spring. But this year, I decided to be more focused. Now I swim at least six days a week. My coach thinks

I have a good chance at a scholarship if I keep it up." I mentally prepare myself for the heart palpitations that typically follow statements about going away to college, but tonight, that doesn't happen.

He looks past me, toward the far end of the pool. "And while you were doing *that*," he says, not even trying to hide the surprise in his voice, "you were writing at the same time?"

"No." I lie. I can't tell him what I wrote. "I didn't write anything this time."

"Yes, you did. I can tell by the look on your face."

"There's no look on my face."

He pivots me around so he's at the deeper end of the pool. We're eye to eye now, and it seems like we're the same height.

"Come on . . . Tell me, Sam."

Sam. I love the way he calls me that, but right now, I wish he wouldn't. It's completely disarming.

"I can't. I wrote it in, like, twenty seconds. It sucks."

He splashes me lightly. "Sorry. I don't have any paper." I try to hide behind my hands again, but he grips my arms and gently forces them underwater, pressing them against my sides. "You saw my songs. I've written some incredibly lame stuff." I start to argue with him, but he doesn't give me any time. "Tell me, Sam." His smile is kind, encouraging, contagious, and that dimple . . . so adorable.

Another "Sam."

I blow out a breath. Close my eyes. Breathe in again.

Everything in me tells me to stop talking, but I don't listen like I usually do. And then another thought takes over.

Tell him.

"I didn't go there looking for you. I went looking for me." My voice is soft, low, and shaky. "But now, here you are, and somehow, in finding you, I think I've found myself."

I start to panic. I said too much. I knew I would. Caroline was wrong about letting my guard down.

Damn blurting.

Before I can open my eyes, I feel him rest his forehead against mine, and his hands slide around my back as he brushes his lips lightly against mine, kissing me like I just said the right thing, not the wrong thing. And this kiss . . . God, this kiss is soft and warm and perfect, and I part my lips as my fingers find the back of his neck. He tastes like spearmint, and his skin smells like chlorine, and I kiss him, remembering all the times I pictured Brandon doing this, and how those moments never ended well. I trail my fingers along his skin. He feels real. I let my hands wander up to his damp hair. That feels real too.

Please, let this be real. Please, don't let me be imagining this.

"You okay?" he asks.

He hooks his finger under my chin and tips my head back so I have no choice but to look up at him. "See, this is where that blurting thing of mine comes in handy," he says quietly. "I'll start. I'm so glad I just kissed you. I've wanted to kiss you for weeks, long before that day at my house, and right now I really want to kiss you again."

He kisses my forehead, my cheek, my mouth, and I kiss him back, but he must sense my hesitation because he pulls away and rests his forehead on mine again. "This isn't fair. I can't tell what you're thinking. Don't worry about getting the words right. Tell me."

This is a mistake. He doesn't like me; he likes the person Caroline turned me into. He thinks I'm a normal girl who swims and writes poetry, but I'm not. I'm obsessed with my thoughts and I can't sleep and I count in threes. He writes music and wears his heart on his sleeve, and I don't deserve him.

"This isn't good." I bite my lips together, pressing them closed to keep the rest of this thought inside me where it belongs. I stare down at the water again, but I can see his reflection. He's watching me, waiting for me, silently asking me to keep going, to keep talking.

"Sam." He runs his thumb along my cheekbone. "What isn't good?"

As soon as I part my lips, I hear the words slip out, like they're floating away from me all by themselves. "I like you too much."

He kisses me again, harder this time. "Good," he whispers. "I like you too much, too."

whatever this is

Once we start, we can't seem to stop.

Other swimmers rarely show up after eight thirty, and we're still the only ones here, but just in case that's about to change, I lead AJ away from the race lanes and back over by the diving board where there's a little more privacy. The water's a lot deeper over here, so we both have to grip onto the side of the pool to keep from going under, and we have to stop kissing every few minutes so we can readjust. Each time we do, we laugh because this whole thing is totally unexpected and more than a little bit funny.

Kurt wasn't a very good kisser. All tongue, jabbing into my mouth over and over again, circling way too fast. Aside from him, I've kissed guys at parties and stuff, but all of them were probably drunk at the time. So maybe it's an unfair comparison, but AJ seems especially skilled.

I try not to think about how much practice he had with Devon. I try not to think about the girls he kissed before Devon, or the ones before that. I employ Caroline's baseball trick, mentally swinging my bat, sending the negative thoughts flying into the distance. It works. Soon they're gone and there's nothing left but AJ and me, mouths and skin and water and . . . I don't want it to end. It feels so amazing to let go and lose myself this way.

He spots the ladder and slides me toward it, lifting me onto the top rung. I take his face in my hands and wrap my legs around his waist to keep him from drowning, and we go right back to kissing again.

Each time one of us makes a move to leave, the other one plants a kiss somewhere—AJ on my back as I'm climbing the ladder, me on AJ's neck just as he's starting to pull himself out of the water—and each time we slide back in, picking up where we left off. When we finally agree to get out, we make a deal and shake on it.

When we're back near the locker rooms, I step into the outdoor shower.

"You coming in?" I ask him. I'm used to rinsing off next to my teammates out here, but this feels different. I stop at a showerhead and flip it on, and he finds one farther in the back on the opposite wall.

I wash the chlorine out of my hair, stealing glances at him

as I do. AJ doesn't have a swimmer's body; his arms and back aren't as muscular, but he's definitely not skinny like I once thought he was. He's balanced, solid and strong all over.

He catches me watching him. He cuts the water and I do the same. I grab my towel and wrap it around his shoulders, and then I ball the ends up in my hands and pull him in close, like I once imagined Brandon doing to me. We kiss again for a long time. Then he wraps the towel around me. "I'll meet you back out here," I say as I head for the locker room.

I get dressed in the post-swim clothes I packed—yoga pants and a fitted sweater, a big step up from the baggy sweats and my faded hoodie I usually throw on when I get out of the pool—and I dig through my bag until I find my makeup kit. I carry it over to the mirror, but it seems weird to put any of it on. He's already seen me without it for the last hour. What's the point?

I gather my things and head for the bathroom door. AJ's hair is still damp, but he's dressed in the clothes he wore here. We walk through the gates and out to my car. He shivers and I crank up the heat.

"Music?" he asks, reaching for my phone. I remind him of my password and he makes his selection so quickly, it's as if he went straight to *Song for You* and pressed play. He tosses my phone in the console and falls back into the headrest.

The first track is an acoustic version of "Your Body Is a Wonderland," and he recognizes it right away. I can tell because his eyes fall shut and he starts plucking at invisible strings.

"Where else do you play guitar?" I ask. "Are you in a band or anything?"

"Nope. I've never played anywhere but downstairs."

"Really," I ask. "Never?"

He opens his eyes and gives me an awkward grin. "Nah. I like playing downstairs. Small group. Extremely kind. Very forgiving."

"You're afraid?" On stage, he's like a performer completely in his element, playing to the crowd, pointing and winking to cheese it up during his funnier songs. He loves being up there. You can tell.

"I can't imagine playing for total strangers. It's not my thing anyway. I love writing songs, plucking at strings, trying to figure out how the words and the notes work together."

We're both quiet, lost in our own thoughts, and neither one of us says another word until I'm at the bottom of his steep driveway. The odometer is on nine, so I tell him I want to hear the rest of this song and drive around the block one time. Then I pretend to miss his driveway. When the digits are lined up correctly, I pull up to his garage door and put the car in park.

His head falls to one side. "Can I ask you something?" I brace myself for a question about my tendency to overshoot driveways.

"Of course," I say.

"When did you start making this playlist?"

Crap. He knows these songs are for him. Or does he? I

start to say something flip, like "Oh, this old thing? Years ago," but that doesn't seem right. Besides, Caroline told me to let my guard down tonight, and when I did, things turned out pretty well.

"After I heard you play the first time."

"Really?"

I feel my face flush. I hope it's too dark out here for him to tell.

"Remember when you came to my house that day?" he asks.

How could I forget?

"After you left, I wrote something for you."

"Really?" I'm relieved to learn that he's been thinking about me, too, and that what happened tonight wasn't a spur-of-the-moment thing for him either. "Can I hear it?" I ask, watching his mouth while I wait for him to reply. I can't help myself.

His lips look so soft when he says, "Maybe."

But inside, I can feel myself starting to panic. I didn't plan any of this. Tonight has been amazing. Now it's over, and I don't know what comes next.

What happens tomorrow?

He twists in his seat and kisses me, and I try to focus on how incredible this feels, but my heart's racing fast and not in the good way it was back at the pool. The thought spiral starts to take control, and I try to ignore it, but it won't let me.

He must be able to tell I'm not fully present, because he pulls away slightly and whispers, "What's the matter?"

Talk to him.

I bite the inside of my lower lip three times. Then I take a deep breath. "What happens tomorrow?"

His hands are warm on the back of my neck. "What do you want to happen tomorrow?"

I want to be alone with you again. Exactly like this.

"I don't know. Tonight has been so . . . unexpected. Perfect. But unexpected."

"And you don't want to tell your friends about me?"

They wouldn't understand.

"It's not that . . . I just . . . I'm not sure I'm ready to share . . . whatever this is . . ."

"'Whatever this is'?" he says, laughing under his breath. He pulls me toward him. "Do you want this?" he asks in his candid way. "Whatever it is?"

So much.

"Yeah."

"So do I." He kisses me slowly, softly, and I slip right back into him, wishing I could slow down time and savor this moment a little bit longer.

"Then let's keep it to ourselves for a little while," he says. "Until we figure it out."

It's like the knot in my chest is unraveling, and now it's a lot easier to breathe. "Okay," I whisper.

"Besides," he says, "it might be kind of fun to have a secret."

Can I handle another secret? I'm already keeping Caroline

from the Crazy Eights, my OCD from everyone but Caroline, and Poet's Corner from Shrink-Sue.

Sue.

I can't keep him a secret from Sue. I'm going to have to tell her about AJ and me, and what happened at the pool tonight. But she'd see this as healthy, right? I slip my fingers under the hem of his T-shirt and touch his skin. He sure doesn't feel unhealthy.

The song changes to one of my favorites, Led Zeppelin's classic "Bron-Yr-Aur," and AJ lets out a sigh as he turns up the volume. "Wow. You know this?" His fingers brush against my waist and he hums along with the tune. "I haven't thought about this song in ages. I'll have to learn to play it for you."

I'm not in any hurry to see his ex-girlfriend-filled bedroom, but I am eager to hear him again. I'd cross the room and kiss him while he played, for real this time.

He grabs his swimsuit from the backseat. "Thanks for showing me where you write."

"Thanks for not laughing at my poem."

"I'd never laugh at you," he says. "Well, not unless you said something funny." He kisses me. And then he opens the door and steps out of the car. "Good night, Sam."

"Good night, AJ."

He gives me a wave before he disappears inside the house, and I sit there for a moment, collecting myself. Then I reach for my phone, set "Bron-Yr-Aur" on repeat, and listen to it all the way home, imagining him sitting on his bed, playing for me.

your best friends

I'm scanning the corridors for AJ while trying not to look like I'm scanning the corridors for anyone. I'm also trying to keep a straight face, but when I think about what happened at the pool last night, I just . . . can't.

AJ's lips were as soft as I thought they'd be, and they were so warm, so wet from the water, and the way his hands moved so fluidly over my body . . . No one has ever touched me like that before . . . and I have no idea how I'm going to get through this day. And he likes me. Too much. How am I supposed to keep him a secret? I swear if I turn this corner and see him standing at my locker, I'm going to press my whole body against his and kiss him hard before he even knows what's happening.

I turn the corner and my stomach drops instead. He's not

there, but the Eights are, each one demonstrating her dissatisfaction in her own unique way: a hip popped to one side, a head cocked knowingly, an eyebrow raised. Hailey's posture is less confrontational, but the nervous look on her face makes me question if she knows which side she's on.

"Hey. What's up?" My voice cracks.

"We need to talk to you." As soon as the words leave Alexis's mouth, the adrenaline kicks in. My armpits already feel sweaty, and my fingers are tingling. As usual, she has taken the role of group representative. The one who will "start the conversation."

"Where have you been?" she asks.

I look around me. "Home. The parking lot. What are you talking about?"

"Not today." It comes out in a huff, and she doesn't add the word "idiot" but she says it with her eyes. She rests her hands on her hips and takes a deep breath. "Samantha, we need to talk to you about the way you've been lying to us."

I start to interject, but she puts her finger to her lips.

"Don't say anything until I'm done, please. You've been lying to us. We just want to know why, because we"—she waves her hands around, indicating the rest of the group—"are your best friends. At least, we thought we were."

This might be a new record. We're barely twenty-four hours away from "Itty-bitty-titty-gate" and it's already a distant memory. They've found a reason to move on. To me.

My hands are shaking, my pulse is racing, and a big part of me wants to take off running right now, bound for the theater or some other dark location where I can sit and breathe and think and prepare for this. I'm no good in an ambush.

Alexis looks over at Kaitlyn. This is the point at which they've agreed to pass the baton to the next person. It's the biggest job, the one with all the heavy lifting. "You told us you were going to start swimming during lunch, but we know you haven't been."

"Your hair is never wet when you get to fifth period," Olivia interjects.

"I wear a cap," I say under my breath.

"We've tried to find you at the pool," Hailey adds. "You haven't been there."

I look at her. This would have been good information to know yesterday. I have a feeling she knew this was coming, and I feel even more betrayed.

I stuck up for her.

"So you've been spying on me?" I ask them.

"No," Kaitlyn says plainly.

"Yes," I say.

Alexis steps forward. "Fine. We were spying on you, but you lied to us and that's so much worse." Her voice pierces the air. Everyone within earshot has stopped collecting their books from their respective lockers and they're all frozen in place, watching the drama unfold, waiting to see what's going to happen next.

Over Olivia's shoulder, I spot Caroline, watching the scene from behind her locker door, and I can read the expression on her face: she's worried I'll tell them about Poet's Corner.

I give her the slightest nod and hope she knows what it means: I have this under control.

"Friends don't lie to each other, Samantha," Kaitlyn says. "Not *ever*."

No. Never.

Not even when they don't like the outfit you're wearing or your new haircut or the new song you like or the guy you think is cute. My friends—especially Kaitlyn—don't lie to each other, not *ever*, even when it's a kindness designed to spare someone's feelings.

"We're giving you a chance to come clean," Olivia says. "Where have you been going during lunch?"

I start to panic, but instead, I think about my conversation with Shrink-Sue last week, when I told her I care a lot less about what my friends think of me these days. I try to reconnect with the part of me that said and truly meant those words. I blow out a breath and lift my shoulders, standing a little taller.

"Honestly?" I say, and they all unconsciously lean in, step forward, move closer toward me. "It's personal."

"Personal?" Alexis asks. "What the hell does that mean?"

"It means it's none of your business, Alexis."

My voice is clear, my words direct, and my hands are already shaking less. Their eyes say everything they're feeling: confused, shocked, humbled, hurt.

This sucks. And it feels good at the same time.

I square my shoulders and step toward my locker. Alexis and Hailey part to let me through.

"Seriously? You're not going to tell us?" Alexis asks, and I can hear the surprise in her voice. This scenario never occurred to her.

"No, I'm not," I say, spinning the combination lock, lifting the latch, gathering my books. Using the opportunity to take a few deep breaths and get my legs to stop trembling.

The bell rings. Thank God.

I sneak another glance over Olivia's shoulder. Caroline is still watching us, but the expression on her face is now filled with relief. She might even look a little proud of me. I glance around at the Eights, wishing they'd leave so I could talk to her, but everyone seems to be in a state of shock.

The picture on the inside of my locker door catches my eye. My gaze travels past the pink Post-it that reads "What you see . . ." and over to the small mirror. I notice that the two expressions are nearly identical. Confidence. That was the word I used when I told Shrink-Sue what I liked about the photo. It's how I felt at the pool with AJ last night. It's how I feel during lunch on Mondays and Thursdays.

I look at that strong, determined expression on my face. I remember exactly what I was thinking when Sue asked me about it. Swim scholarship. A chance to go far away to college. A chance to reinvent myself. And that's when I realize that, as much as I want the scholarship, I don't need to go away to reinvent myself. I've already been doing that.

I turn to face them. "I'm doing some different things during lunch now, but when I'm not, I'd still like to sit with you guys. Is that okay?"

"Of course," Hailey says right away. No one else says a word, until she turns her head and raises her eyebrows at Alexis.

"Yeah," Alexis says. "Of course that's okay. Why wouldn't it be?"

"Cool." I close my locker door. "I'll see you later."

As I pass Caroline, I motion toward the path that leads to the theater. She follows me, and as soon as we duck into a quiet alcove, she gives me a high five.

"Nicely done. How do you feel?" she asks.

"Amazing. But that's only part of the reason why." I scan our surroundings to be sure we're still alone. "Can you keep a secret?" I ask her.

She rolls her eyes. "Of course I can."

And I tell her all about AJ and our non-date.

write about me

I've positioned myself in line so I'll be the last one through the door. When I pass AJ, I feel his fingers brush against my waist, and I slow down so they can linger a moment longer. I want to kiss him right now, right here, right in front of all the other poets. We've been keeping "whatever this is" under wraps for two weeks now, and I'm not sure I can handle it much longer. It's all I can do to walk away from him.

"Are you reading today?" Sydney asks as we head toward the couches.

"No." I can't read. All my poems are about AJ now. They'd know immediately. "You?"

She waves an Auntie Anne's pretzel wrapper in the air, then takes it with both hands and snaps it taut. "You should prepare yourself, my friend, because I'm about to wax poetic on the many virtues of cinnamon, sugar, and butter on warm dough. This—" She snaps the paper again. I can see her handwriting scrawled on it. "This may be my finest work yet."

Sydney sits in her usual chair. Abigail's already taken the seat next to Jessica. Caroline's not here yet, but I see an open spot next to Emily, and I decide to sit with her today instead. She and AJ are friends, and eventually, when the two of us aren't a secret anymore, it would be nice to know her better. She scoots over to make a little more room for me, but she doesn't make eye contact.

Before we start, I take a moment to scan the room and take it all in like I always do. I feel safe here now, not overwhelmed or unworthy, and the familiarity feels comforting. Still, Poet's Corner feels magical. I hope it always does.

I have nine poems on these walls. Nine.

Cameron's on stage alone. I've never seen him up there without Jessica and Abigail. He adjusts his glasses and opens a piece of paper. "I wrote this in my room last night," he says, and then he reads a poem that's heartbreaking and angry, and it takes me completely by surprise. I hold my breath as he reads the last line, wondering what's ripping him apart from the inside out. His face is bright red as he slaps his poem hard against the wall.

"Is he okay?" I whisper to Emily.

She leans in close and tells me that his parents are getting divorced. "He hasn't talked about it in a while. Jessica and Abigail have been trying to take his mind off it with 'The Raven.'"

"I had no idea." He's always so *on,* one of those people who seems to have his life together at all times. Now I have a lump in my throat. I thought I knew him better than this, but I realize I don't really know anything about him at all. I make a mental note to go read his poem now that I have proper context. Maybe it'll help me figure out the right thing to say to him as we're leaving today.

"Who's next?" AJ asks from his usual spot. We all look around. Sydney's directly across from me and I see her start to stand. Her timing's good. After that, we could use some comic relief.

But then I hear Emily say, "I'll go," from my other side.

She steps up onto the stage, and I realize how different she looks today. She didn't even try to cover up the thick dark circles under her bloodshot eyes, and if she brushed her hair this morning, she got caught in an especially strong wind between then and now.

"I've had a really tough week," she says, her voice cracking on the last word. My stomach knots up.

"This is called 'On My Way to You,'" she says. "I wrote it last night in my mom's hospital room."

I'm pretty sure we're all wondering how she's going to get through a whole poem, but she takes a deep breath, sits straight up on the stool, and launches in, voice steady and strong.

I drag my feet on my way to you.
Way over there.
Too far away.
Skin. Thin, practically translucent.
Eyes. Sunken. Skeletal. Bruised.
Tubes. Colorless and everywhere.
You. Not you.
Gone. Not gone.
Not yet.
Hand. Warm. Slack.
But still familiar.
So familiar.
I shouldn't have dragged my feet.

I look back at Caroline. She has her palms pressed into the couch cushions and her gaze fixed on the floor. Sydney has her hand over her mouth.

Tears are flooding down Emily's face when Jessica hurries up to the stage. She hugs her hard, then looks right into her eyes and says something the rest of us can't hear. She hands her a glue stick, and Emily finds a spot on the wall for her poem.

The room is quiet for a long time after that. Across the aisle, I can see Sydney playing with her Auntie Anne's wrapper, folding and unfolding it, before she finally shoves it under her leg.

"Okay, someone please go," Emily says. No one moves or says a word. "I already saw the wrapper in your hand, Syd."

Sydney shifts in her seat, looking around, assessing the tone of the room, trying to figure out what to do. We make eye contact.

You should read, I mouth, and she makes a face, like she's not sure. I gesture toward the stage and mouth *read* again.

Sydney walks to the front. Once she's settled on the stool, she looks out into the crowd. "This is dedicated to my friend Emily. Who, I bet, has never enjoyed the sweet, sweet goodness of Auntie Anne's."

Emily's still dabbing her eyes, but now she's shaking her head, and laughing too.

"I call this one 'Pretzel Logic,' and I'm sure it won't surprise you that I wrote it"—she snaps the bag taut again—"at my favorite aunt's house."

> At Auntie Anne's, I always ask for
> soft, sugary, slippery sweet
> pretzels. Perfectly prepped and pinched,
> rolled into rings and ribbons,
> twisted into tantalizing tastes that tease my
> > tongue and
> deliciously, delightfully destroy my diet.

Sydney pulls her skirt to one side, curtsying while everyone claps and whistles. She looks directly at Emily. "Better, darling?"

"Much."

"I'll bring you a cup of cinnamon sugar nuggets tomorrow. Crappy mall food cures everything."

I cringe at the word "everything" because I'm quite certain nothing they sell at the mall cures *cancer*. But Emily blows Sydney a dramatic kiss, making it clear she wasn't offended by her choice of words.

Sydney runs the glue stick along the back of the wrapper and steps off the stage. She hands it to Emily. "Will you find a home for this piece of alliterative genius, please?"

Emily's smiling as she sticks the poem to the wall next to the one she just read about her mom. Sydney sits next to me.

"Was that okay?"

"It was perfect," I tell her. "And yes, your finest work yet."

"Thanks. I thought so too."

The sound of a guitar pulls my attention back to the stage. I'm still trying to get my bearings after Emily's poem, but AJ's there now, perched on the stool with his guitar slung over his shoulder in that confident musician way that makes me feel light-headed.

He's plucking at the strings, just like he did in his room on that day, but the tune doesn't sound familiar. "I haven't written anything new in a few weeks," he says. "I don't know why. I guess I haven't felt like it."

My heart's already been through enough today, but his words make it sink even deeper into my chest. My yellow notebook is almost full because of him. He's all I think about, all I write about. Doesn't he want to write about me?

"A few weeks ago, a friend of mine reminded me about this song," he says, his music still floating around the room. "I've always loved it, but I didn't know how to play it, so I decided to learn, and it's felt like a bit of an escape, I guess. Like a . . . vacation."

The strings he plays begin to morph into something new, and slowly, I start to recognize the first notes of "Bron-Yr-Aur." I wrap my fingers around the edge of the cushion and squeeze.

"You guys know I love words, but this song reminded me that sometimes they're not necessary." He settles back against the stool and plucks those notes again, but this time he keeps going, playing the next ones.

His eyelids are lightly closed, his head moving gently up and down with the rhythm. Then he opens his eyes and his gaze settles on me, and like the song, he doesn't need any words because that look on his face speaks volumes.

This song is for me.

He gives me the smallest smile and turns away before anyone notices.

When he plays the last note, we all stand, clapping and cheering as he throws his guitar over his shoulder in that sexy way he does, and pulls a scrap of paper out of his pocket. "I wrote out the music," he says. Even his musical notes have that signature AJ slant to them.

He steps off stage and heads straight for Emily. He holds her face in his hands and says something I can't hear, and then she points at a sliver of empty wall space on the other side of the poem she read today. "Right there," she says.

I can't stop watching him. He's so kind to her. And Emily's looking at him with such gratitude.

AJ slaps his song on the wall. Then he pulls Emily into a hug, and she clings to him like she can't let go. I can hear her crying, working hard to catch her breath. AJ tightens his hold on her.

Then Abigail stands up and wraps her arms around the two of them. Jessica joins, and so do Cameron and Chelsea. Sydney grabs my hand and we step into the circle. Caroline's on my other side, one hand on Chelsea's back and the other on Jessica's.

Without thinking about it, I'm moving toward Cameron and tightening my grip on Sydney. Tears are rolling down my cheeks, because my heart is breaking for a girl I didn't even know three months ago.

I glance over at Caroline. She smiles wide and mouths, *Told you.*

this is good

We're sitting on my living room rug, doing homework at the coffee table, when AJ scoots closer, runs his hand around my back, and starts kissing my neck.

"Sam," he murmurs.

"Yeah."

"I think we should tell people."

That's when I realize this isn't the beginning of the typical post-homework making out on my living room rug we've been doing nearly every day for the last two weeks. I don't know how to respond, so I kiss him, but my mind's off somewhere else, caught up in a thought spiral that's a lot like the guilty one I have about Caroline, but worse.

AJ isn't like the guys the Eights go out with. He's not popular. He's not his brother, deemed acceptable even though he's a year younger, because he's not an athlete in *any* way. He doesn't dress like our clean-cut jock friends, especially when he wears that ski hat (which I admit, I find kind of sexy). He walks around campus with his head down, avoiding interaction, and he eats lunch with two people who appear to be his only friends: Cameron and Emily.

Of course, none of this is the real AJ, but that's the AJ they'll see.

He reaches over, grabs me by the waist, and pulls me onto his lap so I'm straddling his hips, and I wrap my arms around his shoulders and bury my fingers in his hair. I look at him, seeing him the way *I* do: slightly scruffy but beautiful inside and out.

"There's a reason I think we should start telling people," he says.

"Oh?" I ask curiously.

"Devon called me last night."

"Oh," I say, already panicking.

She knows I've been researching her. . . . Okay, stalking her.

"Did she call for any particular reason?" I ask, hoping I don't sound jealous, or worse, freaked out.

Caroline's baseball trick works a lot of the time, but I'm still checking on Devon. A lot. And I want to stop, but I can't, because telling someone with OCD to stop obsessing about something is like telling someone who's having an asthma attack to just breathe normally. My mind needs more information. The rabbit hole still hasn't come to an end.

"No. She called to say hi. To see how I'm doing."

Breathe. She called to say hi.

"And you told her about us?"

"No, but I wanted to. I think I should."

Breathe. He wanted to tell his ex-girlfriend about us.

"I'd want her to tell me if she had a serious boyfriend."

Serious.

I bring my hand to the back of my neck and dig my fingernail in three times, but I don't know why I'm upset. This is good.

"What's the matter?" AJ asks.

"Nothing."

"Yes, there is. I can tell. Your forehead gets all crunched up when you're thinking too hard." He kisses my forehead and I feel the muscles relax under his touch.

One. Breathe.

Two. Breathe.

Three. Breathe.

I know what I need: information about the two of them. Information I can't find on my own.

"I need to ask you something," I say, interlacing my fingers behind his head, forcing them to stay still and not scratch against anything. I look right into his eyes. "You loved her. Last time I checked, you weren't sure if you still did."

I bite the inside of my lower lip three times and hope he doesn't notice.

"I did love her," he says. "But I don't anymore, not like that.

I mean, I still care about her, but . . ." He's fumbling through this but he sounds sincere. "Trust me, you don't have any reason to be jealous, Sam."

Not jealous. Just obsessed.

I start to correct him, but then it occurs to me that I'm better off leaving this where it is.

"Seriously, I don't know how to explain it," he says, "but this . . ." He wraps his hands around my waist and kisses me, pulling me closer to him. "This is different."

The thoughts are already losing some of their power. Maybe with a little more information, I can kill them completely. "How is this different?" I ask.

"I never told Devon about Poet's Corner. She never met any of my friends, not even Cameron. She knew I played guitar, but I never showed her my songs or anything." He laughs under his breath. "That day you were in my room and I handed you my clipboard . . . It kind of surprised me. I've never done that before."

"Really?"

"Really. We're just . . . different, Sam. In every way that matters."

We.

He doesn't say we're better. He doesn't say he loves me more than he loved her. And that's okay; he doesn't need to, because now his fingers are in my hair and his mouth is on mine, and my thoughts are all about him and this *different* thing we have, and my toxic Devon-thoughts are scattering away in all directions.

They might return, but I no longer feel the impulse to check on her. The rabbit hole has come to an end—at least for now—and I've landed in wonderland, a peaceful place where my mind can finally relax and quit pleading for information.

"Thank you," I whisper, not necessarily to him, but of course that's how it comes out.

"You're welcome," he says, kissing me with even more intensity. I feel his hands travel underneath the back of my shirt, his fingers pressed into my skin, inching my hips toward him.

"You should stay for dinner," I say, pulling my hands away and attempting to change the subject. "Paige keeps asking about you."

"Will your mom mind?"

"Only if she walks in and catches us like this."

"I'll take my chances." He takes both of my wrists, guiding them around the back of his neck, positioning my arms right where they were. Then he kisses me again, moving slowly from my lips to my cheek to that spot right behind my ear that he knows I can't resist. And when I'm sure he can't see me, I bring one hand to my jeans and scratch my leg three times.

"I think we should tell people," I say.

the tenth thing

"Hey, Colleen. Happy Wednesday!" I say, closing the door to Sue's office behind me. Even from where she sits behind her desk, I can tell Colleen's taken aback, like we're actors in a play and I just went off script. For the last five years, she's had the first line.

"Hi, Sam." She stands, eyeing me suspiciously. "Water?"

"No, thanks." I rest my elbows on the counter and she stares at me, a smile teasing the corners of her mouth.

"Then go on in. She's ready for you."

I feel a bounce in my step as I walk down the hallway toward Sue's office. I've been eagerly awaiting our session, and I can't wait to see the expression on her face when I tell her what I've decided to do.

"Hi, Sam."

"Hey." I kick off my shoes and sit down, folding my legs underneath me. Sue hands me my thinking putty, but I just hold it with one hand and squeeze a few times. I'm not sure I need it today. I'm light, not fidgety. Excited, not nervous. The whole thing feels a little strange.

Sue stares at me for a good thirty seconds before she says anything. "Well, you certainly look happy today. I take it you're having a good week?"

I nod, but "good" doesn't really capture it.

Ever since the lying/spying incident a couple of weeks ago, the Eights have been especially nice to me. Alexis keeps complimenting me on my outfits, and she seems to actually mean it. Last week, Kaitlyn asked me if I wanted to co-chair the junior prom committee with her, and I think she was genuinely happy when I said yes. And when Olivia's dad got last-minute VIP tickets to a Metric concert, she invited me to join them.

Caroline came over to my house after school yesterday, and we sat in the backyard working on a new poem. It was about opening your mind, lowering your walls, and finding friendship where you least expect it. I've been trying to write it on my own for weeks now, but I couldn't seem to find the right words. As usual, Caroline knew exactly how to make it better.

And then there's AJ. I was terrified when he suggested telling people about us, but if I don't think about the "glass half empty" parts—like the Crazy Eights' reaction or making things weird with the Poets—and concentrate on the positive elements—like the two of us walking to class holding hands and kissing whenever we want to—it makes me giddy.

When I fill Shrink-Sue in on everything, she says, "Well, no wonder you're in a good mood." She closes her leather portfolio and leans forward, resting her elbows on her knees, giving me her full attention. I can't read her expression, but she's waiting and listening, urging me to keep talking, without saying a word.

"I've been thinking about our conversation a few sessions ago," I say, forming my putty into a cube. "I told you I didn't care what the Eights think, but that's not entirely true. I do care. AJ and Caroline and the rest of my new friends shouldn't be a secret. It doesn't feel right."

"I like the sound of that." Sue's smile is huge and warm and contagious. She looks so proud of me right now.

And I should feel proud of myself, but there's something below the surface that's nagging me, and I can't pinpoint it.

"Why are you scratching?" Sue asks. I pull my fingernails away from the back of my neck and stab them into my putty instead.

"I'm nervous."

"What are you most afraid about?"

It's a good question. I'm not afraid of the Eights kicking me out of the group, although it's entirely possible they will. And I'm not afraid of them coming after Caroline or AJ anymore. I wouldn't let that happen.

I look at her. "They're not going to understand what I see in him."

God, that sounds so shallow. And horrible.

"Tell *me* what you see in him."

"I've told you," I say, shifting to pull my legs to my chest and resting my chin on my knees. "He's wonderful."

"What's so wonderful about him?"

She's not going to let this drop. I shake my head and look past her, out the window, watching a tree limb whipping around in the wind. "I don't know. I can't explain it." I stretch out my putty and say the first thing that pops into my head. "He plays guitar, and, well . . . that's just hot." I hide my face behind my hand so she can't see my pink cheeks.

"I'm sure it's extremely hot, but I was sort of hoping for something less superficial."

"Fine." I stop fidgeting and give her my undivided attention. "I'll give you ten non-superficial reasons." I hold my thumb in the air and begin counting. "He writes thoughtful, funny, inspiring words. When he picks up his guitar, my heart starts racing before he even touches a string. People pay attention to him when he talks. He's humble. He kisses really well. He thinks my man-shoulders are sexy."

I stop, waiting for a reaction to those last two, but Sue's still in the same position, wearing the same expression. I hold up a seventh finger. "He's kind to people, especially his friends. When he talks about his family, you can tell that he genuinely likes them. He can't swim. At all." I laugh, picturing that hybrid dog-paddle thing he did that night I took him to the pool. Then

250

I blush, remembering how he kissed me in the water that night. How I wrapped my legs around his waist in the deep end, both of us clothed but kind of acting like we weren't.

"That's nine," Sue says.

I drop my feet to the floor and sit up again. "When I'm with him, Sue, I don't feel sick or labeled or broken. I feel *normal*. He makes me feel totally and completely normal."

She leans forward. "Does he know about your OCD, Sam?"

I stare at her. Didn't she hear what I said? Didn't she hear the *tenth* thing?

"Of course not. The second he finds out, I *cease* to be normal. He makes me *feel* normal because he thinks I *am* normal."

Sue doesn't seem to know what to say to that. She crosses her legs and sits back in her chair. "If he's all those wonderful things you said about him, he'd understand, wouldn't he?"

"I'm sure he would, but that's not the point."

I think about that day we stood in his living room and he said, "Everyone's got something. Some people are just better actors than others." I came so close to telling him *my* something. But I chickened out. If I told him back then and it scared him away, that would be one thing, but now there's too much at stake.

I can't lose him.

"You once told me that my OCD was made worse by the people I chose to have in my life. You've wanted me to distance myself from the Eights, to find new, less toxic friends, and I have. We can be the 'Poetic Nine' or some other stupid moni-ker, I don't care. I like them. I like who I am when I'm with them. I'm getting better at saying what I think. I'm not as afraid of my thoughts, maybe because I'm not holding on to them so tightly anymore. I feel like my mind is under control now. Like I'm . . . better."

"What does that mean to you, Sam? To be 'better'?"

Sane. Healthy. Not sick. Not crazy.

"Someone normal! Someone who doesn't need medica-tion to sleep or keep her thoughts under control. Someone who doesn't need *you*."

I clap my hand over my mouth, but it's too late. "I'm so sorry," I say into my palm.

"You have nothing to be sorry about." Sue's expression barely changes, but she's quiet for a long time.

What have I done?

"Have I ever told you about Anthony?" she finally asks.

I shake my head.

"He was a patient of mine many years ago. He had synes-thesia. It's a disorder where, in essence, your five senses have their wires crossed. In this case, Anthony could *hear* in color."

"I'll trade him," I say. "That sounds really cool."

"It wasn't to him. It affected his daily life. He had a hard time concentrating at work, especially in meetings when there were multiple people speaking at the same time. He couldn't tolerate crowds. He felt like his brain was on overload, con-stantly receiving stimuli. It was physically draining.

"We worked together for a long time, and after a while, his perspective started to change. He began to realize no one else heard music quite the way he did. No one else knew that his wife's voice was this really unique shade of purple. 'Normal' people couldn't see the color of laughter, and he began to feel sorry for them, because they'd never get to experience the world the way he did. I think that's a lovely way to look at special minds."

I roll my eyes. "Really, Sue? Special?"

"Very. Your brain works differently, Sam. Sometimes it does things that scare you. But it's very special, and so are you."

"Thank you." I smile at her. It's a kind thing to say. But I know where she's going here. "You're sharing this story to make me tell AJ, aren't you?"

"I'm not making you do anything. Whether or not you tell him is entirely up to you. I'm merely reminding you to embrace who you are and surround yourself with people who do the same."

"Okay."

"And you know what's totally 'normal'?" she asks. "To feel the way you're feeling right now. It's okay to want a life without medication. And a life without me."

"I'm sorry I said that."

"Don't be. I'm incredibly proud of you, Sam. You're doing great."

I am. And it feels good. But I'm still not about to tell AJ my secret.

this one boy

The next night, my phone chirps as I'm sprawled across my bed, doing my French homework. I pick it up and check the screen.

P.C.

"P.C.?" As in Poet's Corner? It's seven forty-five on a Thursday night. That can't be right. I check the recipients of the group message and see the long list of phone numbers.

I wait for someone else to reply, but no one does, so I type:

Is this a mistake?

I press SEND, and AJ responds right away.

No.

My pulse is racing as I leap off my bed and slip out of my sweats and into a fresh pair of jeans and a clean sweater. It's freezing outside, so I throw my swim parka over my arm. I grab my swim bag off the floor and my car keys off my desk.

Mom, Dad, and Paige are sitting together on the couch watching a movie. "I'm going to go swim some laps," I announce, feeding my arms through my jacket and hoping I look convincing.

"This late?" Dad asks, and before I can say anything, Mom chimes in and says, "She always swims this late." She waves me off. "Have fun."

I'm feeling a little guilty as I put the car in reverse and back out of the driveway, and a lot guilty as I drive right past the street that leads to the pool, but guilt turns to nervousness as I pull into the student lot. I drive to a spot that allows me to park with the odometer on three.

AJ's waiting for me inside the gate. He spreads his arms wide. "Welcome to your first P.M."

"Do I even want to know what a P.M. is?" I don't like this. I'm not good with surprises.

"Every once in a while we meet at night, just to shake things up. They're fun. You'll see."

He checks the surroundings to be sure we're alone, and then he reaches out and grabs the zipper on my swim parka. He gives it a tug, pulling me toward him. "You look gorgeous, by the way."

I laugh in his face. "That's not possible. I was doing homework and I rushed out the door. I didn't even put any makeup on."

"Like I said . . ." He slowly unzips my parka down to my waist and slips his arms inside and around my back, pulling me closer, pressing his body against mine. "Gorgeous," he whispers. He tips his head down and kisses me, and my lips part for him like they always do. I'll never get enough of this. I'll never get tired of kissing him.

I want to stay out here, alone with him for the next hour or two, but I know everyone's inside. And besides, it's freezing. He slides his arms away, zips my jacket up to my chin, and kisses my nose.

"That's mean," I say. "How am I supposed keep my hands off you now?"

"You don't have to. We could tell them tonight."

I think about my conversation with Sue yesterday. We could. I want to. But I've been mentally preparing to tell the Eights first. I haven't even thought about how to tell everyone downstairs.

"Never mind," he says before I can respond. He kisses my forehead. "We'll tell them later."

He drops the subject and picks up my hand instead, leading

me to the theater door. I'm surprised it's unlocked, and I give him a questioning look.

"I texted Mr. B and asked him to leave it open tonight."

He drops my hand before we step into the dark theater. I can see them up on stage, all huddled together under the dim lighting, and I do a quick count of the shadows. Seven. Everyone's here.

For some reason, we're all keeping silent, sneaking as quietly as we can through the door and down the stairs. It's strange to be in the theater at night, but it really shouldn't feel that different; these hallways are always dark and dimly lit, even in broad daylight. When AJ unbolts the door, everyone slips inside and heads straight for the lamps, flipping them on until they light up our paper walls.

I sit on one of the couches at the back of the room, and Caroline settles in next to me. "I'm nervous," I whisper when I'm sure no one's paying attention. "This is weird."

She spreads her arms across the back of the sofa, and when her flannel falls open, I can read her T-shirt: CONSIDER THIS DIEM CARPED.

"Stop worrying. This is a good thing. Don't twist it into something else," she warns.

AJ and Sydney both step onto the stage at the same time. When he looks at her sideways, as if he's wondering what she's doing up there, she bumps his hip with hers. "Before we get started, I have an announcement to make." She waves a thin stack of papers in the air.

"There's an open-mic night at this small club in the city tomorrow. All ages. Anyone's invited to read. Or *sing*," she says, looking pointedly at AJ and then back at the group. She gives the flyers to Emily, who starts passing them around.

"Larger stage than this," Sydney says, tapping her foot against the bare wood, "and far less comfortable seating." AJ blows a kiss at his couch. "But we hope the room will be equally friendly."

"Who's *we*?" Emily asks.

"So far, Abigail, Cameron, Jessica, and me. The three of them are doing 'The Raven,' and they're now up to nine stanzas, so you won't want to miss it. And I'll be reading something especially tasty, of course." Sydney folds the flyer in half and fans herself. Then she gets serious again. "Look, none of us have ever read outside this room, and we're all fairly terrified, so come cheer us on. Please."

Then she looks right at AJ. "If you think you *might* perform, and need something like, say, a guitar, you should bring that along." She steps off the stage.

"I'm going to pass," he says. "But I'll be there in the front row, cheering for you guys." AJ plants himself on the stool, resting one foot on a rung and the other on the floor. It reminds me of that day we were down here together, when he told me all about the rules of Poet's Corner and then left me alone to read its walls.

He's only wearing jeans and a T-shirt, but he's so adorable

right now. I want to leap up there and plant kisses all over his face. That'd be one way to tell the rest of them, I guess.

"Okay, take out your notebooks or whatever you write in," AJ says. Sydney holds a jumbo-size plastic bag of wrappers and napkins in the air. I had no idea she had so many poems. It's hard to believe she can zip that thing closed.

"Ideally, everyone should read tonight, but if you don't want to, that's okay," he continues.

Caroline crosses her legs at the ankle and reclines into the couch like she's settling in for the night.

"You're not reading?" She shakes her head. "Why not?" I whisper, and she makes a face. "I should force you up on that stage like you forced me."

"*Pfft.* I'd like to see you try."

"Since Sam's new, I'll explain how it works," AJ says. "One of the other members will join you on stage and randomly pick one of your poems. You read it to the group. If you don't want to read it, ask for another one or just pass. It's not a requirement to read or anything, but this is a long-standing tradition, started by the original founders of Poet's Corner." He shrugs. "As far as I can tell, it's some twisted trust exercise designed to humiliate us in front of each other."

Everyone laughs. AJ looks at me. "Be glad you didn't find us sooner, Sam. If you'd heard the ridiculous song I had to play last time, you wouldn't have stuck around."

That's impossible.

"Okay, who's up first?" He jumps off stage. "Cameron, you read. Abigail, you choose."

I reach for my yellow notebook. The blue poems are my favorites, but the yellow ones are the safest.

Cameron hands Abigail a three-ring binder, and she picks a page from the back. As it turns out, this poem isn't about his parents' divorce. It's about a girl. He's reading so quietly we all have to strain to hear him, but as he describes her long black hair, I think I understand why. I'm pretty sure this poem is about Jessica. They have been working on 'The Raven' together. Maybe AJ and I aren't the only secret down here. Cameron's face is still bright red as he picks a poem for Abigail.

She takes one look at his pick and lets out a whoop. "Yes! Easy." She launches in, reading a totally innocuous little rhyme about the sunset. Lucky.

Abigail picks for Emily. She doesn't show any emotion when she sees what she has to read. And for the first few lines, she manages to keep it together through a poem that's basically about all the things her mom might not be around to see. But after she reads a verse about our high school graduation, she stops. "I'm sorry," she says. "I can't do this tonight. Who's next?"

In a matter of seconds, Jessica is bounding up onto the stage, long black braids trailing behind her like ribbons on a kite, just like Cameron described them.

She hands Emily a bright purple book with a black rubber band around it, and Emily picks a page and hurries back to her seat. Jessica reads a short piece about her math teacher's horrible breath and gives us a much needed mood change.

Chelsea reads next. We're nearing the end of the line and I'm starting to get nervous about my turn. I can feel myself tuning out the voices on the stage and giving the ones in my head far more attention than they deserve.

They could pick anything. I have no control.

The voices are getting louder, closing in, and my palms are starting to sweat. I need to go. I need to get it over with. But when Chelsea finishes, she immediately points at Sydney, calling her up to the stage.

At least it's Sydney.

Chelsea reaches into the plastic bag and pulls out a piece of pink cardboard. She starts to hand it to her, but Sydney won't take it. "Nope. Pick another one, please."

"Syd."

"Another one, please." Sydney can't stand still. I've never seen her flustered. "Read it to yourself," she says, "but then pick again, please. That Taco Bell one is really funny."

Chelsea is quiet as she reads it. Then she leans over and whispers in Sydney's ear.

Sydney considers her for a long time before she finally steps off the stage and collapses into the couch.

Chelsea holds the piece of pink cardboard in both hands. "I've been granted permission to read this lovely poem," Chelsea says. "It's untitled. And I'm going to go out on a limb here and say it was penned in a doughnut shop."

Sydney's face is buried in the couch cushions in front of her, but she nods dramatically.

> I'm not allowed to want you,
> And you're not allowed to want me.
> So I'll just wait here patiently,
> Hoping you'll break the rules.

Whoa. I'm dying to know who she's referring to. Someone older? A teacher?

Everyone's clapping and looking over at Sydney, but she's facedown on the couch now, underneath one of the throw pillows. "Someone go next," she yells. "Quickly."

"I'll go," I say, and I step up on the stage, handing Chelsea my yellow notebook as I perch myself on the stool. She feeds her finger into a random page near the back and hands it to me.

I read the first few lines to myself.

This is bad.

I read the whole thing through in my head two more times. There's a whole lot of crazy in here, but Caroline is probably the only one who will really understand it anyway. After all, I wrote it for her.

"This is untitled, and, I don't know, it's totally random." I stop short of saying it sucks because I don't feel like being pelted with paper tonight. "I wrote it in my room after I said good-bye to a friend of mine." I find Caroline in the crowd and smile at her.

I like it when you're here.

Everything is quiet.
     Peaceful.
          So silent, I almost feel sane.

You take my mind off my mind.

Stay.
     Just one more page.

Please?

Caroline stands and starts clapping hard, and cheering way too loudly, and looking so proud of me, I want to burst. I take a bow, feeling a little proud of myself, too.

I did it. Now they kind-of-sort-of know about the crazy.

Suddenly AJ's on stage next to me, handing me his clipboard, and if he's weirded out by my poem, he's doing a great job hiding it. While he swings his guitar over his shoulder and adjusts it in place, I thumb through his songs and grab hold of a page near the top.

I pull it from the stack and hand it to him. "You can sit," he says with a cocky grin. "I'll play this no matter what it is."

I step off the stage, taking his clipboard with me. He's already plucking at strings, so I sit down on his orange couch instead of returning to my spot next to Caroline.

"Shit," he says, getting his first look at the song he committed to sing. Then he looks right at me. His cheeks are crimson and he's fidgeting with the paper. I've never seen him so uncomfortable, not in Poet's Corner at least.

I watch him, growing even more confused when he removes his guitar and returns it to the stand. He walks right to the front of the stage, past the stool he always sits on when he plays, and roots his feet in place.

"This isn't a song. It's a poem." He jumps up and down a few times, shaking his arms out by his sides. "How do you guys do this? I feel totally naked up here without my guitar." We all laugh as he shuffles into position, feet rooted again, and blows out a loud breath. "Okay, here we go."

He looks right at me. "This is called 'Wondering.' I wrote this in my room a while ago." His eyes never leave mine.

> After you left
>> I stared at the driveway
>> Feeling its emptiness
>> Wondering if you'd return.

> After you left
>> I thought about your questions
>> Wishing I hadn't been so blunt
>> Wondering if I scared you away.

After you left
> I remembered how you felt in my arms.
> How you fit so perfectly there. Like my guitar.
> Wondering if I should have kissed you when I
> had the chance.

After you left
> I sat in my room
> Remembering all the things you said, and
> Wondering about all the things you didn't.

After you left
> I sat in silence.
> Missing you in a way I didn't quite understand.
> Wondering if you'd ever come back.

He drops his arm. "And now you can all see why I write songs and not poetry."

Everyone's staring at him, questioning this poem, curious about his subject, but his eyes are still locked on mine, and that dimple of his is more pronounced than ever.

I nervously glance around the room and watch each of them connect the dots. Chelsea's face lights up. Emily waves her finger in the air, back and forth between AJ and me. Sydney lets out a fake-sounding gasp.

AJ steps off the stage and sits next to me, wrapping his hand around the back of my neck. "They know," he whispers in my ear.

"You think?" I laugh into his shoulder.

"Sorry. That was lame."

"It wasn't lame; it was perfect."

"You're not angry, are you?"

"Of course not." I give him a quick kiss, and we're surrounded by the sounds of whistles and *woots*.

Then it gets awkward. Everyone starts shuffling around, gathering bags and notebooks, heading for the door.

"Wait." AJ stands and addresses the room. "Did everyone read?"

"Everyone but Caroline," I say, gesturing toward her. But I'm not sure AJ hears me. He's already lifting his key out from under his shirt and heading to the back to unlock the bolt. She shakes her head, silently telling me it's okay. She didn't plan to read anyway.

All nine of us quietly climb the stairs, cross the stage, and file out the theater door. Everyone says their good-byes and heads off in groups in separate directions, but AJ and I hang back.

I wrap my arms around his neck and look up at him, feeling euphoric. Buoyant. Like we're back in the pool, floating, kissing, talking, laughing, just us, alone, together. We're no longer a secret. It feels incredible.

"Do you want a ride home?" I ask, winding my fingers into his hair. "You could watch me pull out of your driveway and wonder if I'm devising a plan to sneak into your bedroom."

"Would you be?" He brings his hands to my waist.

"Absolutely," I say. I'm not sure where all this confidence is coming from, but it feels right.

"Then, yes." He unzips my swim parka all the way to the bottom this time, and when he wraps his arms around my back, he pulls me into him, harder than he did before. He kisses me harder, too, and I tighten my grip on the back of his neck, thinking about how much I want this kiss to go on and on. I can't imagine driving him home and saying good night.

"You know what?" I whisper. My voice is shaking, and it's not from the cold. "I think we forgot to turn the lamps off."

"Did we?" he asks between kisses.

"Yeah."

"Hmm. I didn't forget," he says, and I can feel him smiling.

I smile back. "Neither did I."

As much as I've thought about sex, I've always had pretty low expectations about my first time. I know it will be awkward and there will be that whole struggling-with-the-condom moment, and when it's all over, we'll get dressed side by side and won't have a clue what to say to each other. I've pictured my first time as something I'll have to do to get it over with.

So far, this is nothing like that.

AJ kisses my forehead. "Stop thinking," he whispers.

"I'm not." But of course I am. I'm always thinking.

"Yes, you are. Your forehead is all crunched up." He kisses my forehead again and I feel the muscles relax. "We don't have to do this, Sam."

We're lying on the orange couch with a blanket beneath us, our clothes in a haphazard pile on the floor. He's already passed that condom thing with flying colors. I want to do this. We're practically *already* doing this.

"It's okay. I'm just really nervous."

"I know," he says. "Me too."

"You?" I stare at him in disbelief. "Why are you nervous? You've done this before."

"Never with you."

I take his face in my hands and kiss him, closing my eyes, letting his touch clear my mind, following his lead. I force myself to think about nothing but him, to concentrate on what he's doing, and after a while it becomes easier to let go.

His kisses trail down my collarbone, over my chest, across my stomach, each one sending chills through my entire body. When he finally brings his mouth back to mine, I kiss him, trying to lose myself the same way I did in the pool that night. Our hips are pressed together, and I can't believe how incredible it feels to be this close to him.

I didn't expect so much talking. But he checks in a lot, and I like how the sound of his voice keeps me present, bringing me back to him if I start to drift away.

"Are you okay?" he asks.

I slide my thumb over his bottom lip. "Yeah. I'm a lot better than okay."

"I don't want to hurt you."

"You're not. You're amazing."

"I'm not sure about you, but I think I like 'whatever *this* is.'"

I smile. "Me too." He interlaces his fingers with mine, and I'm surprised that such a simple thing can make me feel even more connected to him.

Afterward, we lie there for a long time, face to face, talking and laughing and wondering if we're the first ones to lock ourselves inside the room this way.

"I don't know," I say jokingly as I play with his fingers. "I think you've dramatically overstepped your role as keymaster."

"I blame the couch," he says. "I told you it was inspirational."

That cracks me up. "I don't think I'll ever be able to look at it the same way again."

"Yeah," he says, crinkling his nose. "They probably wouldn't want it back in the prop room now."

"No," I say, laughing harder. "I can't imagine they would."

I kiss him, feeling completely alive and totally normal—saner than I've ever felt before—and now I can't wait to walk through the halls with AJ, holding his hand, kissing him good-bye between classes. I want to know him. *Really* know him. And I want him to know me the same way.

The few lamps we left on softly illuminate the walls, and I think about all the paper around us, all this love and pain and fear and hope. We're surrounded by words. Nothing about this moment could be more perfect, because I'm absolutely in love with this room and the people in it, on the wall and otherwise. And with this one boy in particular.

totally different person

I still have no idea where Caroline eats lunch. I asked her once and she said, "Places," and when I asked her if she eats alone she said, "Sometimes." So I don't expect to see her in the cafeteria today, but I stop at the door and scan the entire room anyway.

I haven't been able to find her, not even at her locker this morning, but I'm still buzzing over what happened with AJ last night, and I can barely stand to keep it to myself another second. I have to tell Caroline first. I wouldn't have known him or any of the Poets if it weren't for her.

Where is she?

The Eights are already sitting at our usual table, Alexis and Kaitlyn on one side, Olivia and Hailey on the other. Olivia moves over to make room for me at the end of the bench.

"Dieting?" she asks as I slide in next to her. I'm confused until she points to the empty spot in front of me. "Where's your lunch?"

"I'm not very hungry," I say, but that's not entirely true. I'm too excited and nervous and elated, too *everything* to eat right now.

"So, what are we doing tonight?" Olivia asks. "I haven't heard about any parties or anything."

"I know. It's too quiet," Kaitlyn says. She takes a sip of her soda.

"Hey, I have an idea." Alexis rests her elbows on the table and looks at each of us. "My parents are going out. Come over to my house. You guys haven't all spent the night in ages." I catch Hailey raise her eyebrows as she takes a big bite of salad.

"I'm in," Olivia says. Kaitlyn follows her with a "Ditto," and Hailey says, "Sure, why not?" Then there's silence. They're all looking at me.

I wasn't expecting to find a perfect opening quite so quickly, but here it is. I dig my fingernails into the back of my neck three times and take a deep breath. "I can't tonight. I have other plans."

Alexis doesn't even try to hide the surprise in her voice. "Really? Hot date?" she asks jokingly as she sips from her bottled water.

"Actually . . . yes."

Now I have their full attention. Kaitlyn pushes her soda away, Olivia returns her sandwich to her plate, and Hailey's jaw drops, along with her chip bag.

"With?" Alexis's eyes are wide as she asks.

I run my thumbs along the edge of the bench three times. "AJ Olsen."

Kaitlyn starts laughing, and at the same time Alexis asks, "Who?" Everyone else looks at her and nods like they're wondering the same thing.

"Wait," Olivia says. "I know him. He's in my English class." She looks at me. "I mean, I don't *know* him or anything. He never says much. But I know who he is."

"You're serious?" Kaitlyn looks at me. She's still laughing. "You're going out with *Andrew* Olsen? You're k-k-k-kidding." She slaps her hand on the table, cracking up at her own joke. "No w-w-w-way." She looks around the table, but I keep my eyes fixed on her. My hands ball up into fists by my sides.

"You guys remember Andrew. From elementary school." When they shake their heads, she sings that fucking Chia Pet jingle again, and then elbows Alexis. "You remember that kid, don't you? He stuttered so badly he couldn't even say his own name."

"Kaitlyn. Stop. Now." Alexis says it like she's scolding her. I've never heard her speak to Kaitlyn that way. I've never heard *anyone* speak to Kaitlyn that way.

I wish I'd been the one to call her out, but I'm too stunned to say anything. Still, I have to speak. It's my job to defend him.

I can't just sit here and let her mock him. "I-I . . ." I choke on my words.

"See? It's contagious." Kaitlyn starts cracking up again but stops when she realizes everyone's staring at her and none of them are joining in. "Oh, lighten up. That was funny."

After a deep breath, I press my palms into the table and lean forward, closing in on her. My voice is shaking. "We were horrible to him, Kaitlyn. We teased him so much, he switched schools."

"Oh, so you're pity-dating him?"

I look at her soda. I consider throwing it at her.

"I am not pity-dating him," I say, picturing AJ on stage in Poet's Corner, guitar swung over his shoulder, singing some line that makes my heart race and my whole body melt. I think about what happened last night, the way he looked at me before, during, and after. "I'm in love with him."

I just blurted it out. I can't believe I did. I look around the table, watching for reactions, but they don't come, not right away at least. The four of them are dumbstruck.

"You're in *love* with him? Do you even *know* him?" Alexis finally asks.

Olivia jumps in before I can answer. "Wait, does he have anything to do with where you go during lunch?"

Everything gets quiet again, and I watch my friends process Olivia's words, seeing their expressions change before my eyes as they clue into the fact that this thing with AJ tonight isn't simply a *hot date* or even a *first date*. It's probably one of many. And that I might have been serious when I said that thing I just said.

"We've been hanging out together for a few months now. First as friends and more recently as, well, more than that."

They all look at each other, but none of them will look at me.

"Well, this explains a lot," Alexis finally says. "We've all been talking about how you seem so different lately. Right?" She looks around the table, addressing them individually. Kaitlyn nods in agreement. Olivia, too. Hailey stares at her food. "You've been acting like a totally different person."

Hmm. Or maybe it's that I'm not *acting.*

Alexis reaches across the table and rests her hand on mine. "You've changed, Samantha. And I think I speak for all of us when I say that it's not for the better, sweetie."

Not for the *better*? How could they not see that I'm a *better* person? I told Shrink-Sue I felt healthier, more in control of my emotions than I ever have. I'm no longer a slave to their words and actions, and that means there's something *wrong* with me.

"We don't feel like we even *know* you anymore," Olivia adds.

"You're right," I say quietly. "You guys did know me, but I don't think you do anymore. Not really." I look around the table as I talk, realizing, maybe for the first time, that I don't know much about them either.

The words are right on the tip of my tongue, and I start to tell them the truth: I need to get some distance from them. But then I take one look at Hailey's face and think about what she said in the bathroom that day, about how she needed me and she didn't know what she'd do if I left like Sarah did. I can't say it. Not today.

I look right at Kaitlyn. "You owe AJ an apology."

"For what? Something I said when I was in *fourth grade*?"

"No," I say as I stand. "For something you said five minutes ago."

That cafeteria door seems like it's miles away, but I throw my shoulders back and march toward it, holding my head a little higher than it was when I walked in here.

all about me

I walk quickly to my locker, glad to be alone in the corridors and back in the fresh air. I'm not sure what made me head this direction, I was sort of on autopilot, but it turns out to be the right call.

As I turn the corner, I let out a relieved sigh when I see Caroline working her combination lock with one hand and holding her backpack strap in the other.

"There you are! I've been looking for you all day." I rest my shoulder against a neighboring locker and come in close, keeping my voice low. "I have so much to tell you."

She continues loading books into her backpack, and I keep talking.

"I told the Eights about AJ, and Kaitlyn made an insanely cruel comment I can't even repeat, but I totally stood up for him." I shake my hands out by my sides. I'm all jittery.

Caroline zips her backpack and hoists it over her shoulder, and when she turns in my direction, I can see her T-shirt: YES, IT REALLY IS ALL ABOUT ME.

"I know," she says. "I was there. You were brilliant."

"What do you mean, you were there?" She couldn't have been. I didn't see her anywhere. I looked. "Where were you?"

She rests her hand on one side of my face. "Close enough to hear everything." Then she steps away and tugs on her flannel shirtsleeve, looking at her beat-up watch. "I have to go now."

"Go where? The bell doesn't ring for another twenty minutes." She stares at me with the strangest expression on her face. "Wait, are you angry because I didn't tell them about you? I meant to. I will. I promise."

"No, I'm not mad. And please, don't tell them about me. Ever." She leans in closer. "But you should tell AJ."

What?

My phone chirps and I pull it out of my back pocket and read the message.

how'd it go?

"Go ahead," she says. "Answer him." Caroline gestures with her chin to the phone. How did she know it was AJ? I give her a funny look and type back:

really good. where are you?

277

I press SEND. And when I look up, Caroline's gone.

"Caroline?" I call out, but there's no response.

I run to the edge of the locker bank and look down the corridor. Lunch is far from over, but it's starting to get a little more crowded out here. I walk down the path that leads to the student parking lot, and then double back to the one that leads to the front entrance. I don't see her anywhere.

My phone chirps again.

downstairs practicing

It looks like he's typing another message, so I don't reply right away.

playing at open mic tonight

I smile at the screen and type:

!!!

I take another spin around campus, still looking for Caroline, and then start heading back toward my locker, typing as I go. I think about what I said to my friends today. What I blurted.

lots to tell you :)

The first bell rings and the halls become more crowded. At my locker, I dial my combination and lift the latch, and then I peek at the far end of the row, hoping to see Caroline.

I'm gathering my books for class when I feel hands sliding over my hips. "Hey," AJ says. My first instinct is to check our surroundings to be sure we're alone, but then I realize I don't have to do that anymore. I recline into his chest, pull his arms even tighter around my waist, and kiss him, knowing that people might be walking by and watching us, but not caring at all.

"I take it you told your friends about us?" he asks when we finally pull away. He's wearing a ski cap pushed back on his head, and his hair is poking out underneath. He looks adorable.

"The Eights know. And everyone else . . ." I crane my neck to see what's happening behind us. People are slowing their steps as they pass, and whispering to each other. "I'm guessing they'll know by the time the final bell rings."

"Wow. That's an amazing picture of you," he says, bringing my attention back to my locker.

"Thanks." I settle into his shoulder, watching his expression change as he scans over everything. He smiles when he reads the little pink Post-it. His eyes shine when he sees the picture of Cassidy and me, taken the day I broke her butterfly record. He's more straight-faced when he looks over photos of me and the rest of the Eights.

"Wow, you've been to a lot of concerts," he says.

After today, I'm pretty sure my collection won't be expanding.

"Is that one of my guitar picks?" he asks.

"Maybe." I smile.

"Robber."

I turn to face him and hook my fingers in the front belt loops of his jeans. "Hey, you didn't happen to see Caroline on your way over here, did you?" I gesture toward her locker. "I just had the strangest conversation with her."

"Caroline?"

"Yeah. It was weird. First she said she heard my discussion with my friends, but that's impossible. She was nowhere in sight. And then she said she had to go. And now I can't find her anywhere. Did she seem upset last night?" I ask.

AJ's expression morphs from confusion to concern. "What?"

"She was the only one who didn't read, but she never does. She didn't seem bothered by it or anything."

The bell rings. AJ doesn't move away from me. There's no one around, but I lower my voice anyway. "I came clean to the Eights. I thought that's what she wanted. She's the one who said I needed 'new friends' and introduced me to all of you. She's the one who brought me down to Poet's Corner in the first place."

I think about all the times Caroline listened to me read my poems and gave me words that she thought might help AJ see me in a different light, like my own personal Cyrano de Bergerac.

"Sam?"

"Yeah?"

"Who's Caroline?"

"Caroline." I say it with a laugh, but he doesn't join me. "*Caroline*. Caroline . . ." It takes me a second to find her last name. I haven't thought about it since the first day of school. "Caroline Madsen."

His eyes grow wider and I watch the color totally drain from his face. "What did you say?" I feel the tug on my fingers as he starts to step away from me, and I release his belt loops, letting my hands fall to my sides.

"I said, 'Caroline Madsen.' As in, our friend Caroline. AJ, what's wrong?"

"Wait. Did you just say that *Caroline* brought you downstairs?" He doesn't stutter, but his voice shakes and it scares me.

"Of course," I say, trying to understand why he's asking. "She was with me that first day, remember?" I've thought about it a million times. I can picture it like it was yesterday. "You weren't going to let me stay, but then Caroline grabbed my arm and you changed your mind."

He stares at me for the longest time.

"She's the reason you let me stay," I repeat. But I can tell by the look on his face that maybe I'm wrong, so I add, "Wasn't she?"

"No." His voice is so faint. He takes a real step backward this time.

Now I'm frightened, and I don't know why, but I know I'm

right to be. My heart starts racing and I want to get out of here, bound for a dark, quiet room where I can catch my breath and think, but I can't leave without hearing whatever it is AJ's trying to tell me.

He takes his cap off and combs his fingers through his hair. "Sam, she wasn't the reason I let you into Poet's Corner that first day."

Yes she was.

"The first time you came downstairs, you were alone. I let you stay that day because you said you thought it might change your life, and I liked that."

I start to tell him that I didn't choose those words, Caroline did. But I keep my mouth shut because I have a feeling that isn't the right thing to say. I squeeze my eyes closed and cover my face.

"No," I say, shaking my head hard. "She brought me there." I open my eyes again and lock them on his. "How else would I have found that room?"

His lips are pressed into a tight line. Then he says, "I have no idea."

"I do. I found it because she brought me there." I say it with more force than I intended to.

He stares at the ground for a long time, and finally, he looks at me again. "Do you know who Caroline Madsen is?"

"Of course I do."

She's my friend. She might be my best friend.

"Sam." I hear a strange hitch in his voice when he says my name. "Caroline Madsen committed suicide . . . in 2007."

I laugh. "Shut up," I say, but he's doesn't look like he's joking. "So, what? You're saying I've been talking to a ghost?" But as soon as the words leave my mouth, I know deep in my gut that's not right.

Now he's taking even larger steps, backing away even faster, and his fingers are impossible to miss, flicking against the stitching on his jeans. "I should . . . I have to . . . get to class," he says, and he's gone before I have a chance to tell him he's wrong. He has to be.

She was just here ten minutes ago.

Wasn't she?

I was standing here talking to her.

Wasn't I?

I slam my locker door and take off running for the parking lot. It takes two hands to start the car, one to bring the key to the ignition, and the other to hold it steady. The engine roars to life and I peel into the street, bound for the only place it occurs to me to go.

recent and raw

*I*n the lobby, I press the button for the elevator three times, and when nothing happens, I press it again, three more times. I slam my hand against the door, and the bell dings as the doors slide open. I press 7 three times.

I burst through the door and Colleen jumps out of her chair. "Sam?"

"I need to see Sue." My voice doesn't even sound like mine, and my legs feel wobbly underneath me. I walk straight for her office and open the door. Colleen is right behind me. "Where is she?" I yell with my fingertips pressed into my temples.

Colleen grabs my arms, pushes me into the chair, and crouches down in front of me. She's trying to pull my hands away from my face, but I won't let her. I'm crying hard and only half listening to what she's saying, but I hear "hospital" and "won't be back today" and "call her." Then "wait" and "water" and "don't move."

When Colleen's gone, I slide my hands down to my cheeks and look around the room. Two days ago, I sat here and told Sue I was better. I was *better*. I know I was. But then I remember Alexis's words, "You've changed . . . and it's not for the better, sweetie."

What's happening to me?

I stand up fast and hurry for the door, into the elevator, back into my car. There's this spot on the top of the hill that looks down on the valley; it's where everyone goes to park and make out, and at this time of day, it'll be deserted.

My hands are tight on the wheel as I wind around the sharp twists and turns, climbing until the road dead-ends. I park next to the big oak tree and cut the engine.

AJ is wrong; he has to be. Caroline *was* there, at every reading, during every lunch hour. She sat next to me. She met me in the theater. She read my earliest poems, told me I was good. She taught me how to let go and write what I felt, and gave me words when I couldn't find them myself. She helped me take the stage. She was one of the—how did I jokingly refer to it the other day—the Poetic Nine?

Wasn't she?

I pull my phone from the cup holder and find the most recent group text, the one AJ sent last night to call the Poet's Corner meeting. His name is right at the top. Next to it: *To Sam and six more . . .*

I know her number won't be here, but I tap the word "more" to help me take inventory. Everyone is a jumble of unidentified phone numbers, and I assign each one a name as I count them. AJ. Cameron. Chelsea. Emily. Jessica. Abigail. Sydney.

Seven total.

"Technology is a trap," Caroline had said, and I believed her.

She never called me. She never texted me. I thought it was odd, but I never questioned it.

My stomach rolls over, and my fingers are shaking so violently, I'm having a hard time holding the phone in my hands.

I open the browser and type in "Caroline Madsen 2007" and within seconds, the tiny screen is filled with links that lead to her story. Headline after headline reading, TEEN'S DEATH RULED A SUICIDE; BULLYING TO BLAME FOR LOCAL TEEN'S SUICIDE?; LOCAL HIGH SCHOOL DEVASTATED BY SUICIDE. The last one contains a picture, so I click through to the full story.

"Oh, my God," I whisper. I remember reading this article, not last summer, but the summer before.

Cassidy had just come back from Southern California to spend the break with her dad. He bought a new house, and she was thrilled to finally have her own room when she came to visit. She'd heard a rumor that a girl had killed herself in the house years ago, and she asked me if I'd heard about it. I hadn't.

Later that week, I went home with her after swim practice and she gave me a tour. We sat in Cassidy's new room, did a quick Internet search for local teen suicides, and didn't find much beyond this one case. We pulled up a bunch of articles, including this one.

Now, I'm looking at the story again, over a year later, this time on my phone. I scan it quickly for the salient points and latch on to words and phrases like "suicide" and "target of bullying" and "history of depression," but the tears are welling up in my eyes.

Her parents were at a Christmas party, only a few houses away. While they were gone, Caroline Madsen threw back a bottle of sleeping pills and never woke up. Her mom and dad didn't realize what happened until the following morning. By the time I get to the quote from her mom, talking about her daughter's witty sense of humor and how she loved to write poetry, the words are so blurry, I can't read any more.

Scrolling down to the photo, I find a girl who looks exactly like the Caroline I know. Hair slightly disheveled. No makeup. She's wearing a flannel, unbuttoned, over a T-shirt.

I zoom in so I can read it: IF YOU COULD READ MY MIND, YOU WOULDN'T BE SMILING.

I run my finger across the screen, laughing at the shirt and fighting back tears at the same time. I remember sitting in Cassidy's room, looking at this photo, skimming this article. We closed the browser, sad for this girl we never knew, and I don't remember giving it another thought.

Now, everything starts to fall into place.

Caroline and I sat together in the theater one day, me complaining about my friends, her telling me I needed new ones.

I confided in her about my OCD and she told me about her struggles with depression.

But Caroline never read on stage. She came to my house, but she always left before anyone got home. We wrote together in the theater, just the two of us, alone in the dark. She never minded being my secret.

She never led me to Poet's Corner.

"She's not real." The words squeak out.

The tears are falling freely now, and I toss my phone hard on the passenger seat and it bounces onto the floor. I throw open the door, walk to the edge of the cliff, and stand there, looking out over the town. It's overcast and chilly, but the bite in the early December air feels good in my lungs.

From up here, I can see my house. AJ's is on the other side of town and harder to find, but I spot the dense cluster of trees that distinguish his neighborhood. Alexis's house is on a hill on the opposite side of the canyon, massive and easy to see. The swim club is easy to find too, and from there, I trace the route I've driven and walked plenty of times—up the hill, round the hairpin turn, straight to the top, until I see Cassidy's dad's house.

Caroline lived there. She died there.

"Depression," she'd told me the first time we sat together in the dark theater. *"Sometimes it feels like it's getting worse, not better."*

I walk over to the big oak tree and throw up in the dirt. And then I sit on the edge of the cliff, my knees to my chest, digging my nails into the back of my neck and scratching hard. I feel the sting on my skin, but I keep going, not bothering to wipe the tears as they stream down my cheeks, feeling empty and cold, mourning the loss of my best friend like it's recent and raw, as if she killed herself this afternoon and not eight years ago. I rock back and forth, scratching harder, crying and muttering "Caroline" under my breath, over and over again.

Like the crazy person I now know I am.

kind of twisted

Once the sun went down, the temperature started dropping fast. I'm not sure how long I've been out here, but my chest feels numb, my eyes are puffy, my face is sore, and there's dirt caked under my fingernails.

I pull myself up off the ground and collapse in the driver's seat. The car door has been open for hours, the dome light on the entire time, so I give the ignition a quick turn to be sure I didn't kill the battery. The engine starts right up. I crank the heat.

My phone is on the floor next to the console. Texts and missed-call messages fill the screen, and I scroll down, past countless pleas from my mom to call her right away. There are three missed calls from Shrink-Sue, the last one only twenty minutes ago.

I hit the call-back button and Sue picks up on the first ring. The tears start falling again when I hear her voice, and I squeak out a faint, "It's me."

"Where are you?" she asks, panic in her voice like I've never heard. I tell her about the hill and give her the cross streets, and she tells me not to move, that she's on her way.

I hang up the phone and stare at the clock on the dashboard. It's 7:12.

Open mic.

I'm supposed to be on my way to the city right now. I'm supposed to be watching my boyfriend play guitar on a real stage, and Caroline's supposed to be next to me, cheering him on. Instead, I'm here in the dark, all cried out, waiting to be rescued. I hope AJ won't tell the Poets; I'll never be able to face them again.

I'll never be able to face him *again.*

I picture the look on his face when he told me about Caroline. What a sharp contrast it was from the expression he wore just minutes earlier, as he stood there, admiring that photo of me on the diving block. The *me* he thought he knew, next to the *real me* he was forced to see for the first time. Once he saw who I really am, he couldn't get away fast enough.

I never wanted him to find out. And now he's gone.

Headlights shine into the back window, and minutes later, Shrink-Sue's guiding me into her shiny black Benz and buckling the seat belt around me. "Your parents are on their way to get your car," I hear her say.

As Sue winds her way down the hill, I stare out the window, wondering where we're going and deciding I don't care. I feel heat on my face. My butt is getting hot from the seat warmer. I rest my forehead against the glass, close my eyes, and don't open them again until we're stopped in a driveway, waiting for a garage door to open.

Sue pulls in and cuts the engine. She comes around to my side of the car and unbuckles the belt, helping me out as if I'm elderly and infirm, and leads me inside the same way.

We arrive in a kitchen, and two girls stop what they're doing. They're a few years younger than me and a lot smaller; like Sue, tiny in every way. Same straight hair. Same delicate features. They've grown up since they took those photographs that sit on Sue's desk, but I recognize them immediately.

"Sam," she says gently, "these are my daughters, Beth and Julia."

Their expressions are full of concern, but I guess I shouldn't expect anything else; I've been crying in the dirt for the last five hours. And they're just staring, like they aren't sure what to make of me, but that doesn't surprise me either. Knowing Sue and her commitment to "professional distance," I'm pretty sure she's never brought a patient into her house.

"Julia, would you get us some tea, please?"

Sue leads me out of the kitchen, past the living room, and through a set of double doors. This must be Sue's home office. It overlooks a perfectly manicured garden, set in a circle with a fountain at the center. It's softly lit. Peaceful. I walk to the glass door. "This sure beats the view of the parking lot."

"It's my favorite place." She's standing right behind me. "I sit right there," she says, pointing over my shoulder to an over-size metal chair with deep cushions and lots of throw pillows. "That's where I think, or meditate, or work on patient files. Unless it's raining, that's where you'll find me."

We're both quiet for a long time. I can hear the sound of the fountain through the glass. It's soothing.

"Are you still cold?" she asks.

I shake my head.

"Do you want to sit outside?" she asks.

I nod.

"Good." She steps forward and twists the lever on the French door, and it swings open. "Let's talk out there until we can't take it." She grabs two blankets from a basket on the floor and wraps one around my shoulders. She tells me to sit in her favorite chair.

Julia arrives holding a cast-iron teapot and two mugs. Sue thanks her and arranges everything on the table in front of us, pouring out a mug of steaming tea and handing it to me. Sue settles into a spot on the couch, and Julia leaves, closing the double doors behind her.

"You can talk whenever you're ready, Sam."

I pull my knees to my chest and hold my mug in both hands, staring down into it, breathing in steam and inhaling the scents of flowers and citrus, thinking about everything that's happened since I sat in Sue's office two days ago. The P.M. Poet's Corner meeting. AJ and me alone downstairs. Telling the Crazy Eights about him. Caroline saying good-bye to me in her own way.

Caroline.

I'm surprised I have any tears left, but sure enough, they start falling again. A tissue appears in front of me, as if by magic, and I dab my eyes and blow my nose.

Shrinks and their tissues.

"What do you already know?" I ask.

"That doesn't matter. I don't know anything unless I hear it from you."

I understand her code. That means she's spoken with Colleen. I think about the urgent calls and texts from my mom, and wonder if she called AJ looking for me. If she talked to him and he told her what happened today, Sue must have a pretty clear picture.

"You asked me to make one new friend," I say, staring into my mug. "And I did. And I liked her. A lot. But as it turns out, she's been dead for eight years, which, as you might expect, can really hinder a friendship." I thought sarcasm would make me feel better, but it doesn't. I start crying even harder.

Sue takes my cup out of my hands so I can pull myself together. I wipe my eyes and blow my nose while Sue tops off my mug. She trades my hot tea for a pile of snotty tissues and doesn't seem to care.

Once I start talking, I can't stop. I've sworn to keep Poet's Corner a secret, but I can't keep it from Sue anymore. I describe that first day I ran into Caroline in the theater, how she settled in next to me, made me laugh, told me that she wanted to show me something that would change my whole life.

"Tell me exactly what happened," Sue says. "Start at the beginning."

"Caroline told me to meet her on the stage, next to the piano." I close my eyes and see the scene a bit differently, like I'm watching it from a bird's-eye view. "I waited for her, hiding on the other side of the curtain until I heard the group pass by."

"And then Caroline met you."

"She told me to follow her, and I did. We went down this narrow staircase, and through the gray-painted halls. She told me where to turn, which doors to open."

I picture the two of us rounding that final corner, just in time to see the door at the far end swinging shut.

"What is this place?" I'd asked her when we were stand-ing in front of it. She ignored my question and pointed to the doorknob.

"I'm going to be by your side the entire time, but this is all up to you from here. You have to do all the talking."

My eyes spring open.

It was *me* all along. I saw the doors in front of me closing. That's how I knew where to go. I turned the knobs—she never did. I saw the mop heads on the wall, swaying as if they'd just been moved. *I* found the hidden seam, the dead bolt.

I followed them.

"Caroline didn't bring me downstairs." I can barely get the words out.

Caroline didn't stand to the side and tell me to knock. I did that on my own. I heard her say it was up to me from that point on, but that wasn't exactly true. It was always up to me.

"I saw them walk across the stage that first day."

"See you Thursday," someone had said.

"I came back when I knew they'd be there again. I waited behind the curtain, by the piano, and then I followed them. Oh, my God, Sue. I followed them down there."

I tell her about the first time I visited the room in the basement. "AJ was really cold to me," I say, picturing the way he stared me down until Caroline grabbed my arm in solidarity. Only she didn't.

I set my mug on the table and wrap the blanket around me tighter. Sue asks me what happened next, and I tell her about the time Caroline came to my house and we hung out in my room together. She told me AJ didn't hate me, but I'd hurt him and he didn't know how to handle that. I suck in a breath, realizing that conversation never actually happened either. *I* knew what Kaitlyn and I had done. I didn't remember it consciously, but I knew all along. I think about the poem Caroline helped me write, and how I used her words to ask him to forgive me. And he did. He let me stay. They *all* let me stay.

I tell Sue about every interaction I had with Caroline and the rest of the Poets, and how that room in the basement calmed my mind. There, I learned how to write and let go and speak up. I became one of them.

Now I'm crying hard again, because despite all the incredible things that have happened over the last few months, I can't stop thinking about the one thing that's wrong with this whole picture.

"I made up a whole fucking person, Sue!" I yell through tears. "What kind of twisted mind makes up a *whole* person?"

"You didn't just make up a person, Sam. You made up a unique and *wonderful* person who was all the things you needed her to be. Funny and smart and kind—"

"And again, Sue. Not. Fucking. Real."

"She was real to you."

Was. Of all those words, that's the one that stings the most. I miss her. Real or imaginary, I don't want her to be gone.

"What's happening to me?" I ask. Sue scoots to the edge of the couch and sets her tea on the table.

"This isn't what you want to hear, Sam, but the truth is, I don't know. It might have to do with your medications, or chemical changes taking place in your brain, or a combination of the two. It could have nothing to do with any of those things." She's trying to keep her voice calm and level, but I can tell she's concerned. A lot more concerned than I want her to be. "What's happening to you isn't consistent with OCD. Something else is going on, and I'm not sure what it is yet, but we're going to figure it out together, just like we always do."

I pull the blanket over my head. I can't look at her. I don't want to listen to her either, but I need the information she's sharing in a way I can't ignore.

"Based on what you've told me tonight, I think Caroline becomes real to you in moments of extreme anxiety." The sound of her voice is soothing me, and I feel a deep sense of relief when she starts talking again. "You met her on the first day of school. You were already highly anxious, but you became even *more* troubled about something Alexis said, and that might have sent your mind looking for . . . a new way to cope."

I pull the blanket off my head so I can see Sue's face.

"And it worked. So after that," she continues, "Caroline came around when you needed her to. After your fights with the Eights. When you were nervous about following a group of strangers down a dark, narrow staircase. When you had to read on stage for the first time. She was there today, after you told your friends about AJ, right?"

I mentally transport myself back to those moments, and then to all the others Sue didn't mention. Whenever I was upset about something and needed to write, Caroline would be right there, waiting at her locker. We'd joke about it, like it was a coincidence. Then we'd go to the theater together.

"Your mind found a solution—a pretty positive one, I might add—and the more it worked, the more real she became to you." Sue reaches for her tea and takes a sip, watching me over her mug, like she's giving me time to let it all sink in.

"Has she been showing up a little less frequently?" she asks.

Now that I think about it, she hasn't been at her locker in the morning, not every day, like she used to be. I never see her between classes.

"Over the past few weeks, I've really only seen her in Poet's Corner."

It fits Sue's theory. I'm always anxious about going down there during lunch. I'm afraid the Crazy Eights are going to follow me and find out about that place, and I'll be the one who exposes the group and the room. It'll be my fault. I'm always a wreck until that door bolts closed. Then I start to relax.

"You read about a girl named Caroline over a year ago, and you thought you forgot all about her, but she stuck around in your subconscious. You gave her characteristics you have a hard time expressing. And she became that kind, caring voice you needed to hear."

All this information is making me feel better in the way concrete facts often do. That last bit even makes me feel a little relieved.

Still, Sue's talking about this whole thing like it all makes perfect sense, like it's perfectly logical, but it doesn't and it's not. This whole thing is completely insane.

"You can go ahead and say it, Sue. I'm crazy."

She's quiet for a full minute, staring into the fountain and trying, I assume, to figure out how to deliver this news.

"Crazy," she finally says, her eyes still fixed on the water. "Do you know the dictionary's definition of 'crazy'?" I shake my head. "It means both 'insane' and 'a bit out of the ordinary.' That's a pretty broad scope, don't you think?"

I nod.

"Crazy is such a subjective word. I'd never use it to label anyone—certainly not you. Look, your brain functions differently from other brains, Sam. And because of the way your brain works, you got to know this wonderful person named Caroline. No one else had that privilege."

"Like your patient, Anthony . . . The guy who could hear colors."

"Exactly."

But I was getting better. Feeling normal.

Two days ago, I wanted Sue to consider stepping down the meds and cutting back my therapy. Now that I'm having full conversations with imaginary people, I'm assuming the opposite is true. More meds. More therapy sessions. No more Caroline.

"We need to be sure Caroline's gone for good, right?" I say, sad about the diagnosis, but proud to beat Sue to the shrink-think.

"Do you want her to go away?"

"No." Caroline felt as real to me as everyone else in Poet's Corner. She's only been gone for a few hours, but I've never missed anyone more. The idea of never seeing her again makes my whole body feel hollow.

Tears start sliding down my cheeks again.

"Remember Wednesday, when you listed all the things that made AJ so incredible?" Sue hands me another tissue. She's giving me that look, the piercing one that makes me feel like she can see right into my soul. "Do the same for Caroline—not the girl you learned about today, but the girl you've come to know over the last few months—your *friend*, Caroline."

My mind starts racing and I feel that same sensation I do when I first step up on stage, my chest tightening, that uncomfortable tingling in my fingertips. Maybe that's why I close my eyes.

I begin counting, starting with my thumb. "She has this energy about her—I can't explain it—but it's kind of contagious. She listens to my poetry, even the really stupid stuff I should never share with anyone, and she never laughs at me. And she doesn't just listen to the words I write, she *hears* what I'm really trying to say and helps me figure out how to express it. She seems to know when I need her."

I open my eyes and bite my lip because, yeah, the reason that one's true is now pretty obvious.

Sue brushes her fingers over her own eyelids, silently telling me to close mine again.

I pick up where I left off, holding up my fifth finger. "She's a little bit damaged, just like me. She doesn't give a shit what people think of her. I love how she doesn't wear makeup. I love her snarky T-shirts." I feel a smile spread across my face. "She always makes me laugh, even when she isn't trying to."

The tenth one pops to mind immediately, and I start to say it like it's no big deal, but I find myself choking on my words.

"That's nine," Sue says.

Caroline told me to knock on that door. She never spoke for me, but she gave me the words to say. When AJ kicked me out of Poet's Corner, she told me to fight my way back down there again. When I was terrified to read on stage, she came up behind me, rested her hand on my shoulder, and said, "Don't think. Just go." And I did. She was always there. And yet, she never was.

"She made me brave," I say.

Sue reaches over and takes my hands, gripping them hard in hers. It strikes me how dainty but strong they are.

"Good. Here's what you do now. You take those parts of Caroline and honor the fact that they're part of *you*. You start being kind to yourself, making decisions that are best for *you*, not best for everyone else. You look around at the people in your life, one by one, choosing to hold on to the ones who make you stronger and better, and letting go of the ones who don't. I think that's what Caroline wanted. She didn't *make* you brave, Sam. You did that all on your own."

We sit there for a long time. I drink more tea. I listen to the water cycle through the fountain.

"She's not coming back, is she?" I ask.

"I don't think you need her anymore," Sue says gently. "If she shows up again, tell me, but don't panic. Let her do her job. She seems pretty good at it."

She's not coming back.

I keep thinking about Caroline and how she left today, and that leads me to a memory of AJ and how he had to be the one to tell me that my new best friend had been dead for eight years.

I'm mortified. I didn't want him to find out. Not now. Certainly not like this.

"I didn't want AJ to know about me," I say.

Sue takes a sip of her tea. "Are you sure about that?"

"What do you mean?"

"Caroline could have left at any time, in a number of ways. She could have told you exactly who she was in the privacy of your room. She could have disappeared without ever saying anything at all. But the way she left, the things she said . . ."

"What's your point?"

"You say you didn't want AJ to know about you, but if you think about it, a big part of you did."

do two things

I didn't wake up feeling brave on Saturday, and I don't feel brave on Sunday either. I feel sad and confused, scared and lonely, missing Caroline more than ever, and wishing everyone would just leave me alone.

Paige keeps knocking on my door to see if I want ice cream, and I can hear Mom on the other side of the door, telling her to give me my space. It's good advice. I wish she'd take it herself, because she keeps checking on me, asking me if I want to talk, and I keep telling her I'm fine and sending her away.

While I was rocking in the dirt last Friday evening, AJ came to my house looking for me. Instead, he found my mom. He told her what I'd said about Caroline, and that he was worried about me. And she politely thanked him, hid her surprise that

I'd never told him about my OCD, and protected my secret like she always has. Then she sent him away, asking him to leave me alone for a few days so I could figure things out.

I'm sure he was relieved. Every time I think about that look on his face when he first heard me say Caroline Madsen's name, I want to be sick.

To distract myself, I've been going through my poems, thinking about the ones Caroline helped me write. Not always, but sometimes, there was that moment at the end, when we finished a piece and read it aloud, and the words were so perfect, so fitting, they gave me chills. I'd feel the urge to hug her, but I never did, and now I wonder what would have happened if I had. Would I have felt her the same way I felt her hand on my shoulder? Or would she have ghosted right through my arms as my body discovered that my brain had been tricking me all along?

I pick up my pen and tap it against my notebook, but I can't write a poem. Not now. I don't know what to say, not even to a blank sheet of paper that no one else will ever see. Besides, poetry isn't going to help me piece all these emotions I'm feeling into a cohesive solution I can wrap my brain around.

I'm scared of my mind's power. I'm angry with Caroline for leaving. I'm confused about all her personality traits, struggling to make sense of the ones I fabricated and the ones that might have existed in a girl who committed suicide in 2007.

I open my red notebook and label the left page "Caroline

Madsen." I label the right page "My Caroline." And for the next two hours, I research everything I can find on the real one, listing it on the left, and detailing everything I know to be true about the one I created on the right.

When I'm done, I see the similarities, but I also spot distinct differences. And I realize that Sue was right: I took a face in a photo and gave her a lot of traits that deep down, I wish I possessed.

I bury my face in my pillow to block out the sunlight. I cry for a long time. And when I finally feel myself drifting off to sleep, I don't fight it.

I hear a knock on my bedroom door. "Sam?" Mom says quietly.

"I'm sleeping," I yell.

"Sam, there's someone here to see you."

I open my eyes and force myself to sit up. My room is dark. My T-shirt is tangled around me, my hair is matted against the side of my head, and I smell like sweat. My notebook is still splayed open across my comforter, and I slam it closed as Mom opens the door and steps inside.

"Please," I say, pointing dramatically at my face. "Tell him I don't want to see him right now."

It's true, but still, my chest feels a whole lot lighter. I knew he'd come over, even though my mom told him not to. I don't want AJ to see me like this, but I'm dying for him to wrap his arms around me and kiss my forehead and tell me to stop thinking so hard. He'll tell me to talk to him, and I will because all he has to do is say those words and my mouth seems to kick into gear before my brain can stop it. I start combing my fingers through my hair, hoping I can force it to comply with gravity.

"It isn't AJ, honey. It's Hailey."

"Hailey." Her name hits me like a punch in the gut. I haven't seen Hailey or any of the Eights since I left the cafeteria last Friday, and none of them know what happened after I did. I'd practically forgotten about our fight. My whole face ignites with the thought, and I fall onto my bed and bury my face in my pillow.

I can't deal with this right now.

"She looks pretty intent on coming upstairs," Mom says as she sits on the edge of my bed. "She even brought flowers."

"Flowers? Why? She didn't do anything wrong."

Mom starts rubbing my back. "Let her come in, Sam. Hear what she has to say. Who knows, maybe she'll cheer you up."

"I don't want to cheer up." I want to see Caroline. I want her to *not* be dead so I can *not* be crazy.

I can tell Mom's not letting up, so I give her a "fine, whatever" as I climb out of bed. I stand in front of the full-length mirror, pulling myself together.

"Hailey has always been my favorite," Mom says as she leaves the room.

A few minutes later, Hailey walks in with her head bowed low. "Hi, Samantha." She hands me a bouquet of cheery-looking flowers.

"Thanks. You didn't need to do this." I bring the bouquet to my nose. The scent reminds me of Sue's garden, and I'm taken aback by the wave of sadness that passes over me when I think about sitting out there, talking about Caroline last Friday night.

I miss her.

"Are these from you? Or from *all* of you?"

Hailey understands what I'm really asking, and I know the answer before she even says a word; I can tell by the way she bites her bottom lip and shuffles her foot on the carpet. She's not here as the group's representative.

"Just me." She glances around my room. "I'm so sorry. You stood up for me and I didn't do the same for you. Twice."

"It's okay."

"Wow . . . It's been *months* since I was in your room. Why is that?" she asks, changing the subject.

"I don't know," I say, but it's not true. The last time she was here, we were preparing for the Valentine's Day fundraiser and my floor was covered with red roses and pink ribbon and sappy love notes.

"I'd forgotten how cozy it is in here. And the paint is really pretty." She walks over to the collage on my wall, runs her fingertip along the words THE CRAZY 8S, and studies the photos. "Wow. Is this really *us*?" Hailey asks. "We were so sweet and happy and . . . we look like we genuinely *liked* each other." She lets out a laugh. "I remember thinking I was the luckiest person in the world to be part of this group. When did we change?"

"I don't know. But I'm starting to think we can't change back."

There's a long pause. "Actually, I did stand up for you. It was a little late, but I hope it still counts."

"You did?"

She nods. "And then I chased after you."

"What?" No. That welcome sense of relief pops like a balloon. Now my mind is racing as I step through everything that happened in the minutes after I left the Crazy Eights in the cafeteria. I went straight to my locker. Caroline was there. She touched my face and told me she'd heard everything. We talked. When she disappeared, I followed her. I yelled her name through the corridors.

Oh, God. Hailey saw me talking to . . . nobody. She knows.

"We all got in a huge fight after you left the cafeteria. I told Kaitlyn she owed you an apology, but you know her. Alexis sided with her, of course, even though she looked a little unsure about it."

What did you see?

"And Olivia . . ." Hailey rolls her eyes. "She could have come with me to find you, but . . . well, she didn't."

What. Did. You. See?

I try to think of a way to ask her without really asking. "Why didn't you tell me this on Friday?" I ask, my voice shaking.

Hailey plops down on my bed and leans back on her hands. "I couldn't find you," she says.

I sit next to her and let out a sigh of relief. "You couldn't?"

"No. I went straight to your locker, but you weren't there."

"Huh," I say.

"You're leaving us, aren't you?" She folds her legs underneath her and sits up straight. "I wouldn't blame you if you did. And you have a boyfriend now, so it would probably happen anyway, but . . ."

"Hailey." I hug her. She squeezes my shoulders so hard, it's like she's being pulled underwater and I'm the only thing she has to keep her afloat. "I don't know what I'm going to do yet. But if I do leave, you can always come with me."

She pulls away, shaking her head. "I'm not sure I could do that."

I know what she's thinking. Leaving the Eights changes everything. No more lunches. No more concerts. No more sleepovers or parties. We wouldn't be included in Kaitlyn's grand plans for Junior Prom, or invited to stay at the hotel in the city afterward. The rest of our high school experience would be completely different from the one we expected.

Or worse, the remaining Eights would give us the same treatment they gave Sarah. We'll be shunned in the halls. They'll start rumors about us, just in case the rest of our classmates consider feeling sorry for us or taking our side instead of theirs.

"How can I help you at school tomorrow?" she asks.

It might be the nicest thing she's ever said to me, but I honestly don't know how to answer her. I can't face the Eights.

I can't go to Poet's Corner. I'm too embarrassed to talk to AJ right now, and my heart can't handle the idea of going to my locker multiple times throughout the day, looking for Caroline at every stop, knowing I won't see her once. My eyes start to well up and I swallow a gulp of air.

"Actually, you can do two things." I walk over to my desk and grab my backpack. "You know my combo. Would you get all my books out of my locker and meet me at yours before first period tomorrow?"

"All your books?" she asks.

I nod. Hailey throws my backpack over her shoulder. "No problem. What's the second favor?"

"Will you please start calling me Sam?"

lock myself inside

I'm not sure I can get through the entire week without accidentally running into any of the Eights or the Poets, but since I couldn't talk my mom into homeschooling me for the rest of the year, that's the plan for now.

I drive around the student lot a few times until I can park on a three. Then I cut the engine and stare at the digital clock, giving myself just enough time to make it to Hailey's locker and then to class. When I arrive, Hailey hands me my overstuffed backpack, and I hug her before I take off for first period.

For the rest of the day, I take circuitous routes to each class and arrive right as the bell rings. As soon as each class ends, I bolt for the door and head straight for the nearest bathroom. At break, I go to the library and eat a PowerBar in the biography section (now I see what Olivia meant; this is an excellent place to make out or otherwise go unseen). At lunch, I head to the pool and swim laps, which turns out to be the highlight of my day. I don't even wear a cap. And I don't race. I swim freestyle in slow, precise strokes, up and down the lane, blocking out all the thoughts, including lyrics and poetry. I concentrate on the peaceful silence and savor the smell of chlorine.

My hair is still damp as I'm heading to fifth period, so of course, that's when I spot AJ walking toward me. My stomach knots up as I duck into a row of lockers and lean against the far wall, hiding my face in my hands like a little kid, assuming, I suppose, that if I can't see him, he can't see me either.

"Sam."

Crap.

My hands fall to my sides as I look up at him. "Hi."

"Hi."

I can tell he has something to say and that he's nervous about it, because in my peripheral vision, I can see his right hand, thumb and forefinger pressed together, strumming lightly on the side of his jeans.

"Are you okay?" he asks.

I shake my head. Then I fix my gaze on his shoes and bite the inside of my lip three times, hard.

AJ keeps his distance, but I wish he wouldn't. I want to tell him everything. And then I want him to slip his hands around my back and wrap me in his arms like he did on campus last

Thursday night. I visualize his mouth on mine, wordlessly telling me that it's all okay and that he still wants me, broken brain and all. But it's not fair to expect that from him. What's he going to do, tell me he thinks it's kind of cute that I fabricated an entire person?

"How was open mic night?" I ask, looking up, hoping to lighten the mood and force him to give me that slow smile of his. It's somewhat effective. The tension's still here, but now so is that dimple. It's all I can do not to kiss it.

"Sydney and Chelsea drove everyone into the city," he says. "Abigail, Cameron, and Jessica did 'The Raven.' They got through the first nine stanzas. Jessica said she totally screwed up, but I'm sure it didn't matter. It sounds like they blew everyone away. Syd read something, too. They wanted to perform their pieces for us today, but then you didn't show up."

He didn't go to open mic.

"You didn't go on Friday?"

"Um. No. How could I go after . . ." He catches himself and changes course. "I couldn't go without you."

"You should have gone," I say plainly. And then I start to panic, wondering what he said to the others. "You didn't tell anyone . . . about me . . . did you?"

"What?" The question clearly catches him off guard. "Of course not. I told them your car wouldn't start. That's why we didn't make it to the city."

We. Are we still "we"?

314

"Thanks. Please don't say anything, okay?"

He's watching me, waiting, I imagine, for an explanation of some kind. And he deserves one. But I can't stand the way he's looking at me right now, his eyes not only full of questions but also full of pity. He didn't look at me this way three days ago.

"Look, I want you to know everything," I say, "but . . . it's hard for me. I've never told anyone but Caro—" It starts to slip off my lips and it's too late to take it back. I hope he didn't hear me. But he did. It's all over his face.

"I've got to get to class," I say as I push past him into the crowd, head down, walking away as quickly as I can, and kicking myself for saying her name.

By Tuesday afternoon, I've become pretty skilled at sneaking around and avoiding people.

Kaitlyn and Alexis were heading my way between first and second, and I started to panic, but then a group of guys on the lacrosse team walked up to them, and that was all I needed to creep by without them ever noticing me. Sydney tried to talk with me after U.S. History, but I pretended I didn't hear her and sped off for the pool. Olivia and I made eye contact a few times during Trig, but I bolted for the door as soon as the bell rang. I haven't seen Hailey since she gave me my backpack yesterday morning.

Even though I'm avoiding all of them, I check my texts

obsessively. Five from Hailey, two from Alexis, and one from Olivia, all saying pretty much the same thing:

> you okay?
> coming to lunch?
> we're worried about you
> sorry about Friday
> we miss you

None from Kaitlyn.

And one from AJ:

> I don't know what to say

I can't decide how to reply to any of them, so I don't.

I hang out in the bathroom near my fifth period class, watching the time on my phone, and I head for the door with less than a minute to spare. I've only taken two steps into the corridor when I spot AJ standing a few feet away, almost as if he's waiting for me.

He starts walking and there's nowhere to hide. Then he stops, looming over me, blocking my way.

"You never read the poems in Caroline's Corner, did you?"

I shake my head. I have no idea what that is.

He reaches for my hand and places the key inside my open

palm. Then he closes my fingers around the thick, braided cord. "Go to the back right corner," he says. He walks away.

Caroline's Corner?

My legs are shaking and I feel light-headed as I open the door to my classroom and slide into my desk. I stuff the key under my leg so no one will see it. But during class, I hold it in my hand, running my thumb back and forth over its sharp edges and deep grooves, thinking about that room.

I'm not sure I can handle going downstairs all alone—I've always been with the group or with Caroline. But then I remember that's not true. Caroline didn't guide me that first time. I followed them, but I was completely alone. I brought myself down those stairs and into that room. That's when I start to understand the connection.

The article I read last Friday night flashes in my mind. *"She loved writing poetry,"* the quote from Caroline's mom had said.

Caroline was a Poet.

After sixth, I don't hide in bathrooms or beeline straight for my next class. Instead, I slowly make my way through the crowd, keeping my head up, returning "hellos" and "what's ups" from the people I pass, and walk to the theater entrance. I've got such a tight grip on the key, I can feel the notches leaving tiny impressions in my palm.

The theater isn't empty—a drama class is rehearsing a play—but no one notices me climb the stairs, creep past the grand piano, and slip behind the curtain. I open the narrow door and close it quickly behind me, waiting to be sure no one saw or followed me. Then I step down.

The air feels thicker and it smells dank, like dirty socks and mold, but I breathe deeply and take it all in like I'm experiencing it for the first time. I let my fingers skim the dark gray walls as I walk down the hallway, feeling the adrenaline pumping through my veins, recognizing how terrified I am right now, and forcing myself to experience every sensation, as if I need to prove to myself I can do this. That I no longer need her help.

Inside the janitor's closet, I push the mops to one side, and the door squeaks as I pull it toward me. I look around at the black ceiling and the black floors and the black walls that hardly look black because they're covered with so many scraps of paper. The stool is where it always is. The guitar stand is in the corner, but it's empty now. I flip the closest lamp on, and then I lock myself inside.

pass it on

I look around, taking everything in the way I always do. The first time I was alone down here, I traversed the room, stopping randomly to read, returning to the poems I liked the most. I remember the sense of calm that washed over me when I finally found the lyrics to AJ's song, and the joy I felt as I read Sydney's fast-food wrappers. I spent hours reading a decade's worth of poetry written by people who'd graduated long ago. My eyes were burning from fatigue by the time I sat on the couch and began writing something of my own. When I left that day, I was in awe of every person who'd ever stepped foot in Poet's Corner.

Now I take slow, measured steps toward the low bookcase in the right corner and flip on the lamp so it illuminates the wall. I never made it over here that first day, and over the last few months, I don't recall planting any of my own poetry here. If I had, I might have noticed what made this spot so unique.

Unlike the other walls in Poet's Corner, everything here is written on the same lined, three-hole-punched paper and penned in the same handwriting—each letter perfectly shaped, each word perfectly spaced.

Next to the lamp, I notice a wooden pencil box. I pick it up, turning it over in my hands, running my fingertip over the intricately carved swirls and waves. On the lid, I see three letters: C.E.M.

I return the box to the bookcase and slowly peel it open. The notebook paper inside looks rumpled, and with shaking hands, I remove it from its home and unfold it along the creases. It's not a poem. It's a letter. My breath catches deep in my throat when I realize it's written in the exact same handwriting I see on the wall in front of me.

Dear Mr. B—

You're going to think that what I did was your fault. It wasn't. And this room didn't do anything wrong. In fact, it saved my life for a long time.

You created a place for me to go and helped me fill it with words and people I could trust. It was the kindest, most generous thing anyone has ever done for me. When I was inside this room, I was happy.

If I could have captured how I felt on Mondays and Thursdays, and carried it around in my pocket for later use, I would have. Believe me, I tried.

You don't owe me anything more. But I hope you'll consider honoring this last request.

Words are beginning to gather here. Just think of what these walls could look like if everyone who needed this room found it. Can you picture it? I can.

Here's my key. Pass it on?

Love,
C

My hand instinctively goes to the cord around my neck, and I squeeze it in my fist.

Caroline's Corner.

That's why Mr. B leaves the theater door open when AJ asks him to. Why he keeps this room a secret. Why he pops in every once in a while to vacuum and empty the trash.

He knew Caroline. He built out this room for her, hid the door, and camouflaged the lock to keep it a secret. She asked him to pass the key along, and he honored her last wish. He's been doing it ever since she died.

Still gripping her letter in one hand, I grab the edge of the bookcase with the other. My knees aren't feeling too stable right now.

Caroline Madsen started Poet's Corner.

I take a step closer and brush my hand along the pages, as if I'm introducing myself for the first time.

These are her poems.

I read the titles and skim over the first lines, but some of them are placed too high and I can't see the words from here. I walk to the front of the room, grab the stool from the stage, and bring it back to the corner, standing on top of it so I can get a closer look.

On the highest point of the wall, I spot a poem titled "Insecurity," and I read it to myself. Then I move to the next one, called "Alone in the Dark." And the next one, which is untitled, but begins with the words, "Alliteration is alarmingly addictive."

They're beautiful and hilarious, and the more I read, the more I cry and the harder I laugh. But something doesn't feel right, and it's not until I'm halfway through her fourth poem that I realize what it is.

I start reading aloud.

As I begin reading her fifth poem, I arch my back and square my shoulders, standing taller, reading louder and stronger and clearer, and it feels good to speak her words—to listen to them come to life again—even if there's no one else around to hear how incredible they are. I read the rest of them the same way, in a loud, booming, confident voice, the way I imagine she would have wanted it.

I've read more than fifty poems, and finally, there's only one left. It's placed low on the wall, closest to the wooden pencil box, and there's something about the way it's mounted, with the black paint still exposed, acting like a thin frame, that makes me wonder if it's special somehow.

It's called "Every Last Word." I read to myself this time.

>
> These walls heard
> me when no
> one else could.
>
> They gave my
> words a home,
> kept them safe.
>
> Cheered, cried, listened.
> Changed my life
> for the better.
>
> It wasn't enough.
> But they heard
> every last word.

I cover my mouth, tears streaming down my face. It's written in threes.

I read it again, out loud this time, even though my voice cracks and I have to stop after every other line to catch my breath. Sometimes I stop because I want to let the meaning of a word or phrase sink deep into my skin. But I keep going, crying harder as I read that final line.

This was her last poem.

And I realize that Caroline *did* bring me here, in her own strange way, to these people, to this room, knowing how much I needed this place.

This room changed her life. And it's just beginning to change mine.

I picture Sydney, sitting alone in fast-food restaurants, writing the funny things she reads to us and the deeper thoughts she never shares. And Chelsea, writing poem after poem about the guy who broke her heart. Emily, sitting at her mom's bedside, watching her slip away and trying to hold her here a little longer. AJ propped up against his bed, playing his guitar and trying to find the perfect words to match the notes. Cameron, watching his parents fall apart and trying not to do the same himself. Jessica and her booming voice in a tiny body, full of contagious confidence. And Abigail, whose poems are deep and astute, who had me at "As if." Now that I know her better, her poetry no longer surprises me.

They're my friends. And I realize I know a whole lot more about them than they know about me.

My next step is so clear. I leap off the chair and head for my backpack, feeling inspired to write for the first time in four days. I reach inside for my yellow notebook, because when Caroline was part of my life, she made me stronger, better, and happier. And that's the part of myself I need to reconnect with right now.

I sit on the orange couch with my feet folded underneath me. The pen feels solid in my hand, and when I bring it to the paper, I'm relieved to feel the words flowing out like someone turned on the spigot.

And before I know it, I've filled the page with a poem for Caroline. It voices what she means to me and how much I miss her and why this room of hers matters, not just to me but to everyone who's ever found it. And, while it doesn't say it in so many words, it's also a poem for my new friends, promising that from now on I'll be a lot braver with my words than I was before.

way too much

I close my notebook, and for the first time since Friday afternoon, I smile. It feels good. As I gather my things, I check the time on my phone. It's 4:18. I've been down here for more than two hours.

Before I leave, I walk to the closest wall and run my hand along the brown paper bags and candy wrappers, the ripped-up scraps of paper and Post-it notes, the napkins and receipts, thinking about all the people who have spent time in this room. Every person with a poem on this wall has a story to tell.

I need to know more.

I feel that familiar swirl start to build inside me, that craving for information, and more information. My breathing speeds up and my fingers start tingling. I want to know every single person's story, and I start to feel excited by the idea of researching each one until I've pieced it all together. And then the swirl stops, as quickly as it started.

I don't need to know hundreds of stories. I only need to know seven.

I've never asked any of them to tell me how they found Poet's Corner. I never asked Caroline. I never even asked AJ.

AJ.

I flip off the last light and race back up the stairs and into the student lot. My mind needs music, and I start to turn on *In the Deep*, but then I spot *Grab the Yoke* and choose it instead.

I think about that day I first drove around with AJ, telling him how I named my playlists. He asked about this one. I told him how I sometimes wanted to "fly the whole mess into the sea," and when I said the words, he looked at me like he was worried I might actually do it. Did my words remind him of Caroline, the founder of his beloved poetry club? She grabbed the yoke.

My mind is on overload and my stomach is in knots as I throw the car in reverse, peel out of the student lot, and make the turns that lead to AJ's house. At the top of his driveway, I pull the emergency brake hard and scramble out of my car.

The wind is picking up, whistling through the trees and stinging my cheeks, and I tighten my jacket around my body as I climb the stairs. I start to knock, but then I hear AJ's guitar coming from the other side of the door. It's too faint to make out the song, but I can picture him with his fingers pressed into the strings, forming chords, sliding up and down along the neck. I knock before I lose my nerve.

The music stops, and few seconds later, he opens the door. "Hi." He looks surprised to see me.

"Hi." I lift the cord over my head and hand it to him. "Thank you," I say. He stuffs it into the pocket of his jeans. I look down at my shoes.

We're both silent for a long time, me trying to muster up the courage to say what I came here to say, and him probably trying to figure out the fastest way to get a psychotic girl off one's porch.

I stand up straighter, cementing my feet in place and looking right at him. "I found her corner." I bite my lip to keep my chin from trembling. "I was kind of hoping you'd tell me more about her. More about that room and how you found it, and how you got the key."

He opens the door wider. "Come in. You're freezing."

Nope. Just terrified.

I haven't been inside his house since that day I drove him home, when he taught me how to play guitar and I learned all about Devon. I step inside and drop my car keys on the entry table where I left them last time.

And that's when it hits me. I jumped out of the car without checking the odometer. For a split second, I consider going back outside, but AJ is already walking toward his room. He looks over his shoulder, sees me hesitating, and gestures for me to follow him.

I force myself to walk down the hallway, trying to think about him and nothing else, ignoring the intense urge I'm feeling to sprint back to the car and park correctly.

Last time, when he closed the door behind us, I didn't know where to go or what to do, but this time, I walk straight to his bed and sit on the edge. I'm relieved when he sits next to me. He leans back on his hands, looking serious. Or maybe he's still freaked out, I can't really tell.

"What do you want to know?" he asks.

I take a deep breath and blow it out slowly. "Everything," I say.

The small smile that forms on his lips makes me relax a bit.

"Mr. B told me the whole story when he gave me the key at the end of last year. He met Caroline when she was a sophomore. One day during lunch, he opened the door to the storage room next to the cafeteria, and found her hiding in there, all alone. It took some doing, but eventually she admitted it wasn't the first time; she had been eating there every day since the middle of her freshman year."

I picture her in one of her funny T-shirts, eating a sandwich while nestled among mop buckets and dustpans, and I want to cry. Or punch something. Possibly both at the same time.

"I guess people were mean to her. She told him she didn't have any friends, and she was too embarrassed to eat alone in the quad, so she ate alone in the storage closet because she couldn't think of anyplace else to go."

My heart sinks deep in my chest. I remember saying almost

329

the same thing to Shrink-Sue at the beginning of the school year. She asked why I wouldn't leave the Crazy Eights. I said I didn't have anywhere else to go.

"Caroline and Mr. B became friends. He started bringing his lunch and joining her. At some point, she told him about her poems, and eventually she let him read some of them. She told him about this crazy idea she'd had to start a secret poetry club.

"Mr. B didn't think it was so crazy. He showed her a room underneath the theater that the drama department hadn't used in years. He installed the lock, hid the seams with paint, and moved some furniture inside. Caroline started filling one corner with her poetry. Over time, she met a few people she felt she could trust. She told them about the room, and by the end of the year, the other walls were filling up, too. I guess she wasn't the only one who needed a place to go."

I came over to AJ's house today because I needed to know what brought him to Poet's Corner, and when he says that last part, things begin to fall into place. My eyes well up.

"*You* needed a place to go," I say, and he nods.

"Emily and I had freshman English together. It was still really hard for me to talk in class, and she caught me doing my strumming-on-my-jeans thing. She asked me about it. Eventually, she brought me downstairs."

"AJ," I whisper. I wipe my eyes, but all I really want to do right now is throw my arms around his neck and kiss him like I've done so many times over the last few weeks. But I'm so afraid of what will happen if I do. Will he push me away? Will he tell me it's over? I don't want to lose him, and I can't tell if I already have. I wish he'd touch me. My heart starts racing, my hands feel clammy, the thoughts are gathering and swirling, and I start panicking.

Why won't he touch me?

And then, as quickly as they began, the thoughts stop. Completely. Inside my head it's eerily quiet. And I know what I need to do.

Caroline's been giving me words, and they've worked. But they were never her words. They were always mine. My words got AJ to let me into Poet's Corner, both times. When I told him how I name my playlists, he paid attention and wanted to know more. When we were at the pool that night, he begged me to talk to him. When I finally told him what I was thinking, he kissed me. Every time I talk to him, he comes closer.

He wants me to talk to him.

And suddenly, I hear Caroline's voice, calm and clear, as if she were sitting right next to me.

Don't think. Go.

I look over my left shoulder, expecting to see her there, but the space is empty. I follow her instructions anyway.

"My mind messes with me," I say, talking in that unfiltered way he likes, not measuring my words and not quite certain about what's coming out until I hear myself say it. I scratch the back of my neck hard three times, no longer caring if he notices. "It's been happening as long as I can remember. I can't turn off my thoughts. I can't sleep without being drugged into it. My mind just . . . never stops working.

"I was diagnosed with OCD when I was eleven. I've been on antianxiety medication ever since. I have this amazing psychiatrist named Sue who is, like, my lifeline, and I see her every Wednesday afternoon."

This is harder than I expected. I take a moment to gather my thoughts, looking around at his posters and his messy desk. I see his clipboard on the floor next to his guitar, and together, they seem to calm me. I shake out my hands.

"For a long time, my friendship with the Eights has been . . . challenging for me. So when school started, Sue and I decided to channel my energy into positive things, like my swimming," I say. "That's been good. Then I met Caroline, and that was *really* good. And then I found Poet's Corner, and started writing poetry, and met a bunch of amazing people, and then there was *you*. And I felt healthy for the first time in years. I thought I was getting better. But as it turns out, I was getting worse."

I study his body language like I do with Sue each week, watching the way he moves in direct correlation to the words I say. It's slight, almost imperceptible, but I notice when he props his hand on his bed and leans in a tiny bit closer to me.

Let your guard down.

"Caroline was my friend," I say as the tears slide down my cheeks. "And now she's gone and I can't quite decide how I'm supposed to feel about that. I'm embarrassed that I made her up in the first place, but I'm also so sad that she's not part of my life anymore."

Keep talking.

"But when I was downstairs this afternoon, I realized something: I don't regret bringing her to life. Not even for a second. Because she's this better part of me, you know? She speaks her mind and she doesn't care what people think about her. I've always been too scared to be that person, but that's who I want to be, all the time, not only when I'm alone with you, and not just on Monday and Thursday afternoons during lunch."

I can tell I'm rambling, but I can't stop now. I'm letting the words tumble out of my mouth, still wishing he'd touch me, hug me, kiss me, do something—*anything*—to make me stop talking. But he doesn't speak and he doesn't move. He just listens.

"It was as if she knew it was time for me to tap into this better person. So she showed me where to find you. *All* of you. These seven amazing people who seem to know how to pull her out of me."

"Sam," he says, and before I can interpret the tone in his voice, he closes the distance, and finally, I feel his thumbs on my cheeks. He rests his forehead against mine, just like he did that night in the pool, and I wait for him to kiss me, but he doesn't.

Keep going.

"I'm sorry I didn't tell you about me. I should have, but all my life, I've just wanted to be normal. You made me feel like I was. I was afraid that if I told you, I wouldn't feel normal anymore."

He laughs. "*I* made you feel normal? You do realize *I'm* pretty far from normal, right?"

"I don't care," I say, brushing my lips against his. "I like you too much. Remember?"

I kiss his dimple first, and then I cover his mouth with mine, kissing him, thinking about how perfect he is, maybe not in every way, but in every way I need him to be. And I'm so relieved when he kisses me back. I feel the thoughts that have haunted me for the last four days pop like bubbles, disappearing into the air, one by one.

"I like you too much, too," he says.

"Still?" I ask.

"Still," he says with a huge smile on his face. "Way, way too much."

After that, we stop talking.

stitched into me

Emily pats the spot next to her and I sit down. I steal a quick glimpse over my shoulder at the couch Caroline and I sat on during the P.M. last Thursday night, but I don't expect her to be there. Cameron's got the whole thing to himself today.

"We missed you on Monday," she says. "Everything okay?"

"Yeah." I see AJ taking his usual seat on the orange couch. He catches me looking at him. "It wasn't, but it is now." I reach down for my yellow notebook and set it on the cushion next to me. Emily's holding a napkin in her hand, presumably for today's reading.

"How's your mom?" I ask.

She doesn't look at me. "She came home last weekend."

"That's great," I say enthusiastically. But Emily shakes her head as she twists the napkin around one finger.

"Hospice," she says, and I feel a pit form deep in my stomach.

"Oh, Emily. I'm so sorry."

"My dad made it sound like a big event, as if her coming home was a good thing, but, come on . . . Like I don't know what fucking hospice is?" She tucks one leg under the other and turns toward me. "The entire living room has been transformed and now it looks *nothing* like the one she decorated, and there are machines everywhere, and that horrible bed is smack in the middle of the window, like she's on display for the whole neighborhood or something. But 'it's a good thing,' right?" she says sarcastically. "Because now she can see our front yard during the day."

Emily rests her elbow on the back of the couch, props her head in her hand, and keeps talking. "I pretended to be happy because I knew it meant a lot to my dad, but now coming home from school every day is absolute torture." As soon as she says it, her eyes grow wide and her whole face turns bright red. She covers her mouth. "That sounded so horrible. I shouldn't have said that."

I picture that cute house she lives in with the cheery paint and the rope swing, knowing that's what her mom is staring at all day, and I can't imagine how excruciating it must be for Emily to walk through that blue door and see her mom lying there, slowly dying.

Emily turns away from me, shaking her head in disgust. "Jesus. What kind of person says that about her own mother?"

I've said those same *what-kind-of-person* words myself. They're especially damaging, the kind of thing that can make a thought-spiral tornado unexpectedly change course, shifting into an entirely new and even more destructive direction. My mom and Sue always have words that help, so I say them to Emily.

"A good person," I tell her. She catches my eye and gives me a trace of a smile. "Someone who loves her mom and doesn't want to see her in so much pain."

She blows out a big breath like she's air-drying her face. "Thank you," she whispers toward the ceiling.

The idea comes out of nowhere, and before I give it a second thought, I start blurting. "Come over to my house after school today. We can talk. Or write. Or listen to music, and not talk, and not write, and not think about anything bad at all."

"I don't know," she says, looking down at the floor, picking at her fingernails. "My dad likes me to come straight home after school."

I point at the phone next to her hip, screen facing up like it always is. "He'll call if he needs you. I can have you there in ten minutes." Emily looks like she's considering it. "You can even stay for dinner if you want to. My mom's a horrible cook, so you'll have to pretend to like the food, but my dad is, like, the king of small talk, and my little sister can be kind of funny."

I force myself to shut up because I can't tell if all this family talk is making Emily feel better or worse. But then she looks over at me and says, "That sounds nice and . . ." She pauses for a moment, as if she's searching for the right word. "Normal."

Normal.

She's right. It does sound normal. My life might not be perfect and my brain might play tricks on me and I might be overwhelmed by my own thoughts, but now that I think about it, I'm lucky to have as much *normal* as I do.

I look at Emily, wondering if I could do for her what Caroline did for me. Wondering if I could pay it forward.

I'll gauge it, but if she comes over today and it seems like she wants to talk, I'll ask her questions and listen—really listen, like Caroline listened to me—and keep her talking until she has nothing left to say. If she wants to, I'll help her write a happy poem about her mom. Something positive. Something she can read to her. And if the moment feels right and she wants a change of subject, I'll tell her my secrets. I'll let her in on my OCD and Shrink-Sue and Caroline and the number three, and I'll talk until she knows everything.

Does she see it in my eyes right now, how much I want to be her friend? Because something shifts in her expression and her whole face lights up, more than I've ever seen it do before. "Actually, I'd love that," she says.

"Okay, who's up first?" AJ asks from his spot in the front of the room.

I look around. Sydney's got a wrapper in her hands, but aside from doing a little dance in her seat, she doesn't move. Emily is still holding her napkin, but she doesn't look ready to go yet. Jessica and Cameron are holding papers in their hands too, but they don't stand up and head for the stage either.

"I'll go," I say, and before I can think too much about it, I'm standing up, walking to the stage, sitting on the stool. I open my notebook to the right page. "I wrote this on Tuesday in—"

As soon as I speak, my mouth goes dry. I take a deep breath, close my notebook on my lap, and look out into the group, letting my gaze settle on each one of them. I remember the first time I sat up here, staring at these total strangers, feeling terrified about how much of myself I was about to expose.

Things are different now.

"I went through something last weekend," I say. "And it made me realize it was no mistake that I wandered down here one day and found all of you. So before I read this poem, I just want to say thank you for letting me stay, even though I probably didn't deserve it and some of you didn't think I belonged."

My notebook is still closed on my lap. I don't open it. I don't need to. I know these words by heart.

"I wrote this in Poet's Corner."

I bring my left hand to my shoulder, exactly where Caroline's was the first time I sat on this stool and read aloud. My eyes fall shut.

You're still here
    stitched into me, like threads in a sweater.

Feeding me words
    that break me down and piece me back
        together, all at once.

Tightening your grip,
    reminding me that I'm not alone.

I never was.
    None of us ever are.

You are still here
    stitched into the words on these walls.

Every last one.

The room is completely silent. Then everyone starts clapping and whistling, and I open my eyes to find AJ standing up, glue stick ready to launch. I give him one of his trademark chin tilts and he sends it flying. I catch it in midair.

It feels good to rip this poem out of the notebook, and even better to cover the paper with glue. I march to the back of the room, and I find a sliver of empty space on the wall near the hidden door. "Thank you, Caroline," I whisper as I bring the page to my lips. Then I press it against the wall, running my hand over the words, securing them in place.

Back on stage, Sydney clears her throat dramatically. "Most of you have already heard this tasty treat, but since some of you missed it because you were dealing with 'car trouble,'" she says with air quotes, locking eyes with AJ, then with me. "I thought I'd read it again."

I sit next to AJ this time, and he wraps his arms around my waist. I recline against his chest and he rests his chin on my shoulder.

Sydney unfolds a paper In-N-Out hat and positions it on her head. Then she launches into a dramatic reading about the secret menu. She praises the Flying Dutchman and the 2x4, makes us hungry with her descriptions of special sauces and spices and grilled onions, and leaves us mystified about the people who order "cold cheese." When she finishes her poem, she passes out paper In-N-Out hats to all of us.

We're all still wearing them as we file out the door. Everyone heads into the hallway, but AJ hangs back.

"What's the matter?" I ask him.

"Your call, but I'm wondering if that poem of yours is in the right home." He hands me a glue stick.

He has a point.

I step back inside, remove the page from the wall, and apply a fresh coat of glue to the back. Then I walk over to Caroline's Corner and find a new spot, right next to her collection.

"Much better," he says as he anchors my hat on my head.

AJ grabs my hand and leads me up the stairs, back into the real world.

that's the thing

My legs feel wobbly and I'm sure everyone is staring at me as I cross the cafeteria. Alexis and Kaitlyn are on one side of the table; Hailey and Olivia are on the other.

Alexis sees me first. She elbows Kaitlyn and whispers something in her ear. I keep taking brave steps across the room, Sue's voice in my head, reminding me to hold on to the people who make me stronger and better, and let go of the ones who don't. Holding on to the Poets was easy. Letting go of the Eights is already proving to be harder than I expected.

"Can I talk to you guys?" I'm asking all of them, but for some reason, I direct the question to Alexis.

"Of course," she replies, scooting down, making room next to her. "Where have you been? We haven't seen you all week."

"We were worried," Kaitlyn says. I must look skeptical because she adds, "Really. We were. In fact, I went to your locker a bunch of times looking for you."

"Why?" I ask.

"I wanted to apologize."

I'm still not sure I believe her. If she wanted to apologize so badly, she could have tried a lot harder to find me. She hasn't texted me once in seven days.

I catch Hailey giving her a stern look. Kaitlyn sits up straighter and leans in closer to me. "I'm glad you're here, because I've been meaning to talk to you. What I said last week wasn't funny. I was out of line and I'm sorry. I hope you'll accept my apology, Sam."

Wait. Did she call me Sam?

I look at Hailey's smug expression, thinking about the conversation we had in my room last Sunday, and I start to realize what's happening. Hailey's been rallying for me from the inside. She doesn't want me to leave. She's convinced them to apologize and start calling me Sam from now on. Then this will all be over. And everything can go back to the way it was.

Am I really such a great friend that they can't stand to lose me? Or are they merely trying to save face? I'd like to think it's the former—that I've been overreacting all these years and they really are true friends who love me for exactly who I am— but I'm not completely sure.

Kaitlyn takes a sip of her soda, and then turns to Alexis. "Did you tell her about this weekend?"

Alexis looks around to be sure no one can hear her, and then she rests her forearms on the table and lowers her voice. "My parents are going out of town. I can't have another party, because if they catch me again, they'll take my car away. So we're keeping it small."

"All the guys are coming over," Olivia pipes in, pointing around the cafeteria as she identifies them. "Travis, Jeremy, Kurt . . . We still need someone for Hailey. And you can bring AJ, okay? So we can get to know him better."

I'm tempted. I don't want to be, but I am. I've been mentally preparing myself to part ways with the Eights all week, but now I'm not so sure I want to leave them behind so completely.

Maybe I was wrong. Maybe I can have both. Now that I think about it, AJ might like being pulled into my circle. I've never even asked him. I picture all of us sitting around Alexis's living room, talking late into the night, everyone getting to know the side of AJ most people don't get to see and . . . Wait. What did Olivia just say?

I turn back to Kaitlyn. "You're seeing Kurt?" For a split second, she looks a little embarrassed, but she quickly recovers. She cocks her head to one side. "Yeah. We sort of bumped into each other at a party last weekend and got back together."

Got *back* together? I'd hardly call making out with my boyfriend in a coat-check room while I was fifty feet away "together." But I'm glad she told me. For a minute, I almost forgot why I came over here today.

"I need to say something to you guys." The mood shifts

instantly. Alexis folds her arms across her chest. Kaitlyn stares at me, eyebrows raised. Olivia bites her lip and fixes her gaze on the table. Hailey brings her hand to her forehead.

"We've been best friends since we were little kids, and there are so many reasons for that. We've always had so much fun together. All of my very best memories include you guys." I'm speaking slowly and clearly, exactly the way Sue coached me. I feel my hands shaking, but I take a deep breath and keep talking. "But we've also changed a lot over the years. And I think that's a good thing. I think we're supposed to change, and when we do, that has to be okay. I've changed over the last few months, and I like the person I'm becoming."

"And who is that?" Olivia asks.

"That's the thing," I say with a shrug. "I'm not sure. The truth is, I don't really know who I am without you guys. But I think I need to find out."

It doesn't come out exactly the way Sue and I practiced, but it's close and I followed all the rules. I intentionally don't mention AJ or any of my other friends downstairs, and I'm careful with my words so they don't think I'm blaming them or anything. We're growing apart. It's time to part ways.

"Did your new boyfriend put you up to this?" Olivia asks.

"He sounds a little possessive," Kaitlyn says to her, as if I'm not sitting right here.

"Stop it," Hailey interjects. "Now." I feel her hand on my shoulder and it catches me completely off guard. "I'm not doing this. Not again."

I know what she means. We all do. She's not going to let them treat me the way we all treated Sarah. And I realize that no matter what happens today, Hailey now knows which side she's on, and it's mine.

"She's right," Alexis says. "You're our friend. We love you. You should do what makes you happy."

Kaitlyn raises her eyebrows. Olivia won't look at me. Hailey still has her hand on my shoulder. Alexis is smiling at me, and it looks genuine.

I'm still trying to get my head around this whole thing. I'm having a hard time believing those words just came out of Alexis's mouth, but she sounds sincere. Maybe it's a game. Maybe I'm about to be the punch line of some big joke, or the focal point of some nasty piece of gossip. Even if I am, I can't do anything about it anyway.

I give Hailey's hand a grateful squeeze as I stand up.

"I'll see you guys later." I walk through the cafeteria doors, leaving my friends behind. Feeling all the pain of letting them go. And knowing I did the right thing.

the first time

"How are you today, Sam?" Colleen stands up from behind the counter as I open the door.

She used to practically sing her "It must be Wednesday" line, but today, I get the same awkward greeting I got last week, her voice dropping into a lower octave when she says my name, her lips pursed sympathetically while she waits for my reply. I tell her I'm fine.

I've already apologized for bursting in here that day, and she insisted I had nothing to be sorry for. That she'd already forgotten all about it. Clearly, she hasn't.

"She's waiting for you. Go on in."

I was kind of hoping Sue would suggest moving our meeting to her backyard oasis, where we could talk in comfortable chairs around a fountain and among flowers, but no such luck.

When I step into her office, she stands up from behind her desk and crosses the room to meet me halfway. "Wow. You look different today," she says, beaming at me.

"Do I?" I ask, like I don't know what she's talking about. But I do. I'm wearing jeans and a plain, long-sleeve T-shirt. My hair is long and straight, but I didn't flat iron it or anything. And I'm hardly wearing any makeup, just a light bit of foundation, some blush, and mascara. I've been scaling back over the last few weeks. This feels more like me. And I have an extra hour to sleep now.

"If it weren't for the holiday decorations all over town and the fact that I have to cook Christmas dinner for twenty people next week, I'd swear it was the middle of July," she says. "You look relaxed. And happy. Like Summer Sam."

I'm not sure how to explain it, but I don't *feel* like Summer Sam. I'm more relaxed, happier than she ever was, because even in July I was dreading August, and finding it hard to be truly happy when the sand was flowing into the bottom half of the hourglass and there was nothing I could do to stop it.

"Summer Sam was always . . ." I pause, searching for the right word, and settle on: "Temporary. But *this* feels pretty permanent."

Sue smiles.

"I registered for the advanced swim program today. Five a.m. practices every morning." I roll my eyes. "But year-round meets, a chance to swim at Junior Nationals, and a much better shot at a scholarship."

Now she's beaming. "Well, that's certainly cause for celebration." Sue glides over to the minifridge and removes a bottle of sparkling apple cider. She pours it into two plastic champagne flutes and returns, handing one to me.

"To Sam," she says, raising her glass in the air.

I clink mine against it and echo her words. "To Sam."

We take our ciders over to our chairs. I kick off my shoes and Sue hands me my putty. I take sips from my glass as I fill her in on my week, and she listens and nods. She doesn't have her leather-bound portfolio on her lap like she usually does, so I have a feeling this is going to be a light session. After the last few, I imagine we could both use one.

Three weeks ago, we spent the entire time role-playing my breakup with the Crazy Eights. The week after that, I spent the whole time crying, wondering if I'd made the right decision. Last week, we switched gears, and Sue convinced me to recite the poem I wrote for Caroline. And then she asked me to read more of my poems, and I cried even harder.

As I was reading, I started to realize how much the number three has been impacting my thoughts and actions, and by the end of our session, I told her I wanted to work harder to control my impulses. Which meant I had to fess up about the odometer.

Sue pointed to the putty in my hands. "What if you took a chunk of that with you today and used it to cover the numbers?" I'd squeezed it in between my fingers and told her that might work. "If you feel like you truly need to remove it before you park, go ahead," she says. "Then put it back. But see if you can keep it on there for good."

I still think about those numbers every time I park, but I haven't cheated once.

We talk about AJ next. I fill her in on everything, and then I tell her he drove me to my appointment today.

"He needed some new guitar strings, and the music store is a couple blocks away." I take a sip of my sparkling cider, thinking about how the whole conversation with AJ played out.

We've talked a lot about Sue over the last few weeks. He knows how important she is to me, and that I want him to meet her someday. I'm not sure I'm ready for that yet, but I liked the idea of him dropping me off. I told him he could meet Colleen if he wanted to.

"I kind of needed him to see where I go on Wednesdays."

I can tell she's proud of me. I'm feeling a little proud of myself, too. It feels good to talk. It feels good to be surrounded by people who make it so easy.

And then she asks me about Caroline, and I get quiet for a long time.

Finally, I tell her how my stomach falls every time I look at the other end of my locker bank and find it empty, and how I often sit in the first row of the theater during lunch, writing in the dark like the two of us used to do. I admit that last week, I started making a playlist of songs that were popular during Caroline's high school years and titled it *Right Beside You* after the lyrics in a Snow Patrol song.

"I miss her. A lot. Every day." The lump in my throat swells and I can feel my eyes welling up. I don't want to cry. Not today.

Sue must be able to tell from the look on my face, because she stands and claps her hands together once. "Hey," she says excitedly. "I have something for you."

She walks over to her desk and returns carrying a box wrapped in bright blue paper with a big white bow around the center. She hands it to me.

"You got me a Christmas present? Let me guess. A shiny new brain? A healthy one this time?" I give it a little shake. Damn. Too light.

"It's just a little something. I couldn't resist. It spoke to me—said you two needed each other."

"Hey, if I can talk to imaginary people, I guess you can talk to inanimate objects." I tug at the bow and it falls to the floor. I pull the lid off the box. "No way," I say. I hold the T-shirt up in front of me so I can read the big block letters: I AM SILENTLY CORRECTING YOUR GRAMMAR.

"Sue, this is awesome. It's so . . ." I stop short of saying the first thing that pops into my head. Then I say it anyway. "Caroline."

I stand up and hug her, even though I'm not supposed to, and she hugs me back, despite the fact that we're breaking her "professional distance" code. I layer my new shirt over the top of my long-sleeved tee and model it for her. "What do you think?" I ask.

"Perfect," she says.

No. It's not perfect. But it's me.

When our time is up, I leave her office and head back to the waiting room, realizing that, for the first time in five years, we didn't talk about the Crazy Eights.

AJ had said he'd meet me downstairs, so I'm surprised to find him in the waiting room. "Hey," he says. "Nice shirt."

"Thanks. It was a gift from Sue." I point to Colleen. "Did you two meet?"

"We did," she says. She's no longer wearing that pity-stare. She's looking at us with the glowing, giddy expression I'm more accustomed to.

"See you next Wednesday," I tell her.

AJ and I walk out the doors and stop in front of the elevators, and once we're out of Sue's office and away from Colleen's curious eyes, he wraps his arms around me. I feel his fingers in my hair and his breath on my neck, and he doesn't say a word, he just hugs me tight for the longest time. I love the way I fit in his arms. How my ear rests perfectly against his chest and I can hear his heartbeat.

"Thanks for coming today," I tell him.

"I'm glad I did."

"Me too."

I reach out and press the elevator button. Once. I feel the urge to push it two more times, but I grab AJ's hand and kiss it instead.

got this one

It's pouring outside. AJ, Cameron, Chelsea, Jessica, Sydney, and I are gathered around a table in the cafeteria. Emily would be here, but her mom lost her long battle with cancer, and she hasn't been at school since we returned from winter break. The funeral is tomorrow and Emily asked AJ to play one of her mom's favorite songs. We'll all be there, of course.

I glance over at the spot where I used to sit. Alexis, Kaitlyn, Olivia, and Hailey are all where they belong, eating and chatting as usual. We haven't said much to each other in the last month, but they all look happy, even Hailey.

AJ rests his hand on my knee. "You all right?"

"Yeah." I push my food around my plate. "I'm not very hungry today." I pull my phone out of my pocket and check the time. We still have another thirty minutes before lunch is over. "I think I'll go write for a bit."

"Have fun," he says, giving my leg a squeeze.

I stand up, grabbing my tray off the table and telling everyone I'll see them later. Before I leave, I wrap my free arm around AJ's neck from behind. "Love you," I whisper in his ear.

The rain is coming down harder, which doesn't matter that much until the covered walkway comes to an end and there's no other way to get to the theater's double doors than to cross the open grass. I throw my jacket over my head and make a run for it.

Once I'm inside, I toss my jacket over a chair in the back row and walk down the aisle to the front of the theater. I sit in the chair I always sit in, open my yellow notebook to an empty page, and fish around in the bottom of my backpack until I find a mechanical pencil. I click it once, twice, three times. And then I hear Shrink-Sue's voice in my head, telling me to click it again, so I give it a fourth click. I stop, resisting the urge to click it two more times.

I scoot back into the chair and slide down low, kicking my legs out in front of me, crossing them at the ankles, staring up at the ceiling and trying to decide where to start. I tap the eraser against the paper. I'm at a loss. I close my eyes and sit like that for a few minutes, breathing in the musky smell of this room, running my fingernails back and forth across the upholstery. I never expected to feel a connection to this place, and now, sometimes it's the only place I want to be.

It's been a tough week. I can't stop thinking about Emily. I want to write a poem for her, something that expresses how sorry I am and tells her how much her friendship means to me, but the words aren't coming today. I let out a groan and look down at my feet.

I see a pair of boots, right next to my shoes. Then legs, crossed at the ankles, mirroring my posture exactly. My gaze travels up slowly, carefully, like I'm afraid any sudden movement will cause me to lose her.

When I reach her face, I suck in a breath. Then I give her the biggest smile.

"Hey. I'm glad you're here," I say, tapping the page with my pencil. "I could use your help with this."

Her head falls to the side and she smiles back at me. "Anytime," she says as she reaches over and takes my hand in hers.

I want to keep looking at her, but instead, I let my eyes fall shut.

"Actually," I whisper, "I think I've got this one."

When I open my eyes again, Caroline is gone.

And I start filling the page with words.

author's note

I became interested in writing a story about a teen with Obsessive Compulsive Disorder (OCD) when a close family friend was diagnosed four years ago, at age twelve. I sympathized with and related to her battle with insomnia, her struggles to interpret her friends' words and actions, and her challenges to control a stream of negative, often terrifying thoughts she simply couldn't turn off.

I knew she wasn't alone. I wanted to learn more about this disorder and to understand what it was like to live inside her mind. She was eager to share her experience, and I was honored when she agreed to work with me on this novel.

Over the last two years, I've done extensive research on OCD and what some refer to as Purely Obsessional or "Pure-O" OCD, where the emphasis is more on internal thoughts and images than external compulsions. I've learned that many professionals consider the term a bit of a misnomer—compulsions are still part of the disorder, they're simply easier to hide— but many people with OCD use "Pure-O" to differentiate an obsession with their *thoughts* from the better-known external behaviors, like ritualized hand washing or lock checking.

I have read hundreds of blogs written by adults and teens, detailing what it's like to live with OCD and Pure-O. I have pored over articles and medical journals filled with exhaustive information about treatments and medications. I've consulted closely with four mental-health professionals to be sure this work of fiction portrays an accurate account of OCD, while also demonstrating the value of a strong patient-therapist relationship. It has been enlightening, inspiring, and heartbreaking.

During my research, I became especially interested in exposure therapy, a subset of Cognitive Behavioral Therapy (CBT). I found it empowering, and wove it into the story when Sam's mother hands her a pair of scissors to prove that she won't *act* on her invasive, fearful thoughts. While there are hints in the text itself, it is important to me that readers understand that prior to this scene, (1) Sue has led Sam through exposure therapy sessions in her office, (2) Sue has formally trained Sam's mother, so she can provide the 24/7 support Sam might require, and (3) Sue and Sam's mother operate as a team and are in constant communication about managing Sam's disorder. My professional resources have confirmed that, while it is atypical to perform exposure therapy outside a controlled office environment or to involve a parent in this process, it is certainly something they have employed under ideal circumstances. However, a professional therapist *always* oversees and is closely involved in any CBT treatment.

CBT can be emotionally and physically intense, with sessions spanning weeks or months. Afterward, practitioners may transition back to traditional "talk therapy," which is what Sue and Sam engage in through the majority of the novel.

While this is work of fiction, the relationship between Sue and Sam in many ways mirrors the relationship between the real-life teen who inspired this story and her therapist for the last four years. Throughout the process of writing this novel, I've become even more moved by their connection, and I've gained a whole new level of respect for mental health professionals, especially those who work closely with teens.

If you or someone you know is struggling with OCD, anxiety, depression, or any other mental-health concern, I strongly encourage you to seek out your *own* Sue. S/he is real and out there, waiting, eager, and able to help. Here are a few reputable places to begin: www.sfbacct.com; www.teenmentalhealth.org; www.beyondocd.org/just-for-teens; and www.kids.iocdf.org.

I want to close with an update on the girl who originally inspired this story. "C" is now sixteen. I can't get her to swim, but she has started writing poetry, and while she doesn't share it broadly, she finds writing extremely therapeutic. She's found true friends who make her feel good about herself, and she's even found her very own AJ. Recently, she decided that she's brave enough to go away to college, where she plans to study psychology and become a therapist herself someday. I am proud of her, beyond words.

acknowledgments

Writing this novel taught me that I need to be braver with my words, and part of that meant sharing the story with other people long before it felt comfortable to do so. I'm grateful to the many individuals who helped me bring *Every Last Word* to life and made it a much better book in the process, including:

The mental-health professionals who provided guidance and insight on this project. It's been such a privilege to work with Dr. Michael Tompkins, Ph.D.; Dr. Marianna Eraklis, M.D.; and Karen Blesius Rhodes, LCSW. I'm also grateful to my mother-in-law, Rebecca Stone, who deeply understands the workings of the human brain and graciously shared her knowledge along the way.

Everyone at Hyperion, but especially: my editor, Emily Meehan, for her valuable editorial direction and for being such a vocal advocate for this story; Julie Moody, for all her insightful feedback along the way; Stephanie Lurie, Suzanne Murphy,

Dina Sherman, and Seale Ballenger, for their tireless support and enthusiasm; Elke Villa, Andrew Sansone, and Holly Nagel, for marketing this book with heart and creativity; my publicist, Jamie Baker, for *all* she does (also, for not pulling me away from "The Raven" that day); and Whitney Manger, for designing such a strikingly simple yet beautiful cover that celebrates the power of words. I'm lucky to work with such talented, passionate, and genuinely fun people.

Lisa Yoskowitz, my first editor, who believed in Sam and her story from the very beginning, and cared so deeply about every last word (see what I did there?). She always seemed to know what I was trying to say, even when I didn't quite know myself, and I will be forever grateful for her encouragement, coaching, and friendship.

Caryn Wiseman, for understanding what I needed this book to be, reading *many* drafts (often on short notice), and helping me improve it at every turn. I'm fortunate to call her my agent *and* my friend. Also, huge thanks to her extended team—my foreign rights agent, Taryn Fagerness, and film agent, Michelle Weiner—who represent my stories with such dedication.

The members of GetLit.org for inspiring me with their brave and powerful voices, and to all the teen poetry organizations around the country for giving young adults a stage so their words can be heard.

The courageous teens who openly share their personal experiences with OCD, anxiety, depression, and other disorders in an effort to raise awareness and offer support. I've learned so much from them (and from the example they set).

The many friends who generously shared their talents and expertise, including Joe Rut, for writing beautiful songs and letting me borrow his words; Andrea Hegarty, for teaching me the finer points of butterfly and competitive swimming; Claire Peña, for sharing my obsession with music and lyrics; Shona McCarthy, for spotting the little things that mattered a lot; Laura Wiseman, for crying at all the right parts; Lorin Oberweger, for helping me pull Sam to the surface; Arnold Shapiro, time-travel fan turned friend, for providing episodes from his MTV series, *If You Really Knew Me* and *Surviving High School* to help with my research; fellow authors Elle Cosimano, Stephanie Perkins, and Veronica Rossi, for reading early drafts and giving such solid feedback; Carrolyn Leary, for coffee talks about mental health and much more; and finally, my forever friend Stacy Peña, who understood how special this story was to me long before I put a single word on paper. She hugged me hard and told me to write it, and because of her, here it is. These are not just my friends; these are my Poets.

My son, Aidan, who shaped this story in unexpected ways and opened my eyes in the process, and my daughter, Lauren, who isn't afraid to speak her mind but always does it with kindness. They are many wonderful things, but mostly, they're *good people*. I couldn't be prouder of who they are.

Michael, who helps me be brave and just plain *gets* me.

When Sam tells AJ she's going to go write, he says, "Have fun." That line is for my husband, because that's what he says to me before I disappear into my imaginary world. It's such a small thing, but those two little words carry the weight of his love and support, while subtly reminding me why I write books. It's no wonder this guy is at the heart of every love story I tell.

And finally, C, my muse and friend: Thank you for letting me in. For you, I have so many words, but in honor of Sam, I'll keep it to three: I love you.